Love
Out of
Reach

Jack A. Saarela

Can't Put it Down
BOOKS

This is a work of historical fiction. The characters and the events portrayed are based on extensive historical research. A few of the characters are composites of multiple people. While there are no recordings or transcripts of many of the personal conversations held between the characters, many of the conversations are paraphrases of statements made to others, or emotions expressed in letters.

Published by
Can't Put It Down Books
An imprint of
Open Door Publications
2113 Stackhouse Dr.
Yardley, PA 19067
www.CantPutItDownBooks.com

Cover Design by Eric Labacz
www.labaczdesign.com

BOOK ONE

First they came for the communists, and I did not speak out because I am not a communist.
Then they came for the trade unionists, but I did not speak out because I am not a trade unionist.
Then they came for the Jews, and I did not speak out because I am not a Jew.
Finally they came for me and there was no one left to speak for me.

—Pastor Martin Niemöller, Confessing Church

Chapter One

Has something happened? I am afraid that something bad has happened or will happen.
I don't know how I know this, but I feel it in my bones. Someone's life is about to change and not for the better.

—Maria von Wedemeyer

Berlin: April 5, 1943

The air over Berlin in this fourth year of the war was charged with fear and pervasive suspicion. It wearied Maria's body as well as her mind and spirit. Despite her misgivings, the day held promise. Any day that she could be with her love, Pastor Dietrich Bonhöffer, was a delightfully cheerful day, no matter what else was happening in the world. She could hardly believe that he was actually, finally, her fiancé. It seemed as if she had loved him almost all of her life. She knew that many people, perhaps including Dietrich himself, found it surprising.

Though Maria was far less reserved than her fiancé, her friends and family had certainly never called her giddy—a word that would definitely describe her on the infrequent days she could spend with Dietrich. He himself was a rather serious and earnest man, and for all the public speaking he did, truly very shy and reticent. It had occurred to her that her own optimistic temperament was one of the reasons he enjoyed being with her.

This day he planned to spend a significant amount of time in the small third-floor room in his parents' new home on Marienburgerallee in Charlottenburg, a suburb of Berlin. He was working on the manuscript of his latest book, *Ethics*, which he had been working on since the day in the previous year when he and Maria reconnected again. Although still very young for his world-renowned status as a theologian, Dietrich had received his doctorate in theology at age 21 years. A prolific writer, he had already gained respect as a theologian as far away as Great Britain and the United States.

And though when she finally met him their relationship had at first been that of pastor and young parishioner, she had always felt a special, secret attraction to him. It had taken many years for the serious theologian to realize that she had grown into a woman who could accept and return his love. It had taken her mother even longer. She shook her head, unwilling to let thoughts of her stubborn *Mütti* get in the way of her enjoyment of today. She knew not to bother Dietrich when he was writing, but she wasn't very far away. They had been invited to dinner by the Schleichers, Dietrich's older sister Ursula and her husband Rüdiger, whose home was right next door to Dietrich's parents'. Dietrich's family had been much more accepting of their courtship and romance than her own family, and she was grateful for their acceptance of her as an equal, even though she was younger by several years than his many brothers and sisters.

It was handy that Ursula lived so close, and truly a miracle, Maria thought, when the two homes were spared from an Allied bomb that demolished the house just across the street a month before. Maria shuddered to think that Dietrich could have been killed that day. That he had been spared seemed like a sign to her that their future together was guaranteed now, despite the roadblocks her mother had put before them. A future with Dietrich—a home and children—was just one more happy thought to dispel the gloomy premonitions she had woken with.

Dinner was scheduled for 2 p.m. Maria arrived at 1:10 p.m. on the tram from her great-aunt's flat where she was staying temporarily while training to be a nurse. She had come early to share in some casual, relaxed conversation with Rüdy and Ursula while lending a hand in the kitchen. Dietrich would walk over to join them when dinner was ready.

The visit was pleasant enough, although the vague cloud of disquiet, which continually tried to penetrate her happy mood, prevented her from focusing on what they were chatting about. She felt as though she wasn't altogether there at the Schleichers'. She would much rather have been next door with Dietrich. She checked the time often to see when he would arrive.

While Rüdy began to set the dining room table, Maria joined Ursula in the kitchen. She stood by the stove from which the aroma of sautéing mushrooms emanated and filled the room. Maria put on an apron and began peeling the cooked beets. They continued their talk about small, inconsequential things as they worked: the difficulty in getting certain foods, news of Dietrich and Ursula's large family, how Maria was enjoying her training. When all was prepared, she and Ursula sat at the small breakfast table in the corner of the kitchen and continued their conversation while they waited for Dietrich. Slowly, Maria's undefined sense of foreboding began to evaporate like steam from the pot of boiled potatoes on the stove.

From their new vantage point, Ursula could see the clock on the kitchen wall. "My goodness, it's already after ten minutes past two. Little Brother has picked up the very un-German habit of being late. I noticed it after he returned from his year at that church in Barcelona in 1928."

Ursula called Dietrich "Little Brother" even though he had turned 37 years old in February.

"I'm sure he's nearing the end of a sentence or paragraph and doesn't want to lose his train of thought," Maria said in her fiancé's defense. "He's wrapping up his work and will be here shortly."

"I'd telephone over to the house myself to remind him, but I don't want to interrupt *Papa* and *Mütti's* midday nap," Ursula replied, getting up to stir the mushrooms again.

Just then, there was a knock at the back door.

"Who could that be knocking at the back door, not the front? Would you go see who it is, please, Maria?"

Eager to appear competent and helpful, despite how scattered she felt, Maria got up quickly and went to the door.

"Who is it?" Ursula shouted from the kitchen. Not bothering to wait for a reply, she came to look for herself.

Maria was both happy and startled by the sight of Dietrich standing on the threshold. Usually he entered his sister's house without the formality of a knock.

"Dietrich, dear, why are you just standing there like a beggar or a door-to-door salesman? Come on in, silly man," Maria said, gesturing for him to enter the kitchen.

"Dietrich, *Gott in Himmel,* you look as white as a clean sheet!" Ursula exclaimed. "I've never seen you like this."

Neither had Maria, she noticed, looking at him more closely. She had barely had ten months to become reacquainted with him, but she knew that it took a lot to rattle Dietrich. Whatever had caused him to appear so shaken must be serious.

She took his almost limp hand and led him through the kitchen to a chair at the table in the dining room where Rüdy was already seated. She sat down beside Dietrich and placed her hand on this forearm, offering her support no matter what had happened.

Looking up from his newspaper, Rüdy said playfully, "My, you look like you've just been hit by lightning or something, Dietrich. Funny, I haven't heard any thunder out there."

Dietrich was slowly starting to emerge from his catatonia. "Rüdy, my call-up orders came in this morning's mail. They were waiting for me on my desk when I got there." He spoke in a near-monotone, his eyes staring ahead almost blankly at the wall behind Rüdy.

"You hadn't been expecting them?" Rüdy asked, surprised.

"Actually, no. Hans said he'd take care of it all, that he would write a letter of explanation and get me an exemption." Dietrich avoided Maria's eyes; he knew what he would see there, and he couldn't bear the thought of falling from the pedestal he knew she had him on. He knew she would be confused and disappointed, and he was right. Though she said nothing out loud, her thoughts were in turmoil.

What? An exemption from serving the *Vaterland? Father and Max didn't get exemptions. Or seek them. In true German form, they obeyed when the Vaterland ordered. And it killed them.*

But this wasn't the time to pursue that line of thought. She knew that. She schooled her face and listened intently to what Dietrich was saying, hoping for an explanation that would make his distress at the thought of fighting for Germany understandable.

"That's why I picked up the telephone to call Hans right away, to see if he had any ideas," Dietrich continued.

Maria was having difficulty keeping up. "You mean your brother-in-law Hans, or some other Hans that I don't know?"

"Yes," Dietrich said, limiting his words, as usual lately, to the bare minimum of what needed to be said.

"And? What did Hans say?" Rüdy prompted.

"That's just it. No one at all answered my first attempt."

"Oh, Dietrich, Hans probably stepped out to retrieve something from the *Abwehr* office," Maria exclaimed. Surely Dietrich was making a mountain out of a molehill, she thought.

"I thought of that. But I was with Hans and our sister yesterday, and I swear he told me he was looking forward to working at home all day today."

There was a pause while Ursula, Rüdy, and Maria looked at one another to see if anyone understood why Dietrich was so concerned about no one answering a telephone. Maria could almost detect the waves of anxiety emanating from Dietrich's gut like radio signals. This was all so strange to her. Dietrich's apprehension seemed much greater than was called for.

"I tried again, and that time someone did answer," Dietrich continued. "But it wasn't Hans or Christel. It was a deep male voice that said, 'The von Dohnányi residence.' I hung up immediately."

This was beginning to feel like a mystery novel. Maria remembered her premonition. *Something bad is happening.*

"So, it turns out someone was home all along," Ursula offered in an effort to get dinner on the table.

"Ursel, I called Hans on his *private* line."

"I didn't know he even had such a thing as a private line."

"Ursel, just think. How can the Deputy *Kommandant* of the *Abwehr* discuss military intelligence matters on a regular telephone line that can be so easily compromised?" Dietrich paused to allow the question to hover in the air. Ursula seemed flummoxed. Maria was, too.

"Now, can anyone tell me why a total stranger should be in Hans and Christel's home, apparently without either of them being home, or able to come to the phone?"

Were the others experiencing the same feeling of dread, Maria wondered.

"Who do you think the voice belonged to, Dietrich?" Rüdy asked nervously.

"I can't say for sure. I didn't recognize the voice. But these days, who else would it be but the *SS* or *Gestapo*?"

"The *Gestapo*! *Mein Gott,* Dietrich!" Maria exclaimed uninhibitedly, raising her hand to her mouth in an expression of horror. "Why in heaven's name would the *Gestapo* be roaming about in Hans and Christel's house?"

Ursula looked inquisitively at her husband. Did he know more about this than she did? He maintained a stoic face, revealing little.

"I suspect they are rooting through their belongings looking for credible evidence that would stand up in their so-called 'courts,'" Rüdy answered.

"Evidence of what?" Maria questioned.

"For anything that ties Hans in any way to the recent failed attempts to kill Hitler."

"Kill Hitler! That seems rather drastic! It's doubtful, *isn't it,* that Hans would ever be involved in something like that?" She stressed the phrase "isn't it," looking for reassurance that no one in Dietrich's family—no one she knew—could be involved in something as dangerous as an attempt to kill the *Führer.*

"There are those who have concluded that killing Hitler is the best solution," Rüdy said slowly and solemnly.

Maria looked around quickly. It wasn't safe to talk about something so treasonous—even in the safety of one's home, was it?

"But doesn't Hans work for the *Abwehr*?" she continued. "I don't understand. Isn't he on the same side of this war as Hitler and the *Gestapo*?"

"Yes, in part, Maria. But I think the *Gestapo* suspects that Hans is buttering his bread on both sides of the slice."

This was out of Maria's league, and her face showed it. Dietrich was familiar with that look of confusion. He continued where his brother-in-law had left off. "It means that while he is working for the *Abwehr*, he's aiding the resistance at the same time."

"The resistance! That's dangerous, isn't it, Dietrich? It means the penalty of death if he's ever caught."

"Of course, Maria." Dietrich was always patient with Maria when she said the obvious—just one of the many reasons she loved him. "That's why I'm so anxious about the voice on the telephone. It threw me for a loop. Not to mention that I have a strong intuition that they will be coming to Marienburgerallee next. Very shortly, in fact."

"Here!" Ursula shouted, in panic, and her hand going to her face again. She looked at her husband, who was finally displaying some urgency on his face. "We love you, Little Brother, but don't get Rüdy and me mixed up with the *Gestapo*."

Maria made a mental note about Rüdy's expression. The *Gestapo* has the power to inspire such urgency in people. *Especially if you think you may have something to hide from them.* Rüdy, it was obvious, knew more than he was letting on about Hans's—and Dietrich's—business.

"No, not here, Ursel. They'll come next door," Dietrich answered.

"Surely, not to bother your parents! They cannot possibly be part of the resistance," Maria said wishfully. Was everyone she knew involved in some great plot of which she had been totally unaware? Maria's earlier feelings of dread were changing to a distinct feeling of falling down the rabbit hole.

"No, Maria," Rüdy said patiently, and clearly for her benefit. "I think Dietrich means that they are coming to inspect his room."

"Dietrich's room! "Maria's voice cracked in a high pitch, her fear in full view. Instinctively, she stepped away from Dietrich and raised her hand over her mouth, unconsciously mimicking Ursula's gesture.

"Dietrich, you see now just what *Papa* and *Mütti* and the rest of us have been fearing?" asked Ursula. At that moment, she sounded more like Dietrich's parent than his sister.

Dietrich nodded and closed his eyes in reluctant acknowledgment. Something told Maria, though, that only a part of him was really repentant.

"Ever since Hitler became Chancellor," Ursula continued, "you've been openly saying things that the *Gestapo* has taken notice of. That radio speech, the lectures at the university, at Finkenwalde, from the pulpit, anytime you have a chance."

"I couldn't remain silent on the sidelines."

"Dietrich, the family has been proud of you for taking a brave stand against the devil's disciple. But you don't seem to know when to keep silent—for your own sake or the sake of your family. I pray to God that you—that we—aren't being asked now to pay the price."

As though knowing his cue, Rüdy added the finish to his wife's point. "This regime considers anything that doesn't support or endorse all that it decrees and does to be treason, or at least the seeds of dissension. Any freedom of speech we've had disappeared a decade ago."

"In a way, you know, I'm not surprised by this," Dietrich interjected philosophically. "I've been expecting it. Hans and I have warned each other to be prepared. For the past few months, I've been stashing papers that could potentially give the *Gestapo* even the slightest cause to be suspicious of me into a file. Before I came over here, I added a few more papers to the file at the last minute. Then I burned it behind the forsythia bushes between the two houses and buried the ashes."

"Little Brother, are you sure you got everything and that you didn't leave anything to chance?" Ursula asked, once again in that older sister tone.

"Yes, Ursel, there's nothing left in my room that even the *Führer* himself would find incriminating. There are certain other files and documents, but Hans has taken care of them. He has hidden them in the safe of the library of the military post in Zossen."

Dietrich looked directly and reassuringly into Maria's eyes and said, "I placed the fake diary of my foreign travels plainly on my desk, as well as the last pages of the manuscript of *Ethics* I was working on today." He chuckled, "The *Gestapo* won't be able to make heads or tails of those, I assure you. They'll be convinced that I am no more than a run-of-the-mill theologian doing what those boring fellows do."

It was past 4 o'clock now, and dinner still hadn't been served. The whole group sat mum at the table, all talked out, exhausted from expending nervous energy. Suddenly, the elder Doctor Bonhöffer appeared, almost stealthily, in the room. He must have let himself in. He nodded his greeting and bowed toward his daughter but wasted no time on pleasantries before addressing Dietrich.

"Dietrich, there are two men at the house asking for you, from the *Gestapo* they told us. They are waiting in your room. *Mütti* is beside herself with fear. It's time to come home, son."

"*Mein Gott!* You must go, Dietrich," Ursula pleaded urgently, "lest they come here instead."

Dietrich stood up immediately, as Maria had seen him do whenever he received an order from his parents or his older sisters. Mechanically, he thanked Ursula and Rüdy for their hospitality, then turned to smile at Maria warmly and place his hand on her forearm.

"All will be well, Maria," he promised.

She wanted to believe him. He seemed so confident now that it was true, despite his obvious distress earlier in the afternoon. Was he just saying this for her benefit? *If he believes that, then I will choose to do so as well.*

As Dietrich and his father opened the door to leave, Maria darted impulsively toward it. "I'm coming with you, Dietrich!"

Rüdy caught her firmly, almost painfully, by the arm before she could get through the door. He shook her. "We understand, Maria, why you wish to accompany him. But you will be able to help Dietrich more if you are not in the custody of the *Gestapo,* too."

Tears of frustration rolled down her cheeks, but she saw the sense of Rüdy's words and fell back, away from the door, leaning on him for support.

Dietrich and his father walked quickly out of sight. They heard the barking of the neighbors' German shepherds as they stood, stunned, in the doorway, beyond speech. *Dietrich arrested by the Gestapo? How unreal. Beyond belief or comprehension. Could this be happening?*

Suddenly, as though each of them had the thought at the same time, they ran almost in unison to the kitchen window and watched in silence as the two men strode across the lawn to Marienburgerallee 42. Maria began to tremble as though chilled. Ursula kindly put one arm around her and squeezed her comfortingly. She lifted her hand to her lips and tenderly kissed it. Maria was overcome by fear and utter disbelief, but the trembling subsided. She would never forget how bravely and with what aristocratic dignity father and son walked homeward together across the lawn, their heads raised high almost defiantly, their posture erect. She would try to be as brave.

They heard no news by telephone from Dietrich's parents' house. They took turns serving as a sentry at the windows. Maria was the first to spot activity next door about fifty minutes later. "I see movement next door!" she exclaimed.

The others rushed to their posts at the windows. In the gathering dusk, Maria caught a glimpse of Dietrich being led away from his parents' home into a waiting black limousine. *God, they had his hands in handcuffs! As though he were just a common criminal!*

It was a scene she would never forget. Ursula drew their attention to the backseat window as the car proceeded slowly down the driveway toward the street. There was Dietrich, trying valiantly to smile, struggling to lift his shackled hands in greeting in the direction of his parents who waved tearfully from the rear veranda of their house. It was a scene too sad for words. The neighbors' German shepherds were roused again by the bright headlights of the car violating the block's darkness and silence and barked their angry protest.

"A black Mercedes, the official vehicle of *Gestapo* brass. I just pray that they aren't taking him to that hellhole of a prison of theirs in the God-forsaken basement of Number 8 *Prinz Albrecht Strasse*," said Rüdy.

That struck a deeper chord of fear in Maria. Perhaps Rüdy didn't intend for her to hear it. But she trusted that she would eventually learn what he meant by the remark. What was this place he spoke of? For now, her uncontrollable trembling returned. She wondered if Dietrich would ever see the inside of either house again. She also wondered when he and she would see each other again—or, for that matter, if.

Chapter Two

Silence in the face of evil is evil itself.

—Dietrich Bonhöffer

Ten years earlier
Pätzig: 1933

Hans von Wedemeyer surprised his younger daughter by calling to her after dinner while she was in the kitchen, helping to clean up.

"Maria, dear. Can you come to the parlor for a few minutes?"

"Right now, Papa? I'm helping Ruth-Alice clean up after dinner. I'm up to my elbows in soapy water, as Inge is fond of saying."

"Now, Mia, if you would, please."

Maria glanced over at her older sister who had been gathering the dinner dishes on the counter next to the sink for Maria to place gently into the water in the sink to wash. Ruth-Alice looked back at Maria, shrugged reluctantly, and nodded in agreement.

"You'd better go, Mia. I can pick up here where you left off," she said in a voice that made it clear she was not happy about having to finish the dishes so soon after the task has been assigned to Maria by their mother, but their father's orders took precedence. Her mother had reckoned that having turned nine years old, Maria was now ready to assume some of the women's household duties. Their servant, Inge, who usually did the dishes, was enjoying a free evening on Friday, her only one of the week.

Maria entered the parlor where her father stood by the family's new radio on the mantle of the fireplace, his left arm resting on the rounded edge of the mantle. He turned and started fiddling with the knobs on the *Telefunken,* turning one slowly to the left and then to the right until he was satisfied that he had set it accurately to the station he wanted.

"There's going to be a lecture on the radio in a few minutes that I'd like you to hear." He nodded his head toward the sofa in the center of the parlor, a silent command to sit there.

A lecture? Maria was dumbfounded. Would a lecture be understandable to a nine-year-old? Her father hadn't invited Ruth-

Alice, four years older than she, into the parlor to hear the lecture, only Maria. Then again, this was not new. Her father took great delight in exposing Maria to new ideas and experiences, and she was open to them. He had taught her to ride horses several years ago and to care for them afterward. Her mother, also named Ruth, thought Maria was too young for that. Hans gave Maria a book of poems by Rainer Maria Rilke. Maria didn't think any of her friends had such a book on their bookshelf. When her friends came to the von Wedemeyer home to play *Kätz und Maus*, Hans could see that as hard as Maria may be trying not to show it to her friends, this game was too easy for her. Later he introduced her to more advanced games, sometimes even ones that usually only the grown-ups played, such as *Doppelkopf.*

Maria and her father adored each other.

"Despite the change in the radio service in the last couple of days," her father explained, "I'm relieved that the *Reichsradio* and Doctor Göbbels will continue the tradition of the informative and uplifting Friday evening lectures. Dr. Göbbels is interested in promoting anything that elevates the minds of Germans, or at least so he says."

"What's the subject tonight, Papa?" Maria asked.

"The schedule in the newspaper says the speaker will be a young professor from Berlin University. He's also a pastor, only 26 years old. His name is Bonhöffer."

Maria had never heard a university lecture before. She was a little nervous about letting her father down. But, she thought, if her father had invited her to hear it, he must have a good reason. He must be confident that she would understand.

"Bonhöffer?" the girl asked. "If you put the French part of his name with the German, it means 'hope life is good,' correct?"

Her father smiled at his daughter approvingly. He had never thought of that. Maria had a proud, self-satisfied glint in her eye.

"That's mighty clever, Mia. I am hoping that tonight especially we hear someone who hopes for good, for the best, in fact."

"What do you mean, Papa?" she asked.

"Shh," he ordered, placing his index finger over his lips. "Let's listen and talk after the lecture."

A deep, terse male voice came on the air to welcome listeners to the program. Without giving any of the usual information about the speaker other than his name and academic title, he passed the microphone to the invisible Bonhöffer.

The speaker began his address in a higher-pitched voice than Maria was expecting of a university lecturer. It sounded to her more like a girl's voice.

"Good evening, Germany. The title of my lecture this evening is 'The *Führer* Principle: The Younger Generation's Altered Concept of Leadership.'"

In spite of his own desire for silence during the lecture, her father said to her, "You are part of the younger generation, too, Mia. That's why I thought it might be good for you to hear this."

Professor Bonhöffer continued. "The War and the subsequent near-collapse of the German economy in the decades since have brought about crises in which the average citizen has lost all confidence in the government such as it was. That is particularly true of my own generation."

Maria interrupted. "Papa, he says 'of my own generation.' I'm not really of his generation, am I?"

"Just be patient, Mia," he responded, although she sensed he was impatient with her interruption. "He may be one of those speakers who anticipates what the future might be for the generation after his, your generation."

Her father was always concerned about "the next generation."

She added, "Some of the other children at school say that *Herr* Hitler is like that." She wanted to give him the impression that she had some familiarity with this topic.

Her father looked at her but didn't say a word. He just nodded his head toward the radio, suggesting for her to be silent again and just listen.

Bonhöffer continued. "It seems to me and to many informed observers of the situation in Germany that since the Great War, Germany's concept of a leader has evolved so that a leader is one who submits to no one and as such is seen as the 'anointed one.' I ask, are the German people leaning so heavily on our political and military leaders to rescue us from the financial chaos and political confusion of the present time? Are we willing to surrender our freedom, to renounce our newly adopted democracy? Will we abdicate our responsibility as free citizens to shape our own future? Or are we allowing ourselves to become dependent on a strong individual, or a party of individuals, to make sense of the chaos and make our decisions for us?

"Even if a leader is selected by the people," Bonhöffer continued, "he needs to know that the voice of the people can be fickle. The *vox populi* is not necessarily always the *vox Dei*."

The look on his daughter's face indicated to Hans that she was puzzled so he explained kindly. "I think the speaker means that the preferences of the people do not always reflect the preferences of God."

Bonhöffer's voice kept on. "There have been leaders in our nation and others who declare themselves before the masses to be one of them. But they are actually despisers of humanity. All the while, such a leader praises himself with repulsive vanity and despises the rights of every individual. He considers them weak and pliable. The more he seeks the favor of those whom deep down he actually despises, the more he rouses the masses to declare him a god. This is how such a nation becomes a tyranny."

Maria noticed her father nodding his head slowly in agreement.

"The real leader must know the limitations of his power," the speaker picked up where he had left off. "He would be misusing his office if he does not continually tell his followers quite clearly about his limited nature and wisdom and of their responsibility as the people. If he allows himself to pander to the wishes of his followers, they would make him their idol. They surrender their own power to augment his. They relinquish to him their independent judgment. Then the image of their leader will evolve into the image of a misleader. He will be acting in a criminal way, not only towards those he leads but also against God, who is the Ultimate Authority before whom all penultimate authorities are accountable. This is what is called 'The *Führer* Principle.'"

"Papa, what does that word the 'penultimate' mean?" she asked hesitantly. She would have preferred to show her father that she understood completely.

She actually had been thinking about a certain girl at school, the one who loved Hitler so much. She wore such nice dresses, Maria thought, and even after recess her blond pigtails were still in place, unlike Maria's own. Suddenly, Maria heard Pastor Bonhöffer pause to take a breath. She became aware that she'd been letting her mind wander during this part of the broadcast.

"What does what the man is saying have to do with us, Papa?" she asked, hoping her father hadn't noticed her distraction.

Her father thought for a while before saying, "I fear for the future that you and Ruth-Alice and Max are inheriting."

Now she looked a little concerned. "Fear" was not a word she heard Hans utter very often. "Fear?"

"Yes, I admit to having some fear. Or maybe it's more regret about what we Germans may be allowing to happen. I know you won't understand this completely now, and I sincerely hope I am wrong."

"You mean that we are already allowing what this speaker fears to be happening?" she asked. She knew her father thought things through carefully. Many times she had found him to be right about something that many others, sometimes even her mother, thought wrong. "That we are following what he calls a 'misleader'?"

"We can't know for sure, of course. No one can know the future perfectly. But this man, Dr. Bonhöffer, makes sense to me."

The speaker wasn't finished. "The current danger, I humbly fear, is that we forget that man stands alone before the Ultimate Authority, and that a leader who lays an unjust hand on any of his subjects to bolster his own power is infringing on eternal law and taking upon himself superhuman authority. This will, I believe, eventually crush him and his people. He sets himself as a god that mocks God. If Germany yields to the temptation of worshiping a Messianic leader, it would be incinerating its own future as a free people."

Suddenly the radio went mute. There were a few initial moments of crackling static, then total silence except for the hiss of the radio itself. The voice was gone. Hans tried to adjust the volume button on the radio, but it was no use. He gave up, sighed, and plopped down on the wing chair opposite Maria. It was his turn to look confused.

"Why did the man stop speaking, Papa?"

"I wonder that myself, Mia. I don't think it was by his own volition. I hope it's not what the darker part of me suspects."

Maria wondered what he meant by "the darker part." Did he mean the part of him that thought evil thoughts, that was instinctively suspicious of others? Or was it the part of himself he didn't like? If so, Maria was beginning to recognize that she had a side like that, too.

"What do you suspect, Papa?"

"Oh, various things. Maybe that some technician at the radio station accidentally pressed the wrong button that cut off the broadcast. It may be something as simple and innocent as that. Or possibly that *Herr* Göbbels was listening at home, decided he didn't think the speech was 'elevating the minds of the German people,' and called the station to order one of his men to terminate the broadcast."

"Should I also fear, Papa?" the girl asked in all earnestness.

"Perhaps not fear, Mia. Nine-year-old girls should not spend their precious days of childhood being afraid. But I'd advise you not to stop thinking for yourself. Inspiring fear in a person can only succeed if we allow ourselves to be afraid."

Chapter Three

The world exercises dominion by force and Christ and his disciples conquer by service.

—Dietrich Bonhöffer,

Köslin: June 1935

This was the morning the von Wedemeyers had been waiting for. Nevertheless, on this morning, Ruth-Alice had to come and wake Maria from sleep and coax her out of bed.

"Get up, you sleepyhead. *Papa* and Max have already left for the church. The rest of the family is waiting on you."

Maria stirred reluctantly. She had known she shouldn't have stayed up so late, that it would be difficult to wake up and get going in the morning. Ruth-Alice had warned her this would happen. She wished that her older sister was less self-righteous and overbearing about things. But she had to acknowledge her own culpability this time. She just couldn't resist staying up late. Several generations of the von Wedemeyers were together under one roof for the first time since Christmas. They were having such a good time singing and laughing and kidding Max about the new suit—his first one—that he would have to wear for his Confirmation that morning. Maria had enjoyed watching her older brother squirm under the bright family spotlight.

The von Wedemeyer family had all come south to spend the night at Maria's grandmother's estate near Köslin. She had moved here after her husband, *Opa*, Maria's grandfather, died. The old, larger estate near Kieckow had become too much for her to oversee alone. Maria's father Hans ran that estate now while in his absence; Maria's mother, Ruth-Alice, and Max oversaw the operations at their own farm near Pätzig almost 300 kilometers to the north.

Maria's grandmother was formally known to the rest of her region of Pomerania as *Frau* Ruth von Kleist-Retzow, but to the von Wedemeyer children, she was just their mother's mother, their *Oma*. All agreed that she was a remarkably strong-minded woman. Even before her husband died, she was the hub of the extended family. When the von Wedemeyer children were younger and their mother had more than enough on her hands supervising the farmhands, taking inventory, arranging for the sale of their crops, and paying the bills on top of raising her children, *Frau* von Kleist-Retzow would invite her grandchildren to come down on their own to the Köslin estate for a large part of each summer. They enjoyed playing in the fresh air and taking trips with *Oma* into Stettin to shop or see a play or visit the library. Ruth-Alice, being the oldest, was given the task of babysitting Max and Maria, but they were so glad to be at their indulgent *Oma's* that there was little motivation for them to misbehave. They wanted to be invited back.

 Frau von Kleist-Retzow would send Max back home to Pätzig each July to help bring in the hay. One summer, Ruth-Alice developed a crush on the young man, just a boy then, who would eventually become her husband. She was often out on Saturdays with him, his older sister as a chaperone. Maria remembered those as the best summer Saturdays. She had her *Oma* all to herself. She would take Maria onto her lap and read her books from her family library. When Maria grew sleepy, her grandmother put her arms around Maria and squeezed her and spoke affectionate words into her ears, making Maria laugh. When Maria had herself learned to read—truly a landmark day in her life when the world opened up to her—Maria would read to her grandmother. Her *Oma* kiddingly pretended to sit on Maria's lap and laughed heartily when Maria protested.

 On many summer Sunday mornings, *Frau* von Kleist-Retzow also took her grandchildren in tow to worship. Max, of course, would rather have stayed at the estate. But Maria went willingly. Most girls her age weren't particularly excited about having to go to church unless they had a new dress to show off. Maria couldn't honestly claim that "excitement" was the proper word to describe her feelings but it was another opportunity to be with her *Oma* and be part of what *Oma* considered important. Maria went along like an eager and grateful granddaughter.

 Maria particularly enjoyed worshiping now that they no longer attended the large church in the center of Stettin, where the imposing Pastor Bühler, a thoroughly toe-the-line pastor in the *Reichskirche*, or National Church, preached.

When Hitler was named Chancellor, he wanted to unify all the various independent Protestant church bodies, which included the majority Lutherans and the Reformed. Protestants had dreamed of just such a tangible sign of Christian unity for decades. The Chancellor convinced the Protestant leaders to agree to write a new constitution for a unified National Church, the *Reichskirche,* or "Church of the Third Reich." A small faction of Lutherans, however, was suspicious of the Nazis' motives. They resisted Hitler's thinly veiled plan to have at his party's disposal a compliant church body that would further his political and military aims. The clergy and lay leaders of this movement within the larger church formed a new Lutheran church body named the Confessing Church. Their aim was not as much political resistance to the Nazi regime for its own sake as it was to advocate for the total and absolute separation of church and government.

Meanwhile, the *Reichskirche* moved ever closer to the government and accommodated to many of the political policies of the Nazi party. The *Reichskirche* and Confessing Church were both *evangelisch*, or Lutheran. The Confessing Church decided that it needed to train its own pastors and no longer rely on university theological faculties. Any professor appearing to question the Nazi government in even the slightest way had already either been warned or relieved of his position, even if tenured. The Confessing Church established one of its seminaries to train pastors near the village of Finkenwalde. The Confessing Church chose rural locations where the seminaries would be off the beaten track and could operate in a low-key, semi-covert manner.

During the brief train ride from Köslin, *Frau* von Kleist-Retzow informed Maria that the name of the pastor who had been Max's confirmation instructor was Bonhöffer. Maria felt her face flush unexpectedly as she heard his name.

"What a small world!" she uttered elatedly. She recognized the name as that of the young pastor who just a little over two years prior had given the infamous radio lecture on the "*Führer* Principle," which was rudely cut off somehow in mid-sentence. Since then, there had been a lot of speculation as to what happened and why and how the speech was cut short, especially among the Confessing Church leaders. However, *Frau* von Kleist-Retzow said that nobody, not even

Dr. Bonhöffer apparently, knew the real reason.

Hitler had been Chancellor for just two whole days on the evening when Dr. Bonhöffer gave the lecture. Hitler wasn't addressed as *Führer* yet at that time. The German people, and even the Nazi officials, didn't start calling him by that title until the next summer when the ailing President von Hindenburg handed over the presidency to Hitler. From that day forward, Hitler demanded to be addressed as *Der Führer*.

Maria remarked to her grandmother, "*Papa* and I often talk about that lecture even though it was two years ago, and I was only nine years old. Wasn't it amazing how accurately Dr. Bonhöffer was able to tell the future? Was he talking about *Herr* Hitler in that speech, *Oma*?"

"Pastor Bonhöffer claims to have written the lecture several years before *Herr* Hitler became Chancellor and was called *Der Führer*," her grandmother informed her. "But I wouldn't be surprised if Pastor Bonhöffer was able to put two and two together and predict where Hitler was headed. I doubt he was shocked when Hitler combined the two offices of President and Chancellor."

Hearing that, Maria marveled even more at Dr. Bonhöffer's courage in that lecture—or was it foolhardiness, as her *Mütti* said?—to speak so openly.

Frau von Kleist-Retzow was a great supporter of the Confessing Church and particularly of Pastor Bonhöffer, with whom she had talked many times. The seminary had attempted a start the previous year in an abandoned schoolhouse in Zingst on the Baltic shore. They found the facility too small. Always willing to help the Confessing Church, especially when asked by Pastor Bonhöffer, *Frau* von Kleist-Retzow granted permission for the seminary community to be housed in the old vacant manor house beyond Kiekow. The estate, no longer active, had been owned by *Oma's* grandfather. In just a few months, the brothers had done a wonderful job of making repairs and restoring the dark, drafty old relic into a home for themselves. Maria remembered wandering over to explore the abandoned manor house and barns with Max years ago. They had found a set of stairs that led to the attic, which still held boxes that seemed never to have been opened. It was still novel and disorienting to her to think that now, just a few short years later, Max was about to be confirmed in that same old repurposed house.

At Finkenwalde, the worship service was not held in a traditional church building, but in the makeshift worship space—the dining room of the new seminary.

The majority of the congregation on a regular Sunday morning at Finkenwalde consisted of what were called "the brothers." These were the young seminarians who lived and studied in the house. But this day was no ordinary Sunday, especially for *Frau* Von Kleist-Retzow and the entire von Wedemeyer family. A young blond-haired boy led the small procession toward the makeshift chancel at the front through the center aisle between the rows of rather uncomfortable wooden folding chairs. He held up a large rustic wooden cross as he processed slowly and deliberately. He looked anxious. The congregation seemed to hold their collective breath and hope that the poor boy wouldn't drop the cross that was taller than he was.

Max and another boy followed the one girl in the procession of confirmands. The girl looked so self-assured and grown up in a delicate white dress that her mother or grandmother had probably made from scratch.

Maria felt a quiver of envy for this girl. Maria was probably two years younger but felt she was ready to be a grown-up in certain respects. Maria wished that, like this girl, she could free her locks from their little girl braids, wear them curled, wrap her body in a beautiful dress, and be a young lady.

Max looked stiff in his new suit, as though the starch from his white dress shirt had somehow penetrated his skin and made it inflexible. The collar of his suit jacket was folded up. Maria was sure that *Mütti* and Ruth-Alice were wondering in unison what they should do: stand up and approach Max in his pew and turn down the collar before the hymn was finished, or just let it be and hope that not many others in the congregation could see it. Maria looked over at her *Oma* and saw the glint of joy in her eyes. She was not going to allow an insignificant wardrobe faux pas detract from her gratitude and gladness at her grandson's becoming an adult member of the church, particularly this church.

The rear of the procession was brought up by Pastor Bonhöffer. Maria had been warned by her grandmother that in this community he did not want to be addressed as Doctor Bonhöffer. Rather, he instructed the seminarians and others to call him *Pfarrer* Bonhöffer, because that was his role here, Pastor. His tall, slightly rotund body was enveloped in a black gown with two bands of white cloth connected to his collar like all Protestant pastors in Germany.

He processed up the center aisle, his body erect, holding his hymnbook directly in front of him. He boomed rather than sang the verses of the hymn, as though he was truly confident of the truth of the lyrics. The corners of his mouth were raised slightly, giving the impression of a permanent smile. His light brown hair was thinning at the top of his head. Yet, for a scholarly clergyman, Maria judged him surprisingly handsome, not in the style of a Max Schmeling, the celebrated German boxer, but in a cute, playful sort of way. Maria muffled a chuckle as she pictured him on the floor of a parlor playing with little children and making them laugh. She couldn't imagine Pastor Bühler ever doing that.

Maria remembered that her father had said Pastor Bonhöffer was 26 years old the night they heard him give his lecture on the radio. That made him 28 years old now; rather old, Maria thought—much older than Ruth-Alice and not much younger than her mother, in fact.

When Maria had listened with her father to the radio lecture two years prior, she had tried to imagine what the man with the high-pitched voice looked like. She hadn't expected to ever see him in person. He looked rather different than she had imagined. She hadn't visualized the slightly balding head, nor the thick lenses of his eyeglasses. He looked more vulnerable somehow than the courageous outspoken man she had heard on the radio. She had pictured a less stocky figure than the one at the end of this procession, someone more heroic-looking, maybe like Charles Lindbergh or the dashing young Prince of Wales whose photos she had seen in magazines.

Maria was so lost in her internal musings that she practically missed the first part of the service as the congregation rose when Pastor Bonhöffer went to the lectern to read the gospel lesson.

"The Holy Gospel according to St. Matthew, the fifth chapter," he intoned. His voice sounded even more authoritative than two years ago on the radio. Though the pitch was still rather high, he came close to reverberating throughout the room, demanding attention.

"You are the salt of the earth," he read, pausing and looking directly at the confirmands in the first row of chairs. He wanted their attention especially.

"But if salt has lost its taste, how can its saltiness be restored? It is no longer good for anything but is thrown out and trampled underfoot."

He paused the reading once again, looking out over his congregation. His voice was not accusatory like Pastor Bühler's. Maria found it more probing; his pause asked his people to ponder if their own saltiness had been lost.

"You are the light of the world. A city built on a hill cannot be hid…" He closed his eyes, and once they opened again his gaze rose from the page and was aimed directly at the rows of chairs occupied by the seminarians. Their eyes were focused intently on him. They probably knew the rest of the verse but they waited mutely for Pastor Bonhöffer to pronounce the words. Perhaps they thought they were more meaningful and powerful when he spoke them. "Let your light shine before others that they may see your good works and give glory to your Father in heaven."

He shut the large Bible on the lectern and closed his eyes again, this time to invite the congregants to pray with him. "May the words of my mouth and the meditations of all our hearts be acceptable in thy sight, O Lord, our Rock, and Our Redeemer."

Oma's eyes were fixed intently on the pastor. Most members of the congregation straightened their posture in their chair and kept their eyes looking straight ahead as though they were expecting some momentous pronouncement. Only the three confirmands' attention and focus seemed to be elsewhere, or perhaps nowhere in particular. Yet, Pastor Bonhöffer's first words were addressed to them. He turned his head toward them again. They lifted up their eyes as if ordered to attention.

"Dear Confirmands. You remember from our study together that Jesus' command at the end of Matthew's gospel is that those who wish to follow him are to go out into the world to make disciples—students, learners, devotees, followers—not church members, not people who occupy a church pew as an audience that watches a pastor or priest, or who take for granted the gifts of grace God has given in Christ. The Creator does not need more passive observers; He needs productive workers in the vineyard, active participants in the re-creation of the world."

He paused for what seemed like minutes. The confirmands looked very self-conscious.

"Jesus' words to us today from Matthew's gospel are very sobering. Confirmands, imagine! To be called the salt of the earth and the light of the world! What could be more important? To be told that your identity as newly formed disciples is to be two substances that are absolutely essential to the world!

"Jesus is saying that as his disciples you are that important. You along with your brothers and sisters in Christ are charged to be the conduit by which God's saving, preserving love and power will sustain the world from all that seeks to destroy it.

"It is precisely you that, as part of the community of Christ called the church, are anointed today to let your good works of love and forgiveness, kindness and justice, to shine as a beacon to show the way through the present darkness to a world that seems hopelessly lost."

He never took his eyes off the three of them. He didn't seem to look down at his notes. His words, and the way he spoke them, were so compelling, so sincere, so urgent.

Maria wondered what he meant by "this present darkness" and "a world that seems hopelessly lost." As though he anticipated Maria's question, he continued. "The faith in Christ you profess today in church will be tested, I warn you. The salt within you will lose its flavor out in the world; the light within you will fade.

"You will discover that though you will be tempted by Satan to serve two masters, you will be able to serve only one. From this day forward you have only one Lord, one Master, Jesus Christ, who is the Lord of the world. But there will be other lords, other masters, who make false claims, who not only try to entice your service and loyalty but will demand and command them. It is possible that they will threaten you with suffering, loneliness, and perhaps violence, until you surrender your loyalty and commitment to the command and holy example of the Lord you choose this day to follow and obey."

The pastor's round face looked sad, worried.

"To serve this Lord as his disciple, and this Lord only, is the highest honor. In his service is the greatest freedom. But, be aware that to your Yes to this Lord belongs an equally clear No to others. Your Yes to this Master demands your No to all injustice, all evil, all lies no matter how high their source, all oppression no matter who it is that is being oppressed, to all violation of the defenseless and the poor, no matter who is doing the violating."

Maria remembered how just a few months after Pastor Bonhöffer's radio lecture, her father had come home to Pätzig from the Kieckow estate in a very strange and sad mood. He didn't greet his children with laughter and hugs and kisses when he arrived as he usually did. He was unusually quiet and taciturn over dinner. His wife broke the silence by asking him if something was wrong at the estate. He continued to chew his food silently. It was as though he didn't hear her question. But he was just pondering how he should answer. The children all put down their knives and forks in nervous anticipation of his answer.

"Wasn't the order to boycott Jewish businesses already causing the Jews enough sorrow and suffering? Now Himmler has ordered his brutes in the *SS* to beat up any Gentile who is caught violating the boycott, and arrest or shoot on the spot any Jewish business owner who dares to sell anything to a Gentile."

Maria thought she heard his voice quavering. "They beat two farmers from Answalde to mincemeat yesterday and took the farm supply merchant Mondschein—you know, the old man on the Bergdorf road—in shackles to who knows where."

Hans von Wedemeyer's strong voice barely succeeded in holding back tears. They were tears of sadness and sympathy, Maria thought, or perhaps anger, too.

Maria wondered, was this what Pastor Bonhöffer had been referring to when he said, "violation of the defenseless?" That we should say no to something like this even if the ones doing the violating are dressed in police uniforms we've been taught to obey and respect?

Pastor Bonhöffer turned his face to the confirmands again. "Dear confirmands, do you understand what is at stake in your profession of loyalty to your Lord you will make today?"

He paused as if to conclude the sermon, or perhaps let the question linger in the room. The wooden chairs made crackling sounds as members of the congregation tried to adjust their sitting position. "Are you prepared to pay the cost of discipleship?"

Maria swallowed hard in anticipation.

"And you, dear parents, grandparents, godparents, neighbors of these young disciples, do you understand what is at stake in your own discipleship of the Prince of Peace?

"May God grant us the courage to follow him and to endure all that may lie ahead. Amen."

After the service, *Frau* von Kleist-Retzow was teary-eyed from gratitude and pride as she greeted and shook hands with Pastor Bonhöffer.

"Pastor Bonhöffer, you will come and join us for a family celebration at Köslin, will you not?"

Maria was overjoyed to overhear the invitation. Shortly after the family arrived at the estate, Pastor Bonhöffer rode up the drive to the house on a motorcycle. Maria looked quizzically at Max. Max returned her glance and shrugged his shoulders.

After a generous dinner, all retreated into *Oma's* garden for more conversation. Magda, *Oma's* kitchen help, carried out a tray of little glasses filled with *Schnapps* and offered a glass to all, including, Maria noted, to Max, who still in his white dress shirt and tie looked taller to Maria, more grown up. He sat between Ruth-Alice and his *Mütti*. His grandmother sat down between their mother and the pastor. Their father took the chair beside Maria's.

Maria was grateful that her father had chosen that particular chair. She was also pleased to have Pastor Bonhöffer sitting directly opposite her where she could glance at him from time to time. She hoped that he would sneak a furtive glance over at her as well.

"The second of my grandchildren to be confirmed, but the very first at Finkenwalde," the lady of the manor remarked with obvious pride.

"I suspect we have you to thank for that and all the material assistance from your neighbors, *Frau*, do we not? You didn't break any arms in persuading them to help, did you?"

The family joined in unison in loving laughter. *Frau* von Kleist-Retzow's face displayed a slightly self-deprecating smile.

"Good Pastor," *Oma* replied shyly, "it's just that we are so grateful to have your new community nearby in the forgotten wilds of Pomerania. We hope that you and the brothers and the Confessing Church will bring positive changes in the church."

"All over Germany, for that matter, Pastor," Hans added

enthusiastically.

Maria wanted to step in and ask her *Oma* what things in the church she would like changed. But *Oma* had more to say. "Even my son-in-law here has started to come back to the church since Finkenwalde opened and you started inviting your neighbors to join the brothers for worship there."

Maria's father's face was beginning to turn red. He was embarrassed by her remark. Maria, looking over at Pastor Bonhöffer, was a little uneasy, too, on her father's behalf. She moved her eyes and focused on a spot in the concrete on the ground. She was surprised at the frankness with which her grandmother commented on her father's erratic church attendance patterns in a pastor's hearing.

"Hans has said that you, Pastor Bonhöffer, are the only clergyman he trusts enough to listen to, haven't you, Hans?"

More embarrassment. Parents and grandparents and mothers-in-law seem to be experts at doing that.

"They need to make more like him," Hans said.

Maria's face registered eager agreement.

"That's what he's endeavoring to do at Finkenwalde, Hans," *Oma* said.

Hans still seemed to be feeling awkward with all the attention so he turned to Pastor Bonhöffer and asked, "So, Pastor, do you always travel on your motorcycle?"

"Much of the time, *Herr* von Wedemeyer. Once I made the original investment in it, travel with it is very inexpensive, especially here on the Pomeranian plains."

"It must be a fast and powerful machine, Pastor. I was afraid you would beat the host family back to the manor today."

"I've been all over Europe on that cycle," the pastor said. "At least those parts where you don't need to cross big bodies of water. I purchased it when I was a vicar in Barcelona."

"From what I've read, they may be preparing for civil war in Spain. Is that true?" Hans asked.

"That would be a tragedy. It could destroy one of the most beautiful countries in Europe," Pastor Bonhöffer replied.

Maria thought that this pastor seemed so adventurous, so worldly-wise. To have been to Spain and other exotic faraway places! In a sermon once he had mentioned his time as a pastor in cozy

England. He often mentioned friends he made as a student in New York.

"New York!" Maria exclaimed in the privacy of her own thoughts. She hadn't even seen much of northern Germany beyond Stettin and Pätzig. She wished someday to go see faraway places for herself. She was sure she would.

Hans pursued the conversation. "It appears our *Führer* is thinking along the same lines. Of war, I mean."

"I'm certainly no fan of the Versailles Treaty," Pastor Bonhöffer said. "Germany was treated very unfairly. But the *Führer* does seem intent on undoing it somehow, even through war if necessary. Or, perhaps more correctly put, especially through war, necessary or not. I doubt that yet another war so soon after the last one will solve anything, don't you, *Herr* von Wedemeyer?"

"I saw enough pointless suffering in the Great War."

His wife flashed a look of disapproval in Hans's direction. She obviously didn't want a conversation about the *Führer*. *Mütti* understood that *Oma* had a strong dissenting view of the *Führer*, and she wanted above all to avoid a contentious family debate to dampen the joy of celebration on Max's big day.

Papa comprehended the silent message. He changed the subject. "Thank you for your confirmation instruction for our Max, Pastor." He glanced briefly in his wife's direction, and then at his mother-in-law's, before continuing, as though for their permission. "Would you do us the same courtesy by giving instruction to Maria?"

Maria had been listening to the conversation intently. As her name was uttered without warning, she became flustered and felt like a little girl. The von Wedemeyers had never discussed the matter of her confirmation instruction before as a family. It seemed to her rather strange for her father to bring up the subject with special company. But she was excited by the prospect.

"Well, I'm always eager to shape new disciples," Pastor Bonhöffer replied, looking a little taken aback by this request, but he didn't seem to miss a beat. He looked in Maria's direction across the space between them. She sat up straight in her chair with her hands folded in her lap as though she was about to be interrogated. She earnestly hoped she wouldn't disappoint him.

"Let me ask," Pastor Bonhöffer began, "How old are you, Maria?"

"I am 11 years old," she boasted, then suddenly felt inadequate and small.

"Well, that's still very young. Perhaps we ought to wait at least another year. A young person needs time to make her decision about entering the process of initiation into the faith."

The suddenly disagreeable look on Maria's young face betrayed her disappointment. It was as though she was taking an examination, a test for his acceptance and approval of her. She suddenly became aware of how much she coveted that.

"But, Pastor Bonhöffer, I—"

Her grandmother cut her off.

"Now, now, Maria. We must go by the schedule the pastor suggests."

Pastor Bonhöffer turned to Maria. "Well, let me ask you, Maria, do you think you are ready to explore becoming a disciple of Jesus?"

"I believe so. I am a good student at school, and I enjoy learning," she added hopefully.

"That's exemplary, Maria. There's nothing I liked more as a youth than school and learning. That's still the case, in fact. But learning to follow Jesus is a different kind of learning than what we learn in school. It's more like training for an athletic contest."

Maria's visage revealed that she was even more let down by his response. She pulled back her hands on her lap as though she had just been rapped over the knuckles for giving an incorrect answer.

Hans entered the conversation again. "We understand, Pastor. There's really no hurry."

Maria's body was animated by her hope and adrenaline. She sat on the edge of her chair and was on the cusp of protesting, "Yes, there is a hurry," but held her tongue and sat back deeper from the edge in her chair. She asked herself whether her sense of urgency was more about letting the enticing opportunity pass to be alone with Pastor Bonhöffer than about the process of confirmation itself.

Her grandmother interjected, "As long, Pastor, as you don't leave here this afternoon without making a solemn promise that our Maria will receive her instruction from you whenever you think the time is right."

Pastor Bonhöffer seemed a little taken aback by *Frau* von Kleist-Retzow's insistence. He thought for a half-minute or so before responding. Maria's eyes grew bigger with hope at the possibility that

Pastor Bonhöffer might still be persuaded to change his mind.

"Well, *Frau*, I think I can promise at least that much. When she is ready, I would be honored to give instruction to a young lady from such a Christ-centered family as this."

Maria gave a wide satisfied smile. She sensed she had won a victory—not a victory over Pastor Bonhöffer, but over all the people who called her a little girl and wanted her to stay that way. He had called her a young lady! No one else called her that unless they were angry with her. His agreement to make such a promise felt almost like a sacred commitment. She wondered if this is what they meant when a man and woman say to each other at their wedding, "I pledge thee my troth."

Chapter Four

Dietrich arrived with an open gash in his soul.

—Maria von Wedemeyer

Köslin: December 1937

Finkenwalde was no more! Gone so suddenly. So sadly.

The little town and train station were still where they had been for years. The old estate of the fledgling seminary still stood, but its doors had been sealed. No comforting light came through the windows at night. Without the laughter and theological disputes among the seminarians, the empty interior of the house was sad and deafeningly still. No sound of Pastor Bonhöffer playing on the grand piano or his favorite student, Eberhard's Bethge, practicing on the pump organ.

When the *SS* closed the seminary, the remaining seminarians scattered to their respective homes like dry leaves in the wind. Maria knew that Eberhard Bethge was still nearby. But where the others were—the ones who had withdrawn prematurely out of disappointment in their director's leadership, or who enlisted—she had no idea.

For Maria, Finkenwalde had been such a happy place. Now her confirmation was uncertain. She and Pastor Bonhöffer had been preparing for the rite to be held the following June when she turned 14 years old. He had vowed to visit Köslin periodically so they could continue their study of the manuscript of his next book, which he entitled *Nachfolge*. Maria was just 13 years old, but she could figure some things out for herself. She could see that the shattering of his dream had disheartened Pastor Bonhöffer. His energy and curiosity diminished sharply. It saddened Maria to see him so uncharacteristically passive. She understood it was probably a temporary adjustment to the loss of Finkenwalde, but it made her wonder whether he would have enough energy or time to provide for Maria's confirmation, despite his promise. He had commitments elsewhere in Europe, as the youth secretary of the World Alliance of Churches, that would take him away from Germany for periods of time.

In their most recent session reading and talking about *Nachfolge*, their last such session after the closing of Finkenwalde, Maria detected something new in him that she had not felt before. An impervious veil of melancholy had been drawn over him, as if he was already gone. She had worked hard to maintain a positive mood throughout that last session and pretend that she didn't notice his melancholy or distraction. But she couldn't deny that the shutting of Finkenwalde had left an indelible bruise on his spirit and that their time together had lost some of its fresh, innocent joy.

Pastor Bonhöffer had visited her and *Oma* one other time after the shutting of Finkenwalde. He had arrived with an open gash in his soul. Maria saw his ashen face out the window as he got off his motorcycle. She sensed that something had gone terribly wrong. She quickly ran upstairs to her bedroom and cried. She didn't want him to see her cry. She wanted him to think of her as a mature girl, a young lady.

He recounted the telephone call from *Frau* Struwe, the housekeeper at Finkenwalde, with the news of the closing of Finkenwalde. He and Eberhard had been on a much-deserved hiking vacation in the Alps. The *Gestapo* had come under the cover of darkness with their dogs and handed the housekeeper papers they claimed were from *SS Direktor* Himmler himself that declared Finkenwalde to be an illegal Confessing Church seminary. Pastor Bonhoffer didn't go into any more detail than that. Maria thought he was afraid of losing his composure and breaking down in tears in front of them. He thanked *Oma* for all her support for him personally and for Finkenwalde. He bowed before them both, bid farewell, stepped back onto his motorcycle, and left for who knows where. He didn't divulge where he was headed. *Oma* understood that he wanted some privacy, at least for now. But the youthful Maria was forced to swallow her bitterness that he seemed to be locking her out of his life.

She was profoundly frustrated. Her grandmother tried telephoning Finkenwalde a few times but was told by an operator that the line was dead. *Oma* and Maria agreed in their suspicion that the *SS* guard had returned to Finkenwalde and ripped the telephone from the wall. Maria would have loved to be able to hear his voice and laughter again. Her eyes filled with tears of longing as she thought of him and the empty seminary at Finkenwalde. It felt as though a death had occurred, irretrievably final.

Chapter Five

We are not to simply bandage the wounds of victims beneath the wheels of injustice, we are to drive a spike into the wheel itself.

—Dietrich Bonhöffer

January 1939

Christmas had passed. As seemed to happen every January after the *Tannenbaum* had been discarded and the sweet songs and carols muted for another year, Maria sank into a sad mood. She wandered aimlessly from room to room in the house, almost pouting. Going to her *Oma's* in Kõslin as *Mütti* suggested didn't relieve her blues. In Pätzig, *Mütti* attributed Maria's restlessness and lack of focus to boredom. But as usual, *Oma* understood her granddaughter better. She correctly diagnosed Maria's condition as lovesickness. She had not seen Pastor Bonhöffer very much since the *Gestapo* had shut down Finkenwalde. *Oma* understood that to Maria's young mind his farewell to them when he left Köslin it felt like a final goodbye. He and Maria had, in effect, abandoned their journey together toward her confirmation. Even if he came to Köslin, she would most likely have not been there. When she had turned 14 years old the previous year she went away to a boarding school in Wieblingen to advance her education beyond what was available in Pätzig.

She had completed her confirmation instruction at the local *evangelisch* church in Pätzig. The red and black swastika flag placed prominently at the front covering the cross clearly showed it was a *Reichskirche* congregation. Maria couldn't imagine that Pastor Bonhöffer would have been very pleased with that.

Maria had not expected that the lessons about Christianity from Pastor Bühler at the Pätzig church would be so irrelevant to her daily life and so thoroughly uninteresting. It made her miss Pastor Bonhöffer's entertaining teaching even more. He was so skilled at helping her apply her faith and knowledge to life in this world and finding God's fingerprints everywhere. She sat sullenly during Pastor Bühler's lessons, not so much as a protest against the boring and conventional nature of his teaching, but with a slow and secretly seething anger at Pastor Bonhöffer for abandoning her.

He had telephoned *Oma* once or twice to give an update on his new unexpected situation. He said he'd call more often if he weren't suspicious that since the closing of Finkenwalde, the *Gestapo* might possibly have been monitoring his telephone calls and his mail. *Oma* told Maria that Pastor Bonhöffer usually asked about her at the end of his telephone calls. It was a pleasant thought, but she wouldn't acknowledge that, not even to herself. In a way, it poured salt into the wound of not having him close, adding to her growing bitterness that he hadn't seemed to try hard enough to find a way that they could continue to keep their relationship developing and flowering. All the same, she missed his humor in the same way she craved his earnestness about the Christian faith.

Maria was sure that Pastor Bonhöffer had no idea that she still thought about him. She was certain that he assumed she had moved on to focus on her studies in her new boarding school, especially her mathematics. To an extent, he was correct. But she thought of him often, what he was doing, who he was with. Maybe he thought her mind was occupied thinking about boys the way most of the girls her age seemed to do constantly. They bored her, however, with their giddiness and silly soliloquies about the wonders of certain boys who caught their glances. Maria didn't find the boys all that interesting. Admittedly, a few of them were rather handsome but she enjoyed more the conversations with her parents—especially *Papa* and *Oma*, and even her brother and sister—than listening to the obsessive bragging of the boys about their exploits on the football pitch. One or two of them had joined the Hitler Youth, which she considered utterly repulsive.

Actually, Pastor Bonhöffer was not terribly far away. He was back in Pomerania, in Schlawe, as the assistant pastor of the village Confessing Church congregation, even though that didn't mean he saw her any more often. When Maria first learned of this, she wondered how he felt about such a "demotion" from his status as director of a seminary. She wrote to *Oma* to say that it was a waste of a very bright mind to be stuck in such a little and insignificant village as an assistant to another pastor.

"He doesn't see it as a demotion at all, dear," *Oma* explained in her next letter. "It's all part of a larger strategy he has devised—a rather clever one, I'd say—to continue Finkenwalde's mission without drawing the attention and suspicions of the *Gestapo*."

After witnessing the abandoned remnants of Finkenwalde, Dietrich retreated to his parents' home in Charlottenburg to rest and recover. He was terribly depressed. Several of his siblings tried to coax him to come downstairs and join the rest of his family in the family *Stube*. He usually refused, even if graciously, except to listen with the others every evening to the 10 p.m. news on the BBC. His parents understood his depression and knew that it was best to just let him be.

After almost two months, Dietrich derived new energy and ambition from somewhere. His depression loosened its claws on him. The other Confessing Church seminaries—Bielefeld, Elberfeld, and Dortmund—had suffered the same fate as Finkenwalde at the hands of Himmler's *Gestapo*. Dietrich came down from his room on the third floor on the day he heard the news, his face scarlet with anger. The very tips of his earlobes were a brilliant red, a sign to the rest of the family that he was either angry or very determined.

"Are we supposed to take these injustices lying down?" he asked forcefully, addressing everyone in the room. "Isn't it high time for the Confessing Church to reclaim its right to train its ministers as the government allowed us to do until these silly new edicts from Himmler's office? Are we going to pass by this opportunity to assert our right and find some way to resist—no, to undermine—the arbitrary authority that they claim for themselves? Damn it! Just as Christ was raised from the tomb, so will our mission be resurrected."

When Maria read about this incident in *Oma's* letter, she allowed herself a smile at the mental picture of Pastor Bonhöffer as a tow-headed boy with the shiny red earlobes trampling up the stairs, on the verge of bitter tears. But somehow she also knew that when he got upstairs to his attic room, he had begun to lick his wounds and channel his holy anger into this new strategy to forward his mission in spite of the obstacles and restrictions. That was very much like him. She was certain that he believed that the power of the Almighty was with him, and that the project of training pastors for the Confessing Church would be blessed.

Yes, the strategy was clever. The loophole in Himmler's policy was that ministerial apprentices working under the supervision of pastors in ministries approved by the state were exempt from the order to take the loyalty oath to the *Führer*. Even as efficient a bureaucracy as the Nazi regime did not have the time and manpower to pay attention to every single clergyman or seminarian. Dietrich's plan was to appoint the remaining seminarians as "apprentice vicars" in congregations throughout Pomerania where the local pastor was known to be supportive of the Confessing Church but were actually members of the *Reichskirche*. These pastors were to be responsible for supervising and directing the practical work of the apprentice vicar in the congregation. Dietrich and some of the other faculty would meet with the vicars in regional groups and provide theological education as it had been taught at Finkenwalde. All the vicars had to do was register with the local police that they were working under the supervision of the particular parish pastor.

This explained why Dietrich was merely an "assistant" pastor. To gain some distance and concealment from the *Gestapo*, he had assigned himself to "apprentice" with Pastor Block of the Schlawe parish. He was hidden in plain sight. The *Gestapo* had begun to lose track of him, or maybe even their interest in him. Out of sight, out of mind.

A few months later, Maria, now 15 years old, was at Köslin on fall break from Wieblingen when Pastor Bonhöffer surprised them by visiting *Oma*. Maria didn't come downstairs right away to welcome him. She didn't want to seem too eager, even though she was exceedingly glad that he had come. But she wasn't sure how she would feel in his presence. Perhaps, she thought, she ought not to give him the satisfaction of seeing her joy. She should be distant since there didn't seem to be much of a relationship with him for her to hope for.

But he was his usual gracious, gregarious self at dinner, and she quickly put aside her silent bitterness. The three of them at the dinner table reminded her of old times. As dinner progressed, Maria began to show signs of becoming her old joyful, outgoing self again. But after dinner, over coffee and cake that Maria had baked, they could tell that something had changed in him. He was refilled with that holy anger.

"The cowardice and naïveté of the damned Chamberlain and

Deladier in Munich had gotten under my skin that I had to start taking pills at night in order to be able to sleep," he said.

Maria had never before heard him curse.

"They handed the Sudetenland, and now all of Czechoslovakia, on a silver platter to Hitler like an early Christmas present," he said. "Couldn't they see through his *ersatz* formal hospitality to the slinking tiger beneath? We are headed straight to war, I can tell. The *Führer* has acquired the taste of blood like a shark encircling a wounded, bleeding swimmer in the sea."

As Maria listened to his impassioned jeremiad, she became aware that she was beginning to agree with his assessment of the *Führer* and his increasingly extremist policies. It was difficult at the boarding school to hear news and keep track of developments in Germany that were changing almost daily. The girls just didn't want to hear it. So, when Pastor Bonhöffer mentioned war, Maria grew both startled and afraid. Was such a thing possible when many of the wounded of the previous war had just begun to heal? Or was this just the dark ruminations of a pastor on the run, prone every now and then to bouts of melancholy?

"Last Wednesday night," he resumed, "I had just fallen asleep in the little cottage that the congregation has provided for me. I was awakened by a violent crackling sound and the boom of wooden beams hitting the ground. It was a spectacle such as I've never witnessed before. Bright luciferous light flared through the window against the wall beside my bed. I jumped out of bed to look outside the window.

"*Frau,* to my horror, the village synagogue next door was up in flames! I thought quickly of taking a pail down to the cottage's well and fetching water, but I could see that it was too late for that. My heart leapt when I saw a burning beam fall toward the cottage. I pulled on my trousers and raced out the door, fearing that the old cottage would burst into flames at any second. It did.

"I stood a good distance away from the almost totally burned synagogue and cottage. I watched in horror at the violent fire, but more at what I suspected was the real source of the evil being perpetrated there. There was a small crowd of villagers on the other side of the road. Some had brought their dogs, which howled in fear of the flames. As one wall after another caved in, I couldn't believe the cheers they were shouting, some too crude to repeat here in your home, dear *Frau*. These were the neighbors of the people of God who gathered regularly on *Shabbat* in that synagogue."

Then, as if leaving the greatest atrocity for the last, he looked directly in *Oma's* eyes and said, "I spotted a few sons-of-bitches standing on the sidewalk and shouting who sit in the pews of the village church on Sunday mornings." He spoke through tightly clenched teeth, his face as red as Maria had ever seen it.

"I fear that the Nuremberg Laws of 1935 are only the beginning of the chaos and effusion of acts of hatred. This is nothing more than an extension of the evil lie that has been vomited on the German people that the Jews are responsible for every problem endured by the Aryan people."

"*Mein Gott*, that's horrible," *Oma* responded. "But, Dietrich, I'm at a loss to know what one can do about this."

"We each have to do our part to stand in the way of those who want to make war. War would be disastrous for Germany right now. For all of Europe, for that matter. For all of humanity. It will mean that we haven't learned a blessed thing since the last one—"

Suddenly, Maria lost her focus. She could hardly bear to look at *Oma* or Pastor Bonhöffer. She was afraid her face would reveal the sudden delightful and unfamiliar tumult within her. She felt a sensation of an unfamiliar weakness in her knees as though they would buckle if she stood up. An electric current buzzed through her veins. It was like hearing the first bars of the *andante* movement of Mozart's Piano Concerto No. 21, her favorite piece of music. She wondered if the strange sensation would ever go away. Did Pastor Bonhöffer have any idea of what she was experiencing, and if he did, would he think ill of her?

Other girls had talked about this sensation—this serendipitous, delicious, burning desire to be in the presence of someone extremely special and attractive. She was feeling the first delectable inklings of a crush.

"I will invite all the vicars in churches in Pomerania to come to Schlawe to minister to the people and help them rebuild the destroyed synagogue," Pastor Bonhöffer continued, startling her and bringing Maria back to the present moment. "They can comfort the loved ones of however many of them were slain defending their spiritual home and protecting the scrolls of Torah. It's beginning to be past the time for people of faith, and all people of goodwill and reason, to simply apply bandages on the wounds of those crushed beneath the wheels of hatred and injustice. It's time to drive a spoke into the wheel itself!"

He rose abruptly and thanked *Oma* and Maria for their hospitality and their willingness to listen to him. As he was going out the door to his cycle, he turned and said, "I will tell the seminarians that he who does not raise his voice and get his hands dirty in support of the Jews has no business chanting at the altar of the church. And I will preach to the Christians of Schlawe that hatred and violence and abusive cheering in the face of the suffering of the Jews is to drive another nail into the crucified Christ."

Maria was astounded by the intensity of his feelings. He usually talked about current social issues much more rationally and calmly, even the rifts in the churches. She didn't have much experience with Jews. The few she had encountered she pretty well ignored. But for Pastor Bonhöffer, it was obvious that the fire and the hostile behavior of the villagers of Schlawe had cemented his commitment to the plight of the Jews, as though their suffering were his own. She admired his capacity for commitment to those who were being treated unjustly, and loved him for it, too. She went to bed wondering what exactly "driving a spike into the wheel of injustice and hatred" looked like.

Chapter Six

If you board the wrong train, it is no use running along the corridor in the other direction.

—Dietrich Bonhöffer

August 1940

Hans von Donyányi telephoned his brother-in-law Dietrich. His wife, Christel, had told him that Dietrich would be alone in their parents' house in Charlottenburg that afternoon. The parents had been invited to a social gathering and wouldn't be home until late—which is precisely why Hans called him on that day.

Shortly after Dietrich's visit to Maria and her *Oma* after the burning of the synagogue, he had been invited as a guest lecturer at Union Theological Seminary in New York where he had enjoyed a year as a visiting student one decade prior. But this time, he did not stay at Union for the duration of a whole year. He returned to Germany barely a few months after arriving. Since he had returned, he had occupied a room on the third floor of his parents' home in Charlottenburg in spite of the Nazi decree that he was barred entirely from being within the city limits of Berlin. The closing of Finkenwalde ordered by the *Gestapo*, and the discovery by the *Gestapo* of his recent clandestine residence in the parsonage of a pastor in Schlawe, had left him essentially homeless.

Hans let the telephone ring many times. He knew it would take Dietrich time to come downstairs to the phone. He would most likely be in his small third-floor room researching or writing his umpteenth book of theology, which he was entitling simply *Ethics*.

"Hello, the Dr. Karl Bonhöffer residence," he answered.

For heaven's sake, Hans thought, Dietrich sounded like the household servant. Maybe he considered himself as such in gratitude to his parents for their hospitality.

"It's only your brother-in-law here. No further need for formalities."

"Oh, hello, Hans."

"It's been a while, hasn't it? You took off so suddenly for America that I didn't get a chance to see you off and bid farewell and Godspeed."

"I apologize, Hans. I didn't intend to ignore or offend you or anybody else. There was just a narrow window to make arrangements with Union Seminary, to buy the ticket, and prepare to board the ship."

"You should have written from New York, *mein Bester Schwager*. At least to your sister, for heaven's sake."

"You're right, Hans. I should have. There was so much on my mind in New York."

"Enough of this small talk. I've got an important matter to discuss with you. Mind if I drive over?"

"Sure, I need a break from writing. Why don't you bring Christel with you?"

"I'm sure your sister would love to see you. But, no. It's not a social call. It's business, but off the record. I don't want to mix her up in all that stuff—for her own sake."

A short time later, Hans entered the Bonhöffers' house surreptitiously by the back door, a habit developed ever since he took this position as the Deputy Commander of the *Abwehr* under the authority of Admiral Canaris. In intelligence and espionage work, especially in military intelligence, you were aware at all times that the opponent had a similar network of agents. You never knew who might be tracking your movements and where. To avoid alarming Dietrich, who had his own reasons for caution, Hans rang the bell at the back door to announce his arrival. When they met in the kitchen, Dietrich opened wide his arms to embrace his brother-in-law.

"I really am sorry, Hans, for not being in touch from New York."

"I accept; but then again, I suspect my mail is being monitored anyway. I wouldn't want them to be secretly reading your personal postcards from the Empire State Building and the Statue of Liberty."

Dietrich grinned, revealing the deep dimples of his cheeks that his older sisters teased him about, and that Hans suspected many women considered attractive.

"Besides, I didn't come here to receive apologies," Hans said. "They're not necessary. I know you had classes to attend and books to read."

"Come, Hans. Let's sit in the parlor. *Papa* and *Mütti* are not here today, and we won't be disturbed."

"I'm aware of that. That's why I came today."

"You can't help being the spy, even on a day off, can you?"

"No more than you can help being the teacher and pastor."

Dietrich held open for him the tall wooden door out of the kitchen so they could retire into the parlor. Hans took the easy chair underneath the large portrait of Paula Bonhöffer's venerated father, the theologian Karl Alfred von Hase, dressed in his military uniform.

"Your grandfather is an imposing figure watching over us. The esteemed *Kommandant* of Berlin. He can't hear us, can he?" Hans asked kiddingly, apparently trying to keep things light.

Dietrich laughed lightly. "I sure hope not. What don't you want him to hear?"

Hans sidestepped his question. Instead, he asked, "When did you get back from New York?"

"At the end of June. I spent some time in London on the way home with Gerhard and Sabine."

"How are they doing in their new land? Grateful to you for helping get them out of Germany, I hope."

"Oh, they're faring as well as can be expected. They miss the family, and Gerhard longs for his old faculty position with the university. They intend to come back to Germany as soon as this Nazi nonsense is past and hope whatever government will follow allows Jewish professors."

"That begs the question, why in the name of heaven would *you* come back when, from what I hear, you could have had a cushy position as a professor in the precious safety of America? Why the hell leave all that?"

"It's complicated, Hans. Already on the ship crossing westward over the Atlantic, I started to have second thoughts about having accepted Union's invitation to come there. I sensed I was making a mistake."

"But wasn't it a fulfilling time for you when you were there a decade ago?"

"You know it was. I never met such devoted Christians as the Negroes in Harlem. They taught me so much."

"They didn't this time?"

"Yes, they did, but in a way different than I expected. They're just as devoted and committed to following Christ as before, maybe even more so. The 1930s have been extremely difficult for the Negroes, especially in the southern states. They've never had it good in America, starting from the years they were transported there as slaves. But everybody's suffering grew in the last decade. It seems as though the white people needed someone to blame for the horrible conditions of the Depression, some scapegoat to blame, and beat, and hang on a rope from a tree."

"That sounds familiar, Dietrich. Things have deteriorated badly here, too."

"When I saw how courageous the Negro Christians are in doing what they can to alleviate the unjust suffering of their brothers and sisters, how outspoken their leaders have become against their oppressors, I felt ashamed, Hans."

"Ashamed?"

"Ashamed, yes, that even in Third Reich Germany, I enjoyed the freedom to leave. That I could escape the chaos and growing terror by simply buying a ticket to New York. There are so many who can't just do that, certainly not the Jews."

"You feel shame and guilt because you have such a privilege and others don't? Is there really shame in taking advantage of an opportunity that's been given to you, of a freedom that is your right? Does coming back to Germany and these shitty conditions result in a single Jew's having it any better? Is this a form of penance?"

"My coming back I consider to be an act of solidarity with those who cannot escape."

"Very noble of you, Pastor Bonhöffer!"

Dietrich's eyes grew larger. He was surprised that Hans would utter such sarcasm at his courage in returning to Germany right at this decisive moment in its history.

"I apologize, Dietrich. I don't mean to belittle your difficult decision to leave America."

"I'm not entirely proud of the reason I went to New York in the first place."

"To study theology, wasn't it? To familiarize yourself further with theological movements in America? What could be more honorable than that?"

"Hans, let's be honest. I need more theological theory like a hole in the head. No, I went there because the month before I committed to Union, I received the same letter as all my cohorts born in 1906 and 1907, an order to register with the military. Hans, I swear I won't serve in Hitler's war. That's for certain."

"But you knew, didn't you, that you'd have to face the same call-up again as soon as you placed your foot back on German soil?"

"Yes, I knew. I applied to the chaplaincy corps but was turned down. They didn't explain why, but I think I could guess. I'm not sure what I'm going to do now. I'm waiting for God to show me where I'm needed next."

Hans was certainly not God, but he sensed this was just the window of opportunity he'd been hoping for. "Maybe, Dietrich, I can be of some assistance to you in that regard."

"Oh?"

Dietrich seemed genuinely interested in hearing more.

"We need you in the *Abwehr*, Dietrich."

Dietrich looked stunned. He was silent for what seemed like the longest time. "Good Lord! In the *Abwehr!?* In the service of Hitler by *spying* for him? Hans, what are you thinking?"

"Dietrich, this is war. In war, you can never trust what's visible just on the surface. You have to read the invisible message between the lines."

"You certainly speak like a spy, Hans. I can't do what you ask. What in hell's name do I know about military intelligence?"

Dietrich repaid Hans's earlier sarcasm by pronouncing the words "military intelligence" with obvious disdain.

Hans was not to be diverted. "I am thinking that what the *Abwehr* can use from you may not be what you know, but *whom* you know."

The last remark caused Dietrich to look away and ponder its significance. Hans allowed the words to sink in by remaining silent. Finally, Dietrich turned his head back to face Hans.

"Hans, what I can't figure out is why my sister's husband, the son of a prominent Hungarian composer, and a *Jewish* one at that, could possibly be in Hitler's service, providing intelligence about the plans and strategic movements of the Allied forces and in that way contribute to the defeat of those forces. I haven't raised the matter before, not even with Christel, out of deep respect for you. But to be

Deputy Director of Hitler's *Abwehr* just seems to me to violate every liberal and humanistic value you inherited from your parents, learned in your youth, and have practiced your whole life as far as I have known you."

Hans was sure Dietrich expected him to feel chastened, but he didn't.

"'As far as you have known me?' Are you sure you know me now, Dietrich? Do you think you know what I do from day to day?"

"Of course not, Hans. I'm not supposed to know. Isn't all that classified information?"

"What if I were to confess to you, Dietrich, that I'm actually working *against* Hitler by working *for* him?"

"All right, I'm thoroughly confused now," he said, lifting up his hands in exasperation. "I have no idea what you're talking about."

"Come on, dear brother-in-law. It's not that difficult to figure out. Nor is it that unusual in wartime. I thought Lutheran scholars were supposed to be familiar with paradox."

Hans looked intently into Dietrich's eyes, and it seemed as though a light went on suddenly in his brain. With Dietrich, Hans had learned a long time ago the language Dietrich knew best was theology.

"Now, dear Pastor, how can a person be *both*?" he asked.

"Are you a *double* agent, Hans?"

"I thought I saw the light go on."

"You're passing information to the Nazi Central Command, and then passing more information to the Allies?" Dietrich still looked disbelieving.

"You've just about got it. But don't think that all of the Nazi Central Command are firmly settled in Hitler's camp. And we're not entirely sure that the Allies find our information trustworthy or use it."

Dietrich seemed to contemplate this two-part answer.

"Hmmm."

"Don't look so surprised, Dietrich. You know as well as I do that Hitler has to be stopped by one method or another. Fortunately, some of the generals recognize that as well. Otherwise, Germany will be defeated despite all the early successes. He cannot be allowed to spout his deadly venom across all of Europe. Already he's added Poland,

Austria, Czechoslovakia, Denmark, Norway, and the Low Countries to his gruesome, illegal reign of terror. He's near the outskirts of Paris now."

Dietrich turned his body away again to think.

"Now he's bombing Britain," Hans added. "Think of Gerhard and Sabine, Dietrich. Was your assisting them to escape to Britain worth it if they are killed by Hitler's bombs instead of in one of Hitler's prisons or work camps?"

"Hans, this is a lot to take in. I may be an accomplished theologian. But I'm just a simple man. A very simple man."

"Dietrich, you expect me to believe that?"

"Just being a simple spy for the *Abwehr* would be strange enough for me and a steep enough learning curve. It would mean a total reorientation of my life, Hans. But to serve *both* the Reich *and* the Allies simultaneously, I'm doubtful that I can pull that off and not bring destruction to myself and you and everybody else who may be in on it."

"Look, Dietrich. You realize, of course, that our conversation today is strictly between you and me. Even Christel is not aware of why I came to visit you today."

Dietrich regarded Hans as though he had already assumed that.

"I wouldn't want you to answer to my invitation in the affirmative or negative right this moment. You could answer 'yes' too soon and then blame me afterward for getting you in a situation over your head. On the other hand, you could also say 'no' too soon. Think and pray about it overnight at least. Come over to Sakrow tomorrow afternoon when Christel has gone to market—not that there's much there to buy anymore. I've got some things to show you that just may help you decide."

Hans was sure that Dietrich followed his advice to pray about the invitation to join the *Abwehr,* particularly the counter-espionage movement. Hans was confident that he didn't pray by rote, or from a book of prepared prayers, or in a routine or casual manner. Last evening, he knew, was a Gethsemane moment for Dietrich and that he prayed all night like Christ after the Last Supper, begging that, if at all possible, this cup might be removed from him.

What Dietrich would be surprised to learn is that Hans had been praying, too. Praying that Dietrich be propelled beyond the pacifism of his younger years, and the principles of nonviolence he adopted while studying Gandhi, and overcome the obstacles of his deep theological convictions.

The doorbell rang. As Hans walked through the vestibule he steeled himself for the very real possibility that his prayer had been denied or not heard. He told himself that he must not be too eager to make Dietrich commit but allow him space and time to come to his own decision.

Behind the threshold, Dietrich looked haggard. Hans shook his hand, careful that it be interpreted as a brother-in-law gesture rather than the Deputy of the *Abwehr*. "Good morning, Dietrich."

Cautiously Dietrich returned the greeting. His voice betrayed a feeling that he wasn't sure he should be here talking with Hans at all, certainly that he didn't want to be.

"Did you sleep well, brother-in-law?"

"Do you want the honest answer? If so, I have to say I did not."

"Pondering and praying about what I said yesterday?"

"Mostly praying. But pondering, too, trying to recall things I thought about after returning to German soil, the way it feels now over a year since war broke out."

"Perhaps you mean before *we* started this war.?"

"Yes, precisely that."

"I will be very interested to hear about those ponderings from July and your impressions of what Germany has become in the year you were in New York. But before that, come with me to my home office in the basement to see what I have to show you."

Dietrich followed Hans obediently down the stairs.

"Come over here and sit with me at the table."

Again, he followed orders. After he was seated, Hans got them each a cup of coffee. Then Hans looked seriously into his eyes.

"Dietrich, you must realize that your options in Germany are severely reduced. The government has banned you from applying for any job as a professor at a university. You have been prohibited from making any public statement criticizing either the government itself or the *Reichskirche* on the penalty of imprisonment. You're even officially forbidden to be found within the boundaries of the city of Berlin. You're in Charlottenburg now only because your mother sought a softening of the ban by convincing her father, General von Hase, to use his influence to advocate for you with the Ministry of the Interior."

Dietrich stared at the floor and nodded his head reluctantly in agreement.

"But haven't I heard you say in a sermon or two that when God closes a door, often he opens another one?"

"True enough," he answered.

After a moment of silence, Hans went over to the filing cabinet against the wall. He pulled out a thick file labeled *Chronicle.* He didn't say a word as he placed the file with the official *Abwehr* red and black cover before Dietrich on the table. Dietrich looked at Hans inquisitively without touching it.

"This is an *Abwehr* file. Are you sure I should be examining the contents?" he asked tentatively.

"For the time being, only this particular file. But *especially this file.* Go ahead. Open it. Read it, my good man."

He opened the file to the first page and began scanning the first five or six pages. He looked stunned and lay the file on the table.

"Hans, what is all this? These photos from Poland?"

"Yes, from Poland after our *Wehrmacht* slashed and burned its way into Warsaw. Gruesome photos, aren't they? But accurate nonetheless."

"This whole file is about the German invasion and occupation of Poland?"

"No, that's just the first part of the file. There's much more there. Go ahead and see for yourself. Here, let me show you a photo that really shocks me."

Hans flipped the pages to a collection of photos from Holland from the German invasion in May. Hans pointed out one of a German soldier pointing his rifle at the head of a naked elderly Jewish man. Another private stood in front of the feeble man pulling the man by his grey beard and cutting it off with a pair of scissors.

"I don't imagine that the man stripped his clothes off by his own volition and asked for a shave, do you, Dietrich?"

Dietrich shook his head without saying a word.

"You're aware of what nakedness represents for Jews, aren't you?"

Now Dietrich nodded his head very slowly and remained mute.

"Can your stomach stand more, brother-in-law?"

"I guess. Go ahead," he said with obvious reluctance.

"I don't want you to think that only the *Wehrmacht* or the *SS* is guilty of this kind of atrocity. Look at this picture of some of the local Polish civilians who have been inspired to brutality so soon after the Nazi occupation."

"But these men are not in *Wehrmacht* or *SS* uniforms?" a bewildered Dietrich asked.

"You're right, Dietrich. That's because they're neither *Wehrmacht* nor *SS*. They are civilians, citizens of the little nearby village, recruited or forced into service by the *SS* to execute their fellow inhabitants of the village, only the Jews or homosexuals and the occasional Gypsy who has made the mistake of lingering in the village. These local men and boys—do you see how young this handsome fellow looks, all of 12 or 13 years old at most, eh?—are called *Einsatzgruppen*, armed by German authorities and ordered to kill so that the Nazi Central Command does not have the dead on its good Catholic or Lutheran conscience."

"Who do they think they are fooling? God?" Dietrich asked.

"Flip the page, Dietrich, and you'll see the fruits of their labors."

Dietrich did so and beheld a huge pile of nude Jewish corpses, layer upon layer, lying on top of one another, face down at the bottom of the huge pit.

"My God! These are all women and children."

"The men have been taken into the woods and executed by a firing squad of the same *Einsatzgruppen*. This is how our *Führer* conducts his war of expansion. The file is full of photos like these of atrocities committed by our leaders. I call it the *Chronicle of Shame.*"

"Where and how did you amass all the information in the file? What do you plan to do with all this?"

"These are photos taken surreptitiously by ordinary soldiers we have embedded in the *Wehrmacht* and *SS* to feed us information. They themselves are horrified by what they have witnessed."

"I can't blame them. So, Hitler hasn't yet succeeded in neutralizing everyone's conscience, even among the troops?"

"Thank God," Hans affirmed. "We hope that the contents will help lead to Hitler's and his criminal gang's eventual demise and imprisonment by the Allies or, for that matter, by their own people who are kept blissfully ignorant of what atrocities are being committed in the name of the *Vaterland.*"

"But Hans, if you are ever caught with this *Chronicle of Shame* in your possession, they will beat you to a pulp and imprison and torture and finally execute you."

"Not just me, Dietrich, but Admiral Canaris and Generals Beck and Oster, and the others who are my colleagues in the resistance. But the *Chronicle* will not be found. In the next week I am going to hand-deliver it myself to the head librarian at the military base at Zossen. It'll be buried deep in a safe place where no one ever goes. The librarian himself will forget where it is. Only I, and now you, Dietrich, will know of its existence. Then, when the time is right, and the wheel of justice has come back around to point to Hitler and Göring and Himmler and Göbbels, I will come to Zossen and retrieve the *Chronicle* as evidence."

Dietrich sat in silence, shaking his head. Hans gave him time for the photographs to penetrate into his heart and mind. Then he broke the silence.

"Are you sufficiently moved to become one of us?"

Dietrich didn't respond right away. He just stared at the floor in disbelief.

"Remember I told you yesterday that I knew of a way to dispense with any call-up from the *Wehrmacht*?"

Dietrich looked up at Hans with anticipation, now mixed with a palpable sadness at what he'd shown him.

"With your affirmative answer to my invitation, I will recommend you to Admiral Canaris as a new member of the *Abwehr*. He will follow protocol and report this to General Jodl at Central Command. Jodl will request the call-up authorities to remove your name from the call-up list because you are serving the *Vaterland* via vital military intelligence. And that will be that. That's how it worked with Klaus."

A look of blank surprise came over Dietrich's face.

"Klaus? My brother Klaus? He's in the *Abwehr*?"

"Yes, your older brother Klaus. He's not only part of the *Abwehr;* he's also one of us in the underground resistance."

"He never mentioned a word of this to me."

"That's understandable; you were in America when we signed him up. But more importantly, he did what he pledged to do: to protect us and himself from being exposed and discovered. That's what we would demand that you do, too, if you come aboard."

"Where do I fit in this, Hans? I surely can't be embedded in the forces."

"Dietrich, you are a valuable commodity to this effort. More valuable than you can imagine. You have all these significant contacts in the churches of our allies. We need to have assurance ahead of time from the Allied governments that they will recognize any new government that arises as the legitimate government of Germany. Even before then, we will need their active support of the resistance. To promise their support, they will need to see some credible evidence that we know what we are doing and that we have a broad enough base of support among the German people and within the military leadership itself to be able to pull off a coup.

"I know you are a colleague and a personal friend, for example, of Bishop Bell in England, correct?"

"Yes," said Dietrich, "I became very close to him while I served the church in London."

"As a member of the House of Lords he has access to top men in Parliament, like Anthony Eden for instance, who in their turn have access to Winston Churchill himself. Those are strategic relationships that we don't have at present. Likewise, your relationship with leaders of the churches in Norway and Sweden. You see what I mean when I say you are invaluable to the resistance?"

"I don't know, Hans," Dietrich stammered. "This is all so startlingly new to me. It would change the nature of my relationships with Bishop Bell and others. I'll have to ponder and pray some more to discern God's will for me."

"And for Germany, Dietrich. And for the future of Germany."

The doorbell rang one afternoon at Karl and Paula Bonhöffer's home. Dietrich happened to be close to the front door. He answered the door. Standing there was a young boy, perhaps 11 or 12 years old.

"A special delivery for the Reverend Dietrich Bonhöffer," he announced very officiously.

"Yes, you're looking at him."

Without a further word, the boy handed an envelope to Dietrich.

Berlin. 16 August 1940

Dear Dietrich,

I have heard from your dear parents that you have returned prematurely from your studies in New York. I am pleasantly surprised by this. You're making the courageous decision to leave behind the comfort, peace, and safety of that faraway continent in order to return to where you belong is a source of joy, particularly for your parents. It signals to me that you are, indeed, firmly committed to the future of your native land.

I have spoken with your brother-in-law as well. You now know that Klaus is an active participant in the resistance against that monster Hitler.

It is because of Hans's invitation to Klaus to join the resistance that Klaus is doing this. Klaus continues his employment as counsel to the directors of Lufthansa but has accepted a lower status in order to work covertly for the resistance. That he is still with Lufthansa makes him a very valuable member of the resistance movement, to be sure. Klaus's work takes him legitimately to many European and even world capitals where the airline has regional offices. While there, he can gather invaluable information about the movements of Germany's allies and enemies that he relays back to Hans at the *Abwehr*. As he told you, then Hans passes on intelligence information to the Allies.

I have taken the risk, prudent or not, of including such potentially lethal information in a letter delivered by the son of a neighbor so that you can know what your brother is up to. More I must not reveal.

To be totally honest, Dietrich, I have shared this information with you so that you may realize what risks your own brother assumes every day of his life. One small misstep on his part could cause Klaus to lose his job, or even be imprisoned or worse by the Nazi officials. I have had to learn to live productively with the dread of such an event bringing Klaus and both of us down. I fully support and bless Klaus's decision to accept Hans's invitation to risk his life and mine in doing what he is uniquely situated to do on behalf of a secure future for Germany than is utterly inconceivable with Adolf Hitler at the helm.

Don't you agree, dear Dietrich, that the future of our country and its citizens is unimaginatively bleak if the current political situation were not challenged and those responsible for the terror and murder are not removed by some means?

You Christians are a duplicitous lot! Forgive me, dear brother-in-law, for speaking my mind openly and freely with you, even one such as you who is committed to the reform of your churches. I speak this way because ever since I met Klaus and your wonderful family, I know that you are one who speaks the truth and hears the plain truth when another speaks it to you.

What I have observed is this: You Christians speak a lot about justice and the sacred value of all human life. You do not withhold your happiness when someone else takes the initiative to work on behalf of those endangered universal liberal values that you know needs to be done, such work as both Hans and Klaus are now doing. But it seems to me also that you Christians are unwilling to get your own hands dirty to do the work. Many Christians are being so spiritually minded that they are no earthly good. I expect more from you, Dietrich.

I pray—isn't it strange how I continue to use such pious language long after I have abandoned my faith in God and have ceased to pray?—that you respond affirmatively as your brother has to Hans's invitation to use your unique strategic qualifications to the advantage of a future in Germany free forever of Hitler and National Socialism.

One more thought before I close. I know preachers often look for an example from daily life to make their theological message understandable by the congregation. I will do so now as well, Dietrich:

Let us suppose that a drunken driver plows intentionally into pedestrians on the sidewalk of a busy thoroughfare like the Kurfürstendamm. Would it not be the ethical responsibility of everyone who witnesses the act to do all they can to prevent the crazy driver from doing it again?

Sincerely,
Emmi Bonhöffer,
Your sister-in-law

Just a few days after receiving the letter from his sister-in-law Emmi, Dietrich informed Hans that he would accept his invitation to join the *Abwehr,* which he understood also to include work for the resistance.

Hans was a key link in the chain of Nazi insiders who were convinced that Hitler's power must be neutralized. The covert group included several disillusioned Nazi military officers including von Dohnányi's immediate superior in the *Abwehr,* Admiral Wilhelm Canaris, Colonel Hans Oster, and most importantly, General Ludwig Beck, chief of the German General Staff, who was fully capable of galvanizing others in the *Wehrmacht* against the *Führer.* These men had been meeting under the cover of the *Abwehr* at its headquarters since 1937.

Meanwhile, independent of the plotting of Oster and the others, there were other attempts to assassinate Hitler in 1938, 1939, 1941, and 1943—all of which failed. In March 1943, a failed attempt to plant a bomb on Hitler's plane on a flight from the eastern front in the Ukraine to the district headquarters in Smolensk involved a cousin of Maria von Wedemeyer's, Fabian von Schlabrendorff.

In June 1942, Dietrich was dispatched to Sigtuna, Sweden, ostensibly to attend a theological conference that would include the bishops of the state Lutheran church bodies of neutral Sweden and Nazi-occupied Norway. Bonhöffer had prior good relations with both. More important for the Oster conspiracy was the fact that an honored guest at the conference was the Bishop of Chichester, England, George Bell.

Bonhöffer was to speak confidentially with Bishop Bell and divulge to him the current details of the Oster plot. He was to convince Bell of the impressive pedigree and status of the participants in the plot. Dietrich was to use his leverage as Bell's friend to convince him to confide in key members of the House of Lords, and in Foreign Minister Anthony Eden. Eden had access to Prime Minister Churchill. Bell promised Bonhöffer to try to convince Eden of the plot's high chances of success and to request Churchill to order a ceasefire in the bombing of Germany for a brief time while the assassination plot was being executed, most likely in the summer of 1944. Eden was to impress upon Churchill the vital need for the

British government to recognize the new German government, to be headed by Oster, once Hitler was eliminated.

Upon receiving Dietrich's report of his meetings in Sweden by way of von Dohnányi, General Oster thought it wisest for Dietrich to lay low and become invisible for a time. Dietrich interpreted that as permission to return to Köslin to work on his book, *Ethics*, in the room that *Frau* von Kleist-Retzow had promised she would keep vacant just for him.

Chapter Seven

I doubt there is an hour in the day when my thoughts don't turn to you.
When I walk through the garden at 6:00 a.m., on my way to the hospital,
and realize that you may even be looking at the same sky.

—Maria von Wedemeyer

Köslin: August 1942

The late summer days in Pomerania were blazing in floral grandeur, but in the mornings there were definite hints that fall was not far off. These were the last precious days of Maria's three-month summer break, perhaps the last such summer break in her life. She opened the huge window in the parlor to breathe in some of the fragrant August air. She downed her breakfast in a hurry and rushed outside to her *Oma's* extensive flower garden behind the manor house to pick a handful of zinnias, asters, and marigolds that were showing off their glory. She thought she heard, faintly at first, the gentle sound of the piano through the open parlor window. The sound became clearer, and Maria recognized a tune by Beethoven.

Who could that be playing the piano? Her *Oma* had played in her younger years, but it was impossible now for her to produce such a gentle and excellent sound on the keys with her badly arthritic fingers. As far as Maria knew, there was no one else at the house but the two of them. As the playing continued, Maria tiptoed up to the open window to peer into the parlor surreptitiously. The piano player's back was turned to her on the piano bench across the room from the window. It was a large balding man dressed in a white summer suit.

Suddenly, the playing stopped in mid-phrase. Maria emitted a muffled gasp as the piano player stood up. She was afraid that whoever it was had heard her footsteps in the grass, or her swallowed cry, and had been alarmed, or at least curious. She held her breath and ducked quickly underneath the window as if playing a game of hide and seek. In less than a minute, a head poked out the open window. He spied the crouched figure. When he spoke, he sounded more amused than confused.

"Oh, hello, stranger. How can I help you?"

Maria didn't stand up or turn her face. He sounded vaguely familiar, but she had not heard the voice of that someone for several years.

"Are you looking for something on the ground?" the man asked, with tongue in cheek, she assumed by his amused tone. "A lost coin or piece of jewelry perhaps?"

Then she was sure she knew the voice. She straightened to stand so that her face was nearly at the level of his eyes. He wore round spectacles, which, though common in Germany in those days, she could pick out anywhere.

"Pastor Bonhöffer! What a total surprise! What are you doing here?"

"I might ask you the same question, *Fräulein*. Do you make a habit of crouching underneath the open windows of people's houses?"

She felt her face flushing warm and red. She was embarrassed beyond bearing.

"I was just looking to see who was playing the piano so beautifully," she stammered. Between her embarrassment and the recognition of Pastor Bonhöffer, she had trouble getting her tongue around words. "I wish you hadn't stopped. The music matches the beautiful weather so well."

"You aren't Maria, are you? *Frau* von Kleist-Retzow's granddaughter? Now that I can see your face more clearly, and not just the top of your head below, I can tell, by God, it *is* you. Maria von Wedemeyer."

He wore a friendly, reassuring smile despite having been spied upon. Nonetheless, she wished the earth would open and swallow her whole.

Maria and her *Oma* hadn't seen him or heard from him in almost four years. Then, through the grapevine, they had learned that he had gone all the way to New York without telling them. Maria had been hurt and disappointed. She thought Pastor Bonhöffer shared, well, if not her secret crush, perhaps then at least a feeling of friendship, despite their difference in years.

Maria had vowed to herself that if she were ever to see him again, she would give him the silent treatment as punishment for his neglect and go on with her life. But the sheer joy of seeing him now pushed aside all feelings of anger and thoughts of punishment. "Might you keep playing, Pastor? I am so sorry that I interrupted you, especially in the way I did. I feel so foolish."

"Or rather so creative perhaps? If you come inside, I may play something. Otherwise, I feel like Romeo trying to speak to Juliet through an open window, except Romeo was the one outside."

"Can you play Mozart? His Piano Concerto No. 21? Not the whole 30 minutes, but just the *andante* movement?"

"It would sound better if we had some strings to accompany it, but I can try to retrieve it from the back of my brain somewhere."

"Oh, good. That would be such a treat. I'll come inside."

She picked up the mixed bouquet she had dropped when she had ducked beneath the window. *Pastor Bonhöffer! I don't think I can believe it. I must be dreaming. Where has he been all these years? Why haven't* Oma *and I heard from him?*

She went inside and stood outside the entrance to the parlor to catch her breath and compose herself. *I must not seem too girlish and juvenile to him.*

She stepped into the parlor, now suffused with the incomparable beauty of the music—or that is what she told herself. In reality it was the presence of the man at the piano that had changed her entire outlook. Such a pleasant and unexpected surprise just when she had lost all hope of ever being with him again. She sat down on an antique straight-backed chair opposite the piano. Dietrich continued with the Mozart piano concerto. Maria used to play the recording of the concerto on *Oma's* gramophone whenever she was feeling sad. Strangely enough, on that day she requested him to play it when she was feeling unspeakably elated. Playing it without the help of sheet music, he was able to interpret the subtle underlying melancholy of Mozart's notes and phrases with feeling. But she discerned a subtext in the music as he played it of undeniable hope somehow. He played it so lovingly.

When he finished, he came over and sat in the wing chair opposite her.

"Maria von Wedemeyer. How many years has it been now? How different you look. Just as beautiful as before, maybe more so, but so much more like a young lady. How old are you now?"

She recalled how he called her that once before. Hardly anyone had called her anything but a girl since.

"When did we last see each other?" he asked unusually excitedly. "Do you recall?"

She shrugged her shoulders and felt a little foolish for not giving a more intelligent answer.

"Was it that night I came over to talk with you and *Frau* about the burning of the synagogue in Schlawe? Yes, yes, it was 1938. Almost four years ago. It turned out that synagogues and Jewish shops were set afire intentionally that night and by someone's explicit order, not just in Schlawe, but all over Germany. 'The Night of Broken Glass,' as it will be known as for generations to come."

"Yes, I remember how furious you were that night. That was before we heard you went back to America."

"Yes, well, that was largely a mistake. But I did stop to see my sister, Sabine, and her husband, Gottfried, in Britain on the journey back to Germany. But enough of me. I want to hear about you. You are still in school?"

"No, I finished my studies at Wieblingen in June. Next, I will do my National Service as a nurse trainee with the Red Cross somewhere. I haven't been told yet where it will be."

"You mastered mathematics I expect? Do you remember that time one Sunday at Finkenwalde when you almost defeated me in table tennis? I was impressed how you figured out the geometric angles involved in the game."

"Yes, I got top honors in mathematics. I would like to study mathematics at the university. But *Mütti* disapproves. She says that is no life for a woman."

"I suspect that your father feels differently."

"If he were here, I think you are right. I feel that he always understands me better than *Mütti*. But, alas, he is not here. He is a captain with Army Group Six now."

"Army Group Six? He's on the eastern front?" His obvious concern frightened her.

"Yes, I'm afraid so. The last we heard from him was that the Sixth Army was moving to Stalingrad. We're all very worried about him."

"And what about Max? I haven't asked about him yet. He must be at the age of service?"

"Yes, Max is away, too, in the other direction. He took part in the occupation of Paris. The last word from him was that he was flushing out remaining French resistance fighters in Jura. He says that the French army was not impressive, but that the resistance fights like a determined bulldog."

"Don't they always? They have more to fight for. Maria, this is an awfully beautiful day, too beautiful to be indoors. Are you in the middle of something, or can we go outside for a stroll in the sunshine? Around the lake perhaps? Just like old times?"

"That would please me, Pastor."

They rose together and stepped out onto the rear veranda. He held out his right arm. She welcomed his old-fashioned gallantry. She proudly placed her arm through his as though they had promenaded together in the sunshine many times. He cupped his palm on top of her arm, and they began heading happily across the lawn toward the lake.

Neither of them said much at the start. Finally, Maria mentioned how thankful she had been when he had worked with *Oma* to invite the wives and children of Confessing Church pastors who had been killed in the Czechoslovakia campaign to spend a brief time at Köslin to recover from their loss. On her breaks from school Maria took care of the children after their midday meal.

"You kindly spelled me relief by taking the children down to the lake to swim on your breaks from writing up in your room. I will never forget the time you led a raucous parade of happy children back up the hill from the lakeshore with your bathing suit on your head like a helmet on a silly general leading the troops in battle. They were having a grand time laughing at your antics."

"Yes, I recall that. The children might not have known it, but we were satirizing our current German militaristic culture by our songs."

"For once, I didn't worry what parents would say if they heard that the childcare worker's friend was teaching their precious German sons and daughters unpatriotic songs."

"We were having too much fun to have it spoiled by needless worry. People think what they think."

"I hope those poor families of the war veterans are faring better now."

"I've managed to maintain contact with a few of them. So many other families, not just of the Confessing Church, but of every stripe, have suffered similar losses as the war has continued and expanded."

"I remember that was a very sad time for you."

"Yes, it was. Many of the pastors who were killed were former students of mine at Finkenwalde. On most days, however, I was more angry than sad, really."

"At the *Führer?*"

"Well, yes, I'm always angry at the *Führer*. But I was a little upset—no, very upset—at those pastors who had volunteered to serve the *Führer's* unjust cause."

Maria was a little taken aback by that comment. What would he say about *Papa's* serving in the *Führer's Wehrmacht* now? Or *Max's?* Granted, they hadn't volunteered but had been conscripted by their *Vaterland*. What else could they do but report for duty? It was their patriotic obligation.

As if they both recognized the potential dangers, they conspired silently to change the subject of conversation.

"Do you really want to further your study of mathematics, Maria?"

Oh no. Does he want to discourage my hope as well?

"As I say, *Mütti* discourages it."

"But what do *you* want, Maria?"

"Well, yes, I love mathematics. It makes all the confusion of this world more orderly and understandable."

"Understandable for you perhaps. Once I got to the higher grades, it was a little too, too incomprehensible for me. I usually got the correct answer but couldn't tell the teacher how I got it."

She chuckled. *He's not afraid to admit a weakness. Some would call that unmanly, but I don't.* "That's a common phenomenon."

"I was a good student in history, music, literature, and theology, though."

"You did receive your Ph.D. before you were 21 years old, I hear."

"Maria, mathematics is more than a worthy endeavor. It's going to be even more important in the future that we have good mathematicians. I don't wish to interfere between you and your mother. But it is *your* life after all. You must choose to live it as it suits you."

He's the only one so far to encourage me. Even Oma, *who usually supports me, is convinced I'd be making a mistake if I chose to go on to study mathematics.*

Just then, she heard her *Oma's* voice calling from the veranda. She sounded a bit irritated that Maria wasn't at home or near the house.

"I had better get back, Pastor. It sounds as though *Oma* needs my help for something."

"We'll both go back. I need to announce my previously unannounced presence at her house."

"Yes, of course. I didn't mean that I would abandon you here in the woods. How thoughtless that would be."

A few minutes later, *Oma* was pleased to see Pastor Bonhöffer emerge with Maria from the woods. They weren't arm in arm anymore. But her welcome of Pastor Bonhöffer was more subdued than usual. Something was holding her back from her customarily effusive welcome of her favorite pastor.

"Pastor Bonhöffer, how nice to see you. What a surprise. Maria, why didn't you warn me he was coming to Köslin?"

"That's because she didn't know either. I just dropped in less than an hour ago. If I am inconveniencing you in any way, I apologize."

"Nonsense, Pastor. You know my door is always open to you, and that the sheets on your bed in your room are always clean in case you drop by for a few days like this. You will stay, won't you?"

"Since your welcome and invitation still stand, I'd be glad to. I just returned from a conference in Sweden and am waiting to see where I'm headed next. I wanted to spend some time on that stubborn manuscript of mine."

"By all means, Pastor."

Oma glanced at Maria. She could see the lines on *Oma's* face become deeper, the look in her eyes become somber.

"Maria, I don't know how to tell you this."

Evidently, Pastor Bonhöffer could discern the sudden change in mood.

"If this is private, *Frau,* I will retreat to that room you have kindly kept reserved for me."

Maria hoped that *Oma* would say something, perhaps that he

could stay, but she stammered too long, and the pastor had gone into the house by the time she was able to speak.

"*Oma,* what's wrong? Tell me!"

"*Papa's* commanding officer from the Russian front wrote to your mother to say that *Rittmeister* von Wedemeyer had—"her voice began to break, "died valiantly after being struck by a Russian shell and that he had been buried in Ukraine."

It was as though Maria herself had been shelled. She was speechless. Her knees began to buckle until *Oma* put out her arms to catch her. She felt dizzy. She placed her open palm over her mouth but made no sound. She couldn't. She had always thought she'd be crying uncontrollably at a time like this, but her tear ducts felt as dry as the desert air.

"*Papa*? Died?"

"What could there possibly have been left of dear Hans to be buried in Ukraine?" *Oma* said as she burst into tears.

In the absence of a body to mourn over, the family held a memorial service at the little church in Pätzig. Maria reminded *Mütti* that *Papa* had been especially fond of Pastor Bonhöffer and suggested that they invite him to preside at the service. Without so much as a thought about it, her mother gruffly denied the suggestion. When Maria pushed her for a reason, she grew irritated. She snapped curtly, "Because in his public statements, he's been anything but supportive of our country's efforts to avenge the past and protect our way of life. I doubt *Papa* would want a man like that to preside at his service."

"I didn't think that would be the case," Maria countered. But she judged that this was no time to go against her grieving mother and try to defend Pastor Bonhöffer.

Instead, much to *Oma's* chagrin, *Mütti* invited Pastor Bühler, that intellectual pygmy and theological fossil who had confirmed her, to come up from Stettin to preside. Maria was not pleased with the choice. But this was, after all, *Mütti's* husband and not her own so she resigned herself to the arrangement.

Pastor Bonhöffer sat by himself in a pew near the rear of the church. Maria knew that *Mütti* was longing to have Max beside her for a shoulder to rest on, and *Oma* missed having her deceased husband by her side in the family pew as well. For her part, Maria wished she could walk defiantly to the back of the church and request that Pastor Bonhöffer sit beside her in the family pew where she would slide her arm through his for solace. His presence could not make up for the absence of her father, she knew, but it had such a serene, uplifting effect on her that she longed for him, especially now in her time of deepest need.

The service felt empty somehow. Perhaps loved ones always experience an emotional numbness at a memorial service, she thought. Maybe it was the lack of a body in a casket at the foot of the altar that made the whole event feel so unreal. Several honored speakers, the *Bürgermeister* of Pätzig and a retired colonel of the *Wehrmacht,* gave glowing tributes to *Papa's* dedicated civic service and his steadfast, valorous leadership of his company at Stalingrad, but they both referred to him in the past tense. Though Maria knew in her mind that *Papa* was gone, the image she clung to in her heart was that of her familiar, dear father as he bid her goodbye at the train station to report to the Sixth Army. He had been teary-eyed: his wet cheeks were the color of living flesh, and his strong body was tall and whole. She could not imagine his broken body mutilated in pieces on the ground in Russia. She expected him to come rushing into the back of the little church, embarrassed because he was late for his own memorial service. She pictured him sliding into a rear pew beside Pastor Bonhöffer rather than continuing up the aisle to join the rest of the family. *Papa* would never want to draw the attention of the worshipers and disturb the solemn decorum of a church service in that way.

Mütti, Ruth-Alice, *Oma,* and Maria formed a receiving line as they were led down the aisle to the back of the church during the closing hymn, *Bleib bei Mir.* Max was unable to attend the service because of his unit's mission in southern France. *Mütti's* eyes were tinged with red from all the tears she had shed in the previous three days, but they were dry now. She held onto Ruth-Alice's arm, who was weeping for the two of them. *Mütti's* face remained gallantly stoic in a Pomeranian way.

Maria was holding up well until the first person came through the line. Rather than shake Maria's outstretched hand, she wrapped her thin arms around her in a sympathetic embrace.

"Oh, precious child. Your dear father would be so proud of you, about entering the National Service with the Red Cross. He would call you a good soldier."

Maria burst into tears and wished Pastor Bonhöffer was closer so she could bury her face in his shoulders. She longed for his near presence more than she ever had before. She appreciated her certainty that *Papa* would be proud of her. But she wept over what was not true in the woman's words: Maria's *Papa* had been a soldier in two world wars and was not in the least proud of it, and she knew he would never call her a "good soldier." In fact, she wondered, if she were a young man, whether or not she'd show up for service in the *Wehrmacht* at all when called up. Everything about this war was so ambiguous, its aims and purpose not at all as clear and straightforward as most Germans, including her mother and older sister, seemed to make it out to be.

Among the last of the mourners to come through the receiving line was Pastor Bonhöffer. Maria had glanced over at him as he waited for the others to proceed ahead of him. His eyes caught her once, and they seemed to say to her, "I know how difficult this must be for you. You're doing well."

Oma embraced him as he greeted her with some words Maria couldn't overhear. Maria watched apprehensively as he proceeded to Ruth-Alice and *Mütti*. He spoke a few short words to each of them. They were formal and polite in their responses, as one would expect. But there was a definite hint of coolness and distance in their half-hearted effort to be polite, and Maria feared that Pastor Bonhöffer could discern it.

When he came to Maria, the last in line, she didn't know what to expect. He was careful not to do more than extend a sympathetic hand. Why did she expect, or hope, that he would do more?

"I'm so sorry. I know how close you are to your father."

Maria noticed that he didn't refer to her relationship with her father in the past tense. He knew it would not die with him.

"I enjoyed watching the two of you together, father and daughter."

Her mother must have overheard him since she had no person to greet at the moment. She took the few steps in their direction.

"I'm afraid her father always spoiled Maria," she said to Pastor Bonhöffer.

Maria was too embarrassed by her mother's unexpectedly thoughtless comment to make any immediate response. What was a guest supposed to say? Pastor Bonhöffer was still holding her right hand in his. He looked at Maria sympathetically after her mother's words and squeezed her palm with his right hand a little tighter as encouragement. Suddenly tired of playing "the good soldier," she spoke loudly to Dietrich, making sure her mother would hear. "Pastor, I so enjoyed our talk the other day as we walked to the lake. I would like to talk with you again. About *Papa*."

"Of course. Will you be coming back to Köslin after you have rested at Pãtzig with your mother?" He understood the tension between mother and daughter, but he agreed to Maria's suggested rendezvous without any evident concern that her mother did not approve. He was taking an understated but defiant stand in Maria's corner.

"I imagine so—in a few days."

Her moment of rebellion had passed but still, she couldn't admit the truth and add the words, "if my mother permits me." She had lost her father and almost lost her crush once. She would do all she could now not to allow that to happen again.

"Then I will look for you again underneath the parlor window?" he asked with a knowing smile.

Chapter Eight

Music...will help dissolve your perplexities and purify your character and sensibilities, and in time of care and sorrow, will keep a fountain of joy alive in you.

—Dietrich Bonhöffer

Pätzig: September 1942

Maria's days and weeks after her father's death near Stalingrad and the memorial service in Pätzig were the saddest of her life. Max had to remain with his unit in France. A week later, the family received a very short and hurried letter from him postmarked from Kiev saying that he and his unit were being transferred to the Russian front.

Remembering what had happened to her father there frightened *Mütti*, *Oma*, and Maria to the marrow of their bones. They had conspired silently to bury their unspeakable grief, unwilling to break the carefully constructed dam that held back their profound sorrow.

Perhaps it was her fear for Max's safety that rendered *Mütti* private and moody, if not outright irritable for days, if not weeks, afterward. Maria wanted to comfort her, talk with her about *Papa*, but she pushed her daughter away. "What good does talking about your father do him now? Or us?" she exclaimed whenever Maria got up the courage to bring up the subject.

The only source of brightness was the sweet memory of Pastor Bonhöffer's promise that he would visit again when his duties as a roving executive for the Confessing Church (or was it the *Abwehr*?) allowed. Maria was very eager to continue the conversation they had started earlier in the summer when he'd returned from Sweden; he knew she could talk with him about her missing her father without being pushed away. He would know what good talking about her father would do for her.

However, the only word she received from him for almost a month was an even shorter and more hastily composed letter than Max's from Kiev, informing her that he had been summoned back to

Berlin by the *Abwehr*. But a much longer and much more satisfying letter arrived in Pätzig only a few days later, postmarked München.

> Dear *Fräulein* von Wedemeyer: In spite of all the dreariness and sorrow of these times, I have continued to treasure the memory of our recent pleasant meetings at your grandmother's in Köslin and your father's memorial service in Pätzig, even if I mourn the circumstances of the latter. I think of you frequently and wonder how you are bearing up to the grief of your dear father's loss. Please know that if you ever need a friend to confide in, I am here.

Maria was overjoyed to receive this letter from him. She sat at the desk in her room, reading it over and over again. Her overflowing happiness made all the sweet words run together so that she had to read the letter many times over to ensure that she hadn't missed a single sentiment.

She was sure that *Mütti* had steamed the envelope open and read the letter, too, as she had every other time Maria had received a letter in her childhood and youth. Her suspicions would have been especially aroused this time because Maria's name and address on the envelope had obviously been written in the hand of a mature gentleman.

Her mother even helped her compose a lukewarm response and signed it with the words: "With regards, your young friend, Maria."

Maria returned her mother's favor by steaming the envelope open herself before taking it to the post office in the village and adding a few short sentences in her own hand: "Mother will have surgery on her eyes at the Franziskus Hospital in Berlin in October. Shall I see you then?"

She met Pastor Bonhöffer by prearrangement at the front entrance of the hospital. She was so glad to see him that she had to stifle her sudden urge to embrace him. He, however, always so proper, held out his hand to shake hers. They took the lift to the fourth floor, the eye surgical floor. As the widow of a war veteran, *Mütti* was granted a private room, unlike most other patients who had beds in a ward.

They stopped before the open door to her room. *Mütti* lay on her bed in what Maria thought was a deep sleep. Her mother's left eye was covered by white bandages, which held a small white egg-shaped plastic eye shield in place. Two sandbag-like bolsters, long and slender like sausages in pillowcases, were placed on both sides of her head to prevent her from moving it.

Maria gently took Pastor Bonhöffer's hand and led him quietly out of the room into the corridor. "I am sure she'll sleep for at least another hour."

He glanced back into the room and said, "I would have brought flowers as I should, but every flower kiosk on the way was either demolished by the British bombs or closed."

"That's thoughtful of you, Pastor. But as you can see, she would have had trouble seeing them. The doctor said that the bandages may come off next week."

"Cataracts?"

"Yes. She's had trouble reading for some months now but delayed doing anything about it. But now after *Papa*'s death, she has missed reading more than ever. She finally listened to our urgings for her to see an eye doctor."

"Would you like to go out for a walk, Maria? Maybe we'll come upon some wildflowers or flowering weeds to bring her when she wakes up."

They both chuckled conspiratorially.

"Yes. That would be nice. I've been in that room for hours already today. September is too beautiful to be confined in here."

He put out his arm and invited her to place her arm in his, feeling her face flush as she did so. He seemed to notice but pretended not to.

She gathered enough courage to say, "I really enjoyed your letter, Pastor. After I read it, I would have liked to come to visit you."

It was now Pastor Bonhöffer's turn to flush with embarrassment and pleasure.

"I made the mistake of mentioning that idea to *Mütti* in passing one day," she confessed, "and she said that it would be altogether inappropriate. She said we haven't known each other very long, and besides, you're already a mature man."

"Won't she think that it's inappropriate that we have gone on this walk without her knowing it?" He looked genuinely concerned.

"She will be told in any case."

"That's the right thing to do, Maria. I don't want to deceive your mother or seem as though I'm taking advantage—"

"I'll tell her in time. I'll say that you came especially to see her, as a pastor. But I'm not a little girl anymore. I don't think she needs to know everything I do."

"She will probably accept that in time. My mother did when my sisters were starting to get a little independent."

"I wager that she made an exception for you from that rule. After all, you were a boy. That's not your fault, of course. But why do we have different rules for girls?"

He laughed quietly, conceding her point.

"You would get along very well with my sisters, Maria, especially with Han's wife, Christina, whom we call Christel. Not only do I think sometimes that you look very much like my sisters, especially Christel and my twin Sabine, with your light brown hair, but you have similar modern ideas."

She chuckled. "Whether they are modern ideas or not, I don't know, but they are *my* ideas, for the moment, at least."

Pastor Bonhöffer laughed heartily, which she interpreted as approval rather than ridicule. He led her along the busy *Budapester Strasse* over the footbridge to *Cornelius Strasse*. They walked past a few apartment blocks until they came to a copse of linden trees set in a garden. It turned out to be a beer garden, and they entered through the wooden gate.

It was a warm afternoon, probably one of the last of the season. They chose an empty table under a linden tree outside in the beer garden.

"You are sitting at a table in an establishment owned by a person with a well-known name, Maria," Pastor Bonhöffer said, trying to look serious. But she detected an effort at humor. "Care to guess who?"

She didn't know how to answer. He smiled when he saw she was stumped. He pointed to the name of the proprietor painted in Bavarian letters on the placard beside the entrance: *Besitzer—Aloïs Hitler.*

Her face registered disbelief. "He can't be of the same family, can he?"

The Pastor let out a "hard-to-believe-isn't-it?" laugh. "Almost the same. Much to the *Führer's* embarrassment, Aloïs is his half-brother."

"Why embarrassment? Does our *Führer* disapprove of drinking? Or of places that serve drinks?"

"It's not that," Pastor Bonhöffer informed her in the patient manner of a teacher. "It's that Aloïs married an Irish woman when he lived abroad in Liverpool but there was a slight problem. He was already married in Germany. When he returned to Germany in the 1920s, he was arrested immediately for bigamy."

"I bet the *Führer* would be just as glad if his half-brother changed his surname," she said laughingly.

"These days, the name Hitler is still good for business. Although I predict the day when the surname will be detested, even by Germans."

The beer garden was crowded in the mid-afternoon. The majority of the customers were wearing *SS* or *Wehrmacht* uniforms. The garden was replete with the sounds of the clanging of plates by the bussing staff and the loud laughter of the almost universally male clientele.

It turned out that this was not Pastor Bonhöffer's first visit to this establishment. The waiter greeted Pastor Bonhöffer very warmly and with familiarity.

"Walter, how have you been?" he asked the waiter in a friendly tone as though the two were not strangers to each other.

"The regular for starters, Pastor?" Walter inquired.

"Yes, Walter, I believe so."

"I'm very impressed, Pastor. You seem to be well-known in this place."

"Ah, so then you've noticed the young officers looking over to capture a glance at our table? I don't think it's me they are looking at. It's *you*. They want to see my attractive young female companion. They're a little green with envy, I think."

She wasn't accustomed to men noticing her. She flushed again, pleasantly flattered by his remark. *Did it mean that he found her attractive, too?*

"No, Pastor, I meant the way the waiter knew you and what you are accustomed to ordering."

"Don't be impressed. Intimacy with representatives of the current regime is no reason to be impressed. I only frequent this place because my work requires that I be in places like this."

"Your work?"

He didn't get a chance to answer. In only a few minutes, Walter was back at the table with a tray with two plates of the thickest black bread she'd seen in over a decade, some liverwurst, and two frosty *steins* of frothy beer."

"*Danke sehr,*" Dietrich said to Walter.

He turned back to her. "I apologize, Maria," he said a little self-consciously. "Over the years I have lost track of your exact age. I ordered beer for you because I assumed that you are of majority age by now."

In spite of the fact that she hadn't put on any makeup for many days because of the hurried trips to the hospital, she was pleased and surprised that he still believed she looked like an adult. *A young lady.*

"Just barely, Pastor. Eighteen years old, finally."

"My congratulations, *Fräulein,*" he said, holding up his stein of beer. "Welcome to the world of adulthood." He sipped a drink of the beer, as did Maria. "I warn you. There may be many days when you'd rather turn back the pages of the calendar and wish you were back in the magic world of childhood again."

"I wish that every day now that *Papa* is gone."

"You and he are very close, aren't you?"

"*Very.* You know, Pastor, he liked you very much."

"I'm honored. I will miss conversing with him about the state of the world."

"Pastor, I think you are very much like him. You both are very intelligent, thoughtful, and patient with me."

He didn't respond right away but looked down at his empty plate. She was thinking that Pastor Bonhöffer was surprised by her openness. He must have been wondering why this young lady before him was so bold as to nudge the conversation in a more personal direction. Ruth-Alice had told her once that the woman must wait for the man to do that if he chooses to.

She was disappointed at first by his reticence to respond and effort to change the subject.

"Your mother is probably awake by now and must be wondering where you are. Shall we return to her?"

If she had been honest, she would have said she'd rather not right then. She was enjoying their conversation. She was feeling so special to be sitting at a beer garden table with this self-confident man who knew his way around the world, who was shown respect by a waiter, who was the object of other handsome men's envy.

Finally, reluctantly, she said, "Yes, you're right. It's time to get back."

They talked less on the walk back to the hospital. She was concerned that she had spoken too much already or said too much too soon. But she knew that during that conversation something in their relationship had tilted. Or perhaps he was just experiencing the mild post-meal lethargy with a stomach full of bread, sausage, and a tankard of Bavarian beer.

He stopped on the block where the hospital was located and turned to look into her eyes. She waited eagerly for what he was about to say.

"Whoever of my family is in Berlin and is free will gather tomorrow at my parents' home in Charlottenburg for an evening of music. We do that almost every Saturday evening. Some of us play the piano or our favorite instrument, some sing, we all laugh. I would be honored if you were to accompany me as my guest. If your mother can spare you, that is."

Maria couldn't hide her pleasure at this invitation. *He's inviting me home to meet his parents. What do I have in the closet to wear? I must not disappoint him.*

"Yes," she said, "I would love to." Almost instinctively, without any forethought, she squeezed and pulled with her right arm enclosed in the crook of his left so that their bodies touched briefly. Then, feeling a little foolish and forward, she relaxed her arm immediately. Yet she didn't at all regret that she had done so. The physical touch of their bodies was wonderful. He didn't seem to be surprised or offended or even embarrassed. Maybe, she thought, he had walked arm in arm with many women older and more experienced than her.

"*Mütti,* it's me, Maria," she said quietly by her mother's bedside. Maria could tell she was not in a deep sleep, just obeying her body's desire to rest a spell after the afternoon meal. The tray of half-empty plates, bowls, and used utensils had been pushed aside from the bed.

Because of the bandages, it was impossible to tell when her eyes were open. When Maria had waited for what she thought had been a suitable time, she spoke again.

"I brought you a familiar visitor. Or, rather, a familiar visitor brought himself here to see you."

"Oh," *Mütti* said in a tremulous voice, "I have no choice but to believe you because I can't see anything but this total darkness. Maybe if she were to speak, I can recognize her by her voice."

Pastor Bonhöffer smiled at the irony but didn't hesitate. "*Frau* von Wedemeyer, it is good to see you, even if under not the best of circumstances."

When her mother realized the familiar visitor was a male, she ceased conversation and just lay on her bed in silence, making Maria more uncomfortable.

"Your daughter and I just took a little walk earlier to let you sleep."

Maria hoped he wouldn't mention the beer garden. She recognized the slight tensing of her mother's lips, never a good sign.

"In my day," *Mütti* began, unable to turn her head because of the sandbags, "it was not appropriate for a man to escort a girl and for them to be alone together until they were engaged."

Maria could feel irritation, even anger, rising. Pastor Bonhöffer kept calm.

"That was my family's custom, too, as far as my sisters were concerned," he said gently, not at all argumentatively. "Though times have changed with the generations, it seems that some of the former ways are still relevant to many people."

Maria cringed nervously inside. This could get explosive. At least, he had said "former ways," not "old-fashioned" ways.

"That may be here in the big capital city. But as far as a daughter of mine is concerned, I still decide if something is appropriate or not."

"Of course, I didn't mean to imply otherwise, *Frau* von Wedemeyer." He relented a little. Maria hoped it was not a surrender. She felt such admiration for his tactful, yet quietly resolute, manner.

"*Mütti,* Pastor Bonhöffer has kindly invited me to his parents' home tomorrow for their family musical evening." Could she have made it sound more innocent than that?

"That's right, *Frau* von Wedemeyer. I assure you that both my parents will be present all evening. And I promise that I will have your daughter back at her aunt's home on *Brandenburgische Strasse* no later than 10:30 p.m. My older sister Christina and her husband, Hans, will drive her there themselves on their way home. Your daughter will be quite safe with our family."

Maria reflected afterward how ironic it was that to convince her mother that Maria would be safe in Dietrich's presence, he had to assure her that there would be a whole host of other adults present to protect her from him.

Chapter Nine

We must be ready to allow ourselves to be interrupted by God. God will be constantly crossing our paths and canceling our plans by sending us people with claims and petitions.

—Dietrich Bonhöffer

September 1942

Dietrich headed to Koslin as soon as he could to visit Maria's grandmother. If he were honest with himself, he thought sheepishly, he would admit that as much as he enjoyed her company, he was visiting *Frau* von Kleist-Retzow in the hopes that Maria would be there. Unfortunately, Dietrich's superior in the *Abwehr,* his brother-in-law Hans, summoned him to headquarters soon after he arrived, and he had no chance to see Maria. "I had been looking forward to spending a few quiet days writing," he told Hans as an excuse for his late return to Berlin.

Dietrich was Hans's passenger as he drove them to Rome to meet with the resistance agent at the Vatican. The Pope had been slow and hesitant to become an active party to any attempt to subvert Hitler, much less a plot to eliminate him violently. They needed to encourage their man at the Vatican to increase the intensity of his efforts to persuade the Pope to support the resistance.

"Hans, I'm impressed. In wartime, the rest of us are doomed to driving ten-year-old Opels and Hitler's Volkswagens with balding tires," Dietrich observed when he awoke from a nap in the front seat beside Hans. "Whereas the Deputy Director of the *Abwehr* has the luxury of driving a Mercedes-Benz."

"It's not my car, of course," Hans responded defensively. "The *Führer* wants his officers and division heads to drive cars that make them look authoritative and important. This car is not so much for the comfort of the driver as for show and effect."

"That seems to sum up the essence of the National Socialist philosophy, doesn't it? All shine and glitz and very little substance," Dietrich replied with a sarcastic chuckle.

"Your stay in Köslin was short. I didn't realize you had gone up to Pätzig, too. Got tired of the old widow?"

"Not at all. She's still a delight. She knows when to leave me to my writing. And she's the feistiest anti-Nazi old woman you'll ever meet."

"You haven't divulged to her the real purpose of these trips, have you?"

"Hans, of course not. It's the one thing pastors and spies have in common: We know the necessity of keeping confidences. My whole life has become one big confidence I can't divulge."

"Then you ought to be well-practiced at keeping secrets."

"When I packed my bags last night, I thought perhaps I was leaving Pomerania for the last time. I'm not sure I will ever see it again."

"Can't take the flat terrain any longer? Look at these mountains here. Such beauties, aren't they?"

"Pomerania has become somewhat difficult."

"Lingering bad memories of the closing of your seminary at Finkenwalde?"

"A little, yes. Especially the breakup of our close community of brothers. They're being killed one by one on the Russian front."

"Those memories and regrets will stay with you wherever you live."

"It's not the place that has become difficult."

"What, then?"

Dietrich hesitated before answering, weighing whether he should reply at all, yet he recognized that he couldn't keep it in any longer.

"A girl. Or, I should say, a woman?"

Hans burst into laughter, startling Dietrich. "Then your delay makes perfect sense. Men have been known to do anything to *stay* where they are if it's a woman they would miss."

"She's not difficult herself. Quite the opposite. But her mother is somewhat of a morally conservative stickler. Not like Christel's and my mother at all."

"You're not flirting with the girl's, excuse me, I mean the woman's mother or worse, are you, Dietrich?"

"God forbid! No!" They both chortled a little naughtily.

Dietrich looked out the passenger window in silence for a long while. Hans knew him well enough to recognize that either he was regretting ever bringing up the woman in the first place, or else strategizing how to proceed on the subject. Hans recalled his own experiences after meeting Christel a decade ago. At times like this, he couldn't stop conjuring her image in his mind, fighting the urge to turn around and head back to Berlin. Hans imagined himself and Christel in bed as a married couple, she twisting her adorable legs around his waist. Perhaps that was the kind of fantasizing Dietrich was doing during this pause in their conversation. He took a furtive glance at the crotch of Dietrich's trousers to see if they revealed any evidence of his thoughts.

Just as suddenly as he had paused, Dietrich launched into an excited monologue about this woman. Her name was Maria von Wedemeyer. Hans remembered her being at Karl and Paula's house for their family music night a few weeks prior. But she seemed so young, just a teenager, but here was his reserved brother-in-law, stammering and blushing like an eager schoolboy. Hans listened without interrupting his enthusiastic soliloquy.

"You say you are attracted to her. Why, then, would you not want to return to Pomerania?"

"It's not that I don't want to go back. I am always a little wary about going back to face Maria's mother's scrutiny. But at the same time, I also *want* to go back."

"Torn between two opposite feelings, eh? My good man, it sounds to me an awful lot like being in love." Hans slapped him playfully on his left shoulder in congratulation.

"I guess so. I mean, I don't know. What do I know about these things?"

"But you had a relationship with that female student all those years through university. You must know something. What was her name again?"

"Elizabeth. Elizabeth Zinn. I knew her well enough to know that my relationship with Elizabeth was not really love. We were friends. Not much more than that. Oh sure, I loved her as a fellow student, a good one at that, and as a fellow human being. She was a wonderful companion. But I didn't feel the kind of uncontrollable tingling in my body, the sweaty hands, and the wildly beating heart as I do with Maria. Believe it or not, Hans. I was still a virgin when that relationship ended."

"As I say, Dietrich, that sounds like love. *Amore*, as the Pope might say."

"Or maybe it's only lust, I don't know."

"Don't underestimate the essential value of 'only lust,' as you call it. There's got to be some wild electricity, some uncontrolled sparks, at least a little bit of inflation of the penis, as a prelude to love, don't you think? If not, how else would two people ever be drawn together so that they can love each other in the first place?"

"I suppose you're right, Hans. You would know. You're married. That's why I've brought up the subject with you." He continued kiddingly, "Do you mean to tell me that it wasn't the sharpness of Christel's mind that attracted you to my sister, but her body?"

"Her intelligence for sure, brother. It didn't hurt one bit, though, that she's very desirable as well."

"Maria is, too. When I look at her sometimes, I'm reminded of Christel's clear complexion, Sabine's full figure, Suse's high spirits, and even Ursula's practicality." He paused to consider his words. "That sounds a little psychologically suspect, doesn't it?"

"That I don't know. You'd have to ask your psychiatrist-father about that."

"My confusion has something to do with the nature of our situation. Danger and secrecy are strong aphrodisiacs for males. The fact that she doesn't know the whole truth about my real work in the *Abwehr* makes my attraction to her seem so, I don't know, so daring, so erotic, I guess the word is."

"It does add a certain amount of excitement to the relationship, doesn't it? I don't see anything wrong with that."

"But it also feels as though I'm deceiving her somehow."

"That's your overly sensitive conscience at work, Dietrich. It sounds to me that you are having a hard time accepting the fact that you are in love. What's so bad about that? You are a normal man in his mid-30s."

"But it's crazy, Hans."

"Crazy? No, I call it normal."

"In love at a time like this? At a time of war and such disorientation, when everything is up for grabs? It's insane."

"All the more reason for the stability of love."

"I must be mad. Her father's body is not yet cold in his grave in Russia. What in the world can I be thinking?"

"I would think she's eager for love in her life right now more than ever. I don't know the woman at all except what I could learn on a short car ride from your parents' home to that of her aunt's. You know her better. But just think about it, Dietrich. There's a big, gaping hole in her life now that she's lost her father. If what you've told me before is true, why *wouldn't* she want to fill it with the love of a man her father respected highly?"

Dietrich looked pensive, carefully weighing Hans's argument.

"I suppose that's worth my thinking about, Hans. But there's still the matter of our ages. She's 18 years old, just barely out of school. Her 18 to my 37 years. How does that look? People will think I'm a pedophile, for heaven's sake."

Hans broke out instinctively into a broad, sarcastic laugh. "What's this? 'How does that look?' Since when have you been concerned about how something appears, or what others think? That's not the Dietrich I know. Think and tell me what *you* feel—"

Once through the narrow Brenner pass, Dietrich said, "We're close to the Italian border, aren't we?" He was trying to change the subject, but it didn't take long before his thoughts and words were of his Maria again.

"It would be absolutely criminal for a man in my situation to take a wife now."

"Criminal? You think it's better for a man to be without emotional entanglements?"

"When I responded to the call to be a pastor, I made a private vow to myself to remain single."

"Oh, you're turning Roman Catholic on me now, are you? A vow of celibacy? We surely must mention that at the Vatican when we get there."

Hans regretted his sarcasm. But he was growing impatient with Dietrich's attempts to deny his feelings. So much like his father and his older brothers, Hans thought. Perhaps this thing with Maria has the potential to save Dietrich from a lifetime of living constantly in his head.

"I renewed the vow when I decided to enter this new line of employment. Spies shouldn't get married, should they?"

"Well, Dietrich, if they shouldn't, then the director of the military intelligence service and his assistant have violated that. Admiral Canaris is happily married, and your sister Christel is my devoted wife. Perhaps things might have been easier for Christel and the children if I were doing something else with my life. But let me tell you, Dietrich, I wouldn't have passed up the opportunity for anything to have missed our life together all these years. That is where I get my strength. And if the worst were to occur, as it very well could, their love for me is what will help me face it. You could do worse, brother-in-law, than fall helplessly in love and marry your heart's desire. There may only be the one."

"You think so? I wouldn't know what to do as a married man. I'm such a fool with domestic things."

"What did I know when I asked Christel to marry me? Boil an egg? Yes. Make a cup of tea or coffee? Ditto. Start the car engine? That's about it. But we learn to adjust, Dietrich; not just adjust, but actually enjoy it. Sex is a part of it, of course. But it's in the little ordinary things of everyday life where the joy is to be found and the love given and received. Don't turn your back on them."

Chapter Ten

When I examine my heart, I acknowledge both a spiritual and physical attraction to Maria. My middle-class, bourgeois upbringing gives me pause about the physical attraction. But even in the Bible we have the Song of Songs; and really one can imagine no more ardent, passionate love than is depicted there.

—Dietrich Bonhöffer

Berlin: October 1942

Pastor Bonhöffer came by the hospital every day after his first visit. Whenever Maria didn't need to be by her mother's bed, she and he took walks and had wonderful talks and interesting conversations about everything under the sun. They lost count of their days together, and of time itself.

One morning, when Pastor Bonhöffer and Maria arrived at her room, *Mütti* was sitting anxiously on the edge of her bed with the bandages removed. She informed them that she had arranged to be picked up and taken home that very afternoon. *Frau* von Wedemeyer had persuaded the doctors at the *Franziskus* Hospital to discharge her as soon as the bandages and eye cover were removed. Maria did not think that was a good idea for the health of her eyes, but *Mütti* was persistent and stubborn in her decision to go back home to Pätzig. "My own physician can take care of me just as well at home," she argued. Maria knew there would be no discouraging her.

A part of Maria's disappointment, of course, was the fact that she would have no reason to remain behind in Berlin. "I've enjoyed our talks very much, Pastor. Perhaps when you have some free days, you can come and visit us at Pätzig," she told him.

Maria knew the look of gladness he gave was an assent. But before he had had a chance to respond to her invitation, her mother took the liberty of answering for him. "I'm sure the Pastor is quite busy with his duties here in Berlin and elsewhere, Maria."

Dietrich understood their mother-daughter dynamics and attempted to help her assert some independence. "Of course, I would look forward to coming again to Pätzig," he said in contradiction to her mother's obvious disagreement with the idea. "Whenever Hans can spare me."

Pastor Bonhöffer pushed *Mütti* in a wheelchair to the lift to take them down to the exit from the hospital. Maria and the pastor exchanged glances in which they communicated their mutual disappointment that the moment had come too soon. *Mütti* glanced in Pastor Bonhöffer's direction, expecting him to bid her and Maria farewell and wish them a safe journey home. But he lingered outside the door, just as Maria hoped he would. When the driver arrived and assisted *Mütti* into the car, Maria was planning to lean over and kiss the pastor, even if only on his cheek, for the first time ever. The fact that he hadn't left before *Mütti* had been distracted by being helped into a car indicated to Maria that he had a similar plan. Unexpectedly, *Mütti* ordered the driver to wait as he started to push the wheelchair closer to the vehicle and said, "Maria, why don't you step in first so that you don't have to walk out into the traffic and try to open the other door in moving traffic?"

Maria heard it as a command and obeyed just as she always had, even though there was no other traffic at all. So much for her mother's pretense. Quickly, Maria turned toward Pastor Bonhöffer and gave him such a hurried little innocent peck on his cheek that afterward she wondered if his cheek had sensed anything it all.

Maria's *Oma* called on the telephone barely after sunrise on the morning of October 26. To let her mother sleep, Maria picked up the receiver.

"My dear Maria," *Oma* said without prefacing her remarks. "I cannot believe this could happen twice within just a few months." *Oma* paused as though gathering her courage.

What had happened once recently that now has happened again? Maria had only a few seconds to wonder as her grandmother rushed on.

"My daughter does not deserve to lose two strong men from her life in short order like this. No wife or mother does."

Maria's mind, so scattered and distracted in recent weeks, finally hit upon the obvious happening *Oma* was referring to: *Papa* had been killed near Stalingrad. Instinctively, Maria sat down with the telephone receiver balanced on her lap, braced for the worst.

"Maria, your brother has been shot on his company's way to relieve the troops near Stalingrad. He was dead instantly, his commander assured me when he telephoned just a few minutes ago."

Maria was rendered absolutely numb by her grandmother's news. Afterward, she couldn't remember how long she stood silent and motionless in her bedroom, replaying a tragic scene from the same play for a second time. Maria couldn't believe it: Her family whittled down to just three defenseless women? The big, strapping hulk of a young man, Max, dead and gone? Two strong men cut down in frozen Russia? How was she going to tell her *Mütti,* her poor, desolate *Mütti*?

Oma's voice changed from nervous to irrepressible anger. "There's no one else to blame except Hitler. Once the Russians surrounded our boys, the generals requested permission to retreat to safety beyond the Don. But Hitler withheld permission and ordered the generals to hold their positions. 'Do not stop until we have their unconditional surrender of the city,' he called back. The next morning, thousands of Catholic soldiers requested their last rites from the chaplain."

Maria was too overcome by her personal loss to contemplate what and whose military tactics were to blame. All she could think of was the reaction of her poor mother when she told her. She'd been dealing with *Papa's* death courageously. But how would she find the strength to cope with the loss of her son? Her only son?

When Max's personal effects were sent to Pätzig from the front, Maria volunteered to take the horse and wagon and bring them back from the station. The package contained a torn and bloodstained leather pouch, which might have been the same one Max had had when he had been a Boy Scout before the war. Maria had to fight back nausea as she saw the dried blood—Max's blood—on the pouch. Maria looked into the package again, and all that remained were items that Max had probably carried on his person and had on him when he was shot: a small Bible, the locket his girlfriend Anna had given him the past summer, his penknife, and a dog-eared pack of playing cards. Because it was lying flat against the side of the package, Maria almost missed seeing an envelope stamped in Berlin and addressed to Max in familiar handwriting, which appeared to have been folded and unfolded many times. It was a letter that Pastor Bonhöffer had sent to

Max in France the day after *Papa* died. Maria read it several times:

> Dear Max
>
> You have lost your father, for which I am sincerely sorry. I believe I can sense what that means to you. At age 20 you are still too young to lose a father. But you have learned from him to honor the will of God in everything. He also told you that a person's strength comes solely with being at one with God's will. You know that God loved your father and that God loves you, especially now. It was your father's prayer that you continue to love God no matter what God sends you or requires of you.
>
> Dear Max, as heavy as your heart must be right now, let that which by his love and goodness your father planted in you now grow strong. Pray for your mother and siblings that they may persevere in this most difficult time in their lives. They will be able to help you persevere, too, but help them as well as you are able.
>
> Your brother in Christ,
> D. Bonhöffer

Maria could hear Pastor Bonhöffer's voice clearly in the words he had written, gentle and soothing. She reread the letter once more, then stretched out on her bed, weeping softly, the letter beneath her, and fell asleep to the sound of his voice in her ears.

They delayed Max's memorial service a few more days until *Mütti* had regained enough strength to leave her room and sit for a significant length of time. At the dinner table she looked so thin and silent, so utterly defeated. Maria wrote to Pastor Bonhöffer in Berlin to share the news about Max. Since *Mütti* had seemed so reticent about making specific plans for the funeral, Maria took the initiative to invite him to attend and perhaps conduct the service.

Mütti was trying to peel the shell off a hard-boiled egg at the table when she said, "I'm sure he will answer as soon as he gets my letter."

"Your letter?" Maria asked, thrown off balance.

"I wrote to say that we are sorry we cannot accommodate him here at Pätzig at this time."

Maria couldn't believe her ears.

"What do you mean that we cannot accommodate him?" she asked, raising her voice. "We have all kinds of room. Besides, he is a very undemanding guest."

"You've already invited Pastor Bonhöffer to lead Max's service against my wishes. I don't want him," she said point-blank without looking up from her egg.

"You don't want him?"

Maria lowered her voice to prevent her mother from being overly defensive. "Well, even if he cannot sleep here in our home, it would mean a lot to me if he could say a few words at Max's service."

"I've taken care of that. I've invited Pastor Bühler to come up from Stettin with *Oma*."

Maria's heart sank. Maria knew that as Max's only living parent, *Mütti* had every right to plan his funeral service. But Max was *her* only brother. She felt strongly that she ought to have a say in how the service ought to be conducted. She bridled at *Mütti's* thoughtless insistence that everything was to be arranged according to her own wishes alone.

"But, *Mütti,* I had already invited Pastor Bonhöffer to conduct the service. I thought you'd seen and steamed open the envelope. I don't want that old stick in the mud Bühler to do the service for a boy he didn't even know. Pastor Bonhöffer confirmed Max. They were close."

Maria cut her injured complaint short for fear she would allow her whole boiling cauldron of anger to spill out of her mouth.

"I don't want that man under my roof," she said bluntly and stood up. "You've already invited Pastor Bonhöffer to lead Max's service?"

"Yes," Maria answered hopefully, thinking her pleading with her might have been successful.

"I'm not surprised, Maria. You've been going against my clear wishes a lot in the past few months, especially after meeting with Pastor Bonhöffer again. I have sent Inge into the village to send a telegram to Pastor Bonhöffer disinviting him to the funeral. I'm sorry if that is awkward for you, but the next time you'll need to consult with me, Maria. Max is my son."

"And Max is my only brother. And Pastor Bonhöffer is my best friend."

Mütti turned and stomped out of the kitchen as though the matter were settled. Maria heard her grumble under her breath something like, "As if that's all he is to you." She slammed the door leading to the stairs.

Maria wrote immediately to Pastor Bonhöffer to apologize for her mother's inexcusable lack of hospitality toward him and for having the rudeness to disinvite him.

Maria walked every day to the village post office in the hope that there would be a letter from him accepting her apology. But day after day, their box was empty except cards and letters of consolation for *Mütti*. She was sure Pastor Bonhöffer was done with her and her family after such a disgraceful rejection from her mother.

A few weeks after Max' service, however, Maria's mood was altered radically in a way she never could have imagined. A long-awaited letter from Pastor Bonhöffer was waiting for her in their box at the post office. The envelope containing it was a thick one. It could only mean one thing, Maria was certain. A farewell. A withdrawal from their relationship. An end to her world. She ran out of the post office onto the road leading back to her home. She located a very private, partially hidden spot in the shade of a linden tree beside the road, known to the locals as the Lovers' Linden because couples could find privacy there to kiss. Even fearing what Pastor Bonhöffer might have said, she tore open the envelope. She felt it would be better to read the bad news there in the privacy of the space under the tree than at home.

> My dearest Maria,
>
> I can no longer hold back but must tell you all. I have been concealing many things in the privacy of my heart, not in order to be secretive or to mislead you, but because I have not been certain about how you might receive my sentiments. The point is, I love you above anyone. More than that, I want to marry you. Of course, it would be best to ask you in person, but my work took me to Geneva for several weeks. That is why I never responded to your letter informing me of your mother's decision to prevent me from attending Max's funeral.
>
> I must have an answer as soon as you have one to give. If the answer is as I truly hope it will be, I will make arrangements as soon as possible to come and speak with your mother personally.
>
> Yours always,

Dietrich

Maria reread the letter again and again. She couldn't believe it. It was not at all what she had been expecting. *He wants to marry me! Marry me!* I don't deserve such happiness. It is surely an act of God! What else could explain a famed theologian proposing to an 18-year-old virgin in every sense of the word?

She was too shaken to look at the letter again for several days. She placed it in the very back of the drawer in the desk that had been hers since she was a little girl. When she had finally absorbed Pastor Bonhöffer's proposal, she retrieved the letter one morning and plopped it down on the breakfast table right in front of *Mütti* as though it were too hot to handle. Maria was still resentful that *Mütti* had tried to manipulate her. When *Mütti* saw the envelope, she looked at it as if an alien object had fallen from the sky, and then at Maria. From the front of the pocket of her apron, she took out the reading glasses that she had received at the hospital. She opened her glasses very gingerly, picked up the envelope, pulled out the letter, and began reading. When she was done she put the letter back into the envelope and left it on the table without a word. Maria began to weep and started to run out of the dining room.

As she turned just before exiting the room, *Mütti* said to her bitterly, on the verge of tears, "I suppose you are taking great pleasure in defying me?"

"That is so unfair, *Mütti*," Maria managed to get out through her tears. "To both Pastor Bonhöffer and myself. You know *Papa* loved Pastor Bonhöffer. He really did. Or do you prefer to forget?"

"Yes, I'll admit your father was fond of Pastor Bonhöffer. That is different from 'loving him,' however. After all, *Papa* didn't know much about him when he said that."

"That's not true. Pastor mentions something about *Papa* in every letter he sends me."

"He obviously knows what nice things to say to a young, unattached, grieving girl who is available, Maria. He's old enough to be your father."

"I don't care! He's so much more fascinating, more substantial, than boys my age, so much wiser."

"Maria, with the war, you've hardly had a chance to get to know many boys your age. All along I hoped you would."

"That's because I had my heart set on Pastor Bonhöffer."

"For such a young woman like yourself that's a very foolish thing to do, Maria. To put all your eggs in the one basket."

"*Mütti,* don't you understand? I love him, love him enough to marry him."

"Love is difficult to understand. Happiness in marriage is a difficult matter to predict. You're new to this kind of love that seems to sweep you off your feet. Why wouldn't you love him since he knows that you hang onto his every word? Why wouldn't you love him when he holds the promise of replacing your father and Max?"

"That is totally unfair! No one will replace my father or brother. Pastor Bonhöffer is wiser than to try to replace them in my life. He gives me space to grieve."

"What will you do, Maria, on the day when you enter a room and you notice that he no longer lights up like a *Tannenbaum*? Even in marriage, that is bound to happen, you know."

"Mütti, let me ask you the same question. What did you do when *Papa* no longer worshiped the ground you walked on?"

"That's impertinent!"

"Why don't you tell me? Aren't mothers supposed to teach their daughters about marriage?"

Maria turned to look the other way, regretting that she had spoken without thinking first. She didn't want *Mütti* to feel that she thought she was a failure as a mother. She wanted to make amends and reached out for her hand. *Mütti* pulled away immediately, then reached back to take Maria's hand after all.

"Oh, sweet baby of mine," she said, kissing Maria's hand. "Marriage is more than your heart fluttering in your breast or the sensation of the earth shaking under your feet every time you think of him. *Papa* and I enjoyed feeling like that but that was a long time ago. You've witnessed domestic life around here. You know your father and I loved each other deeply. But marriage is listening to your husband even if you disagree with him; it's nursing your husband when he falls ill, and then nursing the children you've made together when they get sick, too. Marriage is making sure your husband's best shirt is washed and ironed and ready to wear to church the next day and then finally getting to your own wardrobe when his and the children's clothes are clean and pressed. Marriage is agreeing to make love with your husband even when you're exhausted after a long day and don't feel like it in the least."

Maria saw her wipe a tear from her eye and added, "Sometimes marriage is burying your husband and standing at the foot of the grave of one of your children."

No matter the empathy she felt for her mother's loss, Maria resented the remark as well. It was another less than subtle form of manipulation. She chose not to be diverted.

"If you refuse us, you will make me a miserable woman for the rest of my life. I love him, and he loves me. What does age have to do with love?"

Mütti was silent. That threw Maria off. She was expecting another comeback that she could counter. Instead, *Mütti* stood up silently and said in a tone of wounded umbrage.

"So, you will go up to your room and spend the night weeping and accusing me of treating you unfairly? I suppose it's what I will have to endure even after *Papa's* and now Max's death."

"You aren't the only one who has lost them. You seem to forget that. Pastor Bonhöffer has supported and comforted me and helped me in my grieving." Maria and *Mütti* both wept in sorrow and frustration.

Again, Maria was about to leave the room, figuring that they had gone as far as they were going to go on that one night. But before she got to the door, *Mütti* said, "Very well, then. You may write to Pastor Bonhöffer and tell him he is welcome to come to Pätzig if he wants to talk to me."

Maria's tears turned to a glow of joy as *Mütti* put her arms around her and said gently, "I am not making any promises, mind you, just a commitment to listen to Pastor. We'll have to wait to see how that goes."

Chapter Eleven

I've never made it difficult for Mütti *and my sister to see into the innermost depths of my heart, but it has been a different story since Father and Max were killed. Now neither of them understands me anymore. They fail to grasp that there are things that belong to me alone, to me and to you.*

—Maria von Wedemeyer

November 1942

It wasn't until late November that Dietrich was able to get away from his *Abwehr* duties to come to Pätzig to talk with *Frau* von Wedemeyer. He was anxious about how he would be received by the pious woman who had disinvited him from her son's funeral. He was defensive but also optimistic that he could use his verbal skills to negotiate a truce with her.

To his relief, she received him graciously. She thanked him for making the time to travel the long distance to Pätzig, though she didn't fail to mention that she would have preferred to have had this conversation before he had, as she put it, "planted the notion of marriage in Maria's head." She was calm and friendly, although Dietrich experienced the conversation as tense. She pointed to the easy chair for him to take a seat while she settled into one facing him.

Dietrich was struck by-the large portrait of her late husband on the wall. He was dressed impressively in his *Wehrmacht* uniform, standing tall and erect. On the other wall there was a smaller portrait of a smiling Max, also in his uniform, holding up his rifle in the air in a stance of victory. The photo had obviously been taken in Paris, with the *Arc de Triomphe* in the background. Dietrich couldn't look at Max's portrait for very long. It reminded him bitterly of how tragically young Max had been when he was killed. He was also still acutely aware of the sting of being excluded from Max's funeral by the woman before him without having an idea why.

"Let me begin, *Frau* von Wedemeyer, by assuring you that I have full respect for your prerogative as Maria's mother. If my proposing to your beautiful daughter seemed a little rushed to you, I apologize sincerely."

"Well, yes, you certainly did move things along more rapidly than I would have wished. A little premature, I think. But I have been in love, too, Pastor, and I think I understand the impatience of the young when they are overcome by deep feelings that are difficult to understand, much less control."

This woman was barely a few years older than he, but she had a way of making him feel like an inexperienced boy. But she had been married for a long time, and he felt that he ought to honor her seniority by considering her words. He suppressed any hint of the resentment that welled up in his chest.

"Yes, you are correct, *Frau*. Once I came to the conclusion that I want to spend the rest of my life with Maria, I was unable to keep the decision to myself. My work for the *Abwehr* has taken me to many places in the past few months. But wherever I traveled, it was Maria I looked for in the crowd at the train station, in the restaurants, and on the busy sidewalks of the city. I want you to know how much I love your daughter and intend to do all I can humanly do to make her happy."

"It's not your love for my daughter that I am anxious about. It's the difference in your ages and experience that makes me hesitant to give my wholehearted blessing to your plans for a union."

"That's totally understandable. It's one of the first questions that I had to answer for myself before I proceeded to propose to her."

"And? What answer did you come up with?"

Dietrich paused and thought about how he might answer the question honestly. He chose his words carefully. "I don't consider myself to be ancient, by any means. Nonetheless, I do feel the clock ticking more rapidly now in my mid-30s. I notice every month and year, every minute and second, passing more quickly now. I have discovered within myself a profound need to have someone by my side whom I love and who loves me with whom to share those precious moments."

After Dietrich said this it dawned on him that she had lost that person in her life only recently and was now set adrift alone. The look in her blue eyes confirmed that she had the same realization.

"I can understand such a feeling, Pastor. It's often not until you lose the person you love and who has been by your side for many years that you come to appreciate how important that is."

"Again, *Frau*, I offer my most sincere condolences."

She paused to accept his offer of sympathy before she continued.

"Pastor, you are willing to risk that an 18-year-old girl with no previous experience in love can serve as that someone you love who stands with you throughout your life? Perhaps you have a higher level of confidence in her than I do."

"Perhaps that's the case, of course. Or is it possible that you have a lower level of confidence than I in her abilities and amazingly precocious intuitive insight about how to be supportive of a man?"

"That's always possible, of course. Some days I think of her as the baby I held in my arms and the little girl who needed direction not so very long ago. Then it startles me that she's not that helpless little girl any longer."

"She's grown up into a fine young lady. You can be proud of how you and your husband have raised her."

"Sometimes our children just grow up to become who they are meant to be, irrespective of what their parents do or don't do."

"Then we can agree that she has grown up to be her own person, capable of her own decisions about her life?"

"I think that only time will tell. The two of you haven't allowed yourselves much time to get to know each other."

"Well, *Frau*, you must also count the years when I taught her confirmation. I realize that she was a girl six or seven years ago, but a very mature one. I formed a good and I think accurate assessment of the essential person that she was and continues to be. I'm not at all surprised that she has grown up to be who she has become."

"I have concluded, Pastor, that more time is what you and Maria need before marriage. You concluded likewise, you recall, when you decided to delay Maria's confirmation instruction for a year because you judged at the time that she was too young to comprehend fully what you called 'the cost of discipleship.'"

He did recall. He had no comeback to her observation. His heart sank in anticipation of what he feared she might propose.

She continued. "I would like to request that the two of you wait for the period of one year. And that during that time you pursue your lives separately without seeing each other. If at the end of that time you still feel confident in your decision that you and Maria should marry, we can announce the engagement publicly, and things can proceed from there. That's how these things are handled in families here in Pomerania."

Pensively, he weighed her words.

"Well, if that is the condition for having Maria as my wife for the rest of my life, dear *Frau*, I will agree to it. But, with all due respect, please allow me to make a comment about your request."

"Of course. That's why we are here to discuss this."

"I've noticed that since the war started, time is measured differently than before. In one week enough life-changing developments can take place that would take years to occur were we not at war. A year in our circumstances is no longer just one year. That's my only hesitation about your request for a one-year waiting period."

Frau von Wedemeyer seemed prepared for this last-minute pushback. "One year it shall be, Pastor. That's my final offer. You yourself accepted it just a few moments ago."

Dietrich could only nod his reluctant agreement. He thanked *Frau* von Wedemeyer and got up from the easy chair to take leave.

"I've got one more thing I'd like to add, Pastor," she said before he was on his feet.

"Yes, of course, *Frau*. As you say, that's why we're together discussing this matter."

"I must admit that I am more than a little anxious about your work. With the *Abwehr,* I mean."

He was taken aback and very quick to respond. He tried to control and mask his rising anxiety whenever anyone got close to "the secret."

"These are dangerous times, *Frau*. The risks I take in the service of the *Abwehr* are no greater than those your late husband and son took on the eastern front."

"That's part of my anxiety, yes. Were you to be discovered by our opponents to be part of the *Abwehr,* you would very likely be killed. I wouldn't want my little girl to become a war widow at such a young age."

Dietrich thought of the middle-aged man whom he had spotted on the train coming back from Geneva and at the airport in Oslo who seemed to be watching him intently. Was he an *SS* or *Gestapo* agent sent to observe and report to superiors about his every movement? Had the man been sent to neutralize him? Or was he being paranoid? Was it just a coincidence that this same man was traveling back from Geneva on the same train as him, or traveling through Oslo on the same day?

"The *Abwehr* has a detailed strategy for the safety of its agents. There are no guarantees, of course, but I put trust in the systems of security that men smarter than I have put in place."

"As I say, that's part of my anxiety, but only one part. The other part is, how do I put this? With all due respect for your service to our country, your participation in the intelligence services of the *Abwehr* is a little suspect in my mind. I suspect that there's more to your work than appears on the surface."

Again, he was very eager to put her suspicions to rest. *How much of my work does she know? My real work?*

"Suspect, *Frau*? In what way? Why would you think that? Frankly, I am surprised and frankly, a little disappointed."

"At the moment they are only suspicions without the benefit of evidence to make them more. I think it's the way your clandestine seminary—"

"You mean Finkenwalde?"

"Yes, the way Finkenwalde was suddenly closed and outlawed by the *Gestapo* is a source of doubt for me. That the *Gestapo* had their eye on you means that they probably continue to do so today, years later. If they have you in their sights, then they will have anyone closely attached to you in their sights as well. That means my daughter— your wife—should you marry her, Pastor."

Dietrich did not see Maria during the visit with her mother. The Red Cross had assigned her as a nurse to the Bethel Institution in Bielefeld in Westphalia.

He was familiar with the Bethel Institution. It had been founded in the middle of the previous century for the compassionate care and healing of epileptics. Its primary founder was Pastor Friedrich von Bodelshwing, Sr., who became its first director. Bodelschwing had greatly expanded the facilities at Bethel and its mission so that by the turn of the century it had become a haven for the poor and sick of Westphalia.

Shortly after Hitler's assuming power in 1933, Pastor Bodelshwing, Jr., the son of the founder, invited Dietrich and several other pastors and theologians of the Confessing Church to Bethel to draft a new confession for the church. In this early form of resistance to Hitler, the signers of the Bethel Declaration proclaimed their rejection of Christian anti-Judaism and anti-Semitism throughout Germany.

He heard by letter from Maria a little over a week after a crisis there.

Oh, Pastor Bonhöffer, how rapidly the genteel environment of Bethel has been destroyed by forces of our own government! People were being healed here, and the patients who could not be cured were receiving the very best of compassionate care. I was very proud and grateful to have been assigned here.

You are aware, however, that in 1940, the *Führer* ordered the gassing of all mental patients in German hospitals. Not long after I arrived here in October, the government sent a medical commission to inspect Bethel or, should I say, to inspect the patients of Bethel. Pastor Bodelschwing, Jr., put up noble resistance. "You can put me into a concentration camp if you want," he reportedly told the head of the commission from Berlin. "But as long as I am free, you shall not touch a single one of my patients. I cannot change to fit the times or the frankly shocking whims of the *Führer*. I stand under the orders from our Lord Jesus Christ."

But Pastor Bodelshwing's appeal had no practical effect, unfortunately. The commission left Bethel and was replaced by hundreds of *SS* and *Wehrmacht* personnel who proceeded to carry out the illest patients and force those who were ambulatory to march in rows into ambulances and vans outside the hospital with their motors already running.

It was a frightfully sad sight. I was in tears, along with many others of the staff. The innocent patients from the mental wards were led to believe that they were going on a day trip to a site of interest in the surrounding countryside. Some of them even waved innocently to us as we watched them enter the ambulances.

I went to bed that night terrorized, but grateful that the seizure of the patients was over. Only, it was not. At breakfast the very next morning, we heard the sound of the lorries entering the grounds carrying the soldiers back to the institution. Even though they had been sternly ordered not to do so by Pastor Bodelschwing, some of the ward clerks pointed out the incurable epileptic patients to the inquiring soldiers. The epileptics were led out of the wards by soldiers holding a gun to their backs.

The soldiers returned to the wards again and asked for any Jewish patients or staff. Half-dressed Jewish patients were paraded through the corridors and outside the institution toward the waiting vans. Someone on the staff identified Dr. Morgenstern as a Jew; he was then placed in handcuffs and forced at gunpoint to join the patients in the transports. Dr. Morgenstern had a reputation among the rest of the staff of being the best psychiatrist on the Bethel staff. It wasn't until they took Dr. Morgenstern that it began to dawn on me where the patients were being taken. Horrific!

In such an unexpected way my dream of being assigned here turned in just a matter of days into a horrible nightmare. Some of my fellow Red Cross appointees have been so traumatized that they have asked and been granted permission by the administration of Bethel to return home. I will complete my assignment, however, even though the joy of serving here has been stolen from me.

This whole tragic episode has made me long even more profoundly for you and to anticipate even more eagerly a peaceful and happy future together after our marriage.

I know personally now how violated you felt when several years ago you came to Köslin to tell my grandmother and me about the burning of the synagogue at Schlawe. But to watch this tragic injustice perpetrated by the very government we have been taught to respect and obey! Shameful.

What on earth can be done about the *Führer* and what I have come to see are his viciously cruel, violent policies and practices?

We are not supposed to see each other this year, of course, according to our agreement with *Mütti*. You were prudent to agree to her conditions, no matter how much I resent them. I don't think we have any choice.

But let me say that if your work brings you in the vicinity of Bielefeld, I would be extremely disappointed if you did not make an effort to come quietly and visit me. But I realize how you don't want to deceive *Mütti* or anyone else—for which I love you dearly.

    Yours always,
    Maria

BOOK TWO

The great masquerade of evil has played havoc with all our ethical concepts in Germany. For evil to appear disguised as light, charity, historical necessity or social justice is quite bewildering to anyone brought up on our traditional ethical concepts, while for the Christian who bases his life on the Bible, it merely confirms the fundamental wickedness of evil.

—Dietrich Bonhöffer

Chapter Twelve

You, Lord, have granted me many blessings; let me also accept what is hard from your hand.

—Dietrich Bonhöffer

Tegel Military Interrogation Prison
Berlin: April 5, 1943

A single, low wattage light was suspended from the holding cell ceiling. The concrete floor felt to Dietrich's bare feet as though it hadn't been swept in years. Against the wall stood a tiny porcelain sink displaying the telltale brown stains left by streams of hard water from the cold water tap, the only one it had. A horrible odor of human waste filled the tiny space. Dietrich looked in the corner and saw the offending slop bucket with clumps of feces floating in unpleasantly colored fluid. Clearly, the bucket had not been emptied when the previous inmate had been moved out.

The foul smell of sulphur and burning brimstone. This is the cave of Satan. I must find a way out of here before Satan victimizes me with his bitter and ceaseless attacks on the soul.

Dietrich had always known arrest and imprisonment by the *Gestapo* was a possibility, but it hadn't really felt real. Arrest and imprisonment had remained a largely theoretical possibility. He had thumbed his nose at the government for so long, his anti-Nazi activities had been so public—first through his seminary with the Confessing Church, later by speaking out against injustice whenever he could—and nothing had ever happened to him. Oh, he had been banned from Berlin, but he had even gotten around that when he began working with the *Abwehr*. For much of his life, he had taken it for granted that he was somehow immune from life's worst consequences and would be exempted from the most serious pain and suffering.

For the first 37 years of his life, Dietrich had enjoyed upper-middle-class privilege and security. His status as the son of a well-respected psychiatrist provided for him and his siblings certain creature comforts and advantages that many of his contemporaries did not enjoy. His father's reputation opened the doors of many fascinating scientists, medical experts, and other intellectuals who enriched his intellectual life. The Bonhöffer family was squeezed by the spiraling inflation of the Weimar era but possessed sufficient independent financial resources to escape the most disastrous effects or make the most painful sacrifices.

Dietrich inherited from his parents and older siblings an unexamined assumption that there would always be someone nearby with the power or influence to exempt them from the routine difficulties of normal people, a divine right to protection by virtue of their father's industriousness and success, and the family's good name.

But on the night of June 5, 1943, Dietrich could not be cheered or comforted by the good fortune of his life to date. As the members of the *Gestapo* threw him unceremoniously into a holding cell in the basement of the Tegel Military Prison in northwestern Berlin, he thought his store of good fortune had either been exhausted or had been a foolish, arrogant illusion to begin with.

Exhausted, Dietrich walked hopefully in the direction of the cot that had a single blanket on it. It had no mattress, only its metal grid to lie on, and his hope turned to dust when he picked up the blanket to pull over himself and detected the overwhelmingly foul odor of human sweat. He discarded the blanket onto the floor and lay down on the metal grid.

Remnants of the Satanic enemy at every turn. I can't endure this.

Before he closed his eyes to sleep, he noticed an end piece of a loaf of bread on the utilitarian wooden desk against the whitewashed wall. He felt a pang of hunger; he had, of course, missed his dinner with Maria at Ursula's. The thought of Maria nearly destroyed him again. *What would happen to her? Would she be caught with him in this trap?* The Nazis were known to threaten loved ones.

But resolutely he struggled up from the flimsy cot, reached for the piece of bread, and took a bite. He spit it out on the floor immediately. It was covered with mold and tasted absolutely putrid.

If there is a hell on earth, it's this place.

He took into his hands his jacket, which he had laid down on the arm of a wooden chair. He folded it neatly into a square and placed it under his head as a pillow to soften the sharp impact of the metal grid of the cot against the bare skin of his head.

He laid his spectacles with the round lenses on the floor beside the bed at a sufficient distance from where his feet would step in case he had to get up suddenly in the middle of the night.

He lay on his back on the cot; he needed to turn his head to one side and cover his eyes with his elbow to shield them from the light. He could not find a comfortable position but tossed and turned with no relief.

No one who loves me or whom I love can reach me here in this darkness. Not my parents. Not my siblings. Not Eberhard. Not Hans. Not even dear Maria. All so close, yet so infinitely far away. I fear forever. In my most horrific imaginings, I never pictured my short life coming to a bitter end in a God-forsaken monument to the forces of death like this.

In short order, he heard a sound like one piece of wood sliding against another. Dietrich sat up on the cot, opened his eyes, and tried to see where the noise was coming from. He saw nothing but the wall until he heard the sliding sound once again. A wooden covering about ten inches by six inches or so slid across an opening in the wall. Dietrich looked carefully at the empty opening and was certain he spied two peering human eyes observing him from outside the cell.

Satan has his cynical eyes on me. I can try to sleep but I can't escape his prying eyes. Those demonic eyes are more powerful, more penetrating, more oppressive than the two feet thick walls of this fortress that suffocates me. Oh Maria, save me. Forgive me for this. I can't blame you for any confusion or disappointment in me. Is there still even the slightest reason for me to hope that our engagement is not off? If it is, I cannot go on. I cannot.

When the observer noticed that he had been discovered, he rapidly pulled the wooden covering closed, covered the opening, and disappeared as strangely as he had appeared. Dietrich leaned back on the cot and closed his eyes to sleep.

Come, welcome sleep, come. Come carry me directly to heaven on your compassionate wings of mercy from this horrid pit. And do not allow terrifying dreams to come over me.

Twenty-four hours later, the same thing happened again. The two eyes reappeared. This time, however, the eyes seemed to beckon Dietrich closer. A voice said, "Take the tray. This is your dinner."

Having announced himself, the man pushed a plastic tray through the slot in the wooden covering onto a small platform that extended into the cell. Dietrich approached slowly and glanced at the food. He still had the lingering bad taste of the moldy bread on his tongue, and the cell had a more obscene fecal smell than the previous evening. Dietrich looked at the two eyes in the slot and shook his head to decline what was being offered.

Are these the sinister eyes of Satan? Or the eyes of God mocking me? I have placed myself into God's hands. But where is God now?

"In case you get hungry and change your mind, I will leave the tray on the platform and pick up the used dishes on my rounds tomorrow. Goodnight."

On the next evening, his third in the cell, the wooden cover over the opening in the wall was slid to the side and another tray was pushed through.

The voice with the eyes spoke. "I noticed that you didn't eat a bite yesterday or the day before. You need to build up your strength, friend. I'd advise you to take the tray this evening and replenish your energy."

Dietrich was plenty hungry by now and considered the wisdom of the man's advice. He stood up, approached the tray in the slot cautiously, and prepared to pull it into his cell. However, it was too big to slide all the way through the slot. Dietrich tried rearranging the angle of the tray to get it to slide through, but it didn't work.

"I see we have a little problem," said the man on the other side of the slot. "I can solve that in a minute or so."

In a few seconds, Dietrich heard the jingle of keys behind the solid metal door leading in and out of the cell. A key turned the lock, and the door opened. A stocky uniformed man held out the tray to Dietrich. Dietrich took hold of the tray and looked into the man's eyes.

The man seemed to be in no hurry to exit the cell, lock the door once again, and leave Dietrich to his meal. Dietrich was in no mood to be with people.

I just want to be left by myself with my thoughts.

The guard didn't give any hint that he was afraid of being taken down by the prisoner in an attempt to escape. Instead, the burly man smiled in an unexpectedly friendly manner and spoke to him genially.

"It's Pastor Bonhöffer, isn't it? Ever since I observed you on your first night here I've been racking my brain trying to remember your name. I checked the prisoner list in the central office, and there was the name I was trying to recall: Rev. Dr. Dietrich Bonhöffer."

As the man spoke, Dietrich examined his face and listened to the timbre of his voice, but neither provided a hint as to who this man was who recognized him. He noticed the small metal name tag pinned to the guard's shirt. "Knobloch." Still no recognition.

"I am Knobloch, Corporal Knobloch," the man said. "You knew me as Kurt. You were our youth group leader many years ago at our church."

"Kurt. Kurt Knobloch," Dietrich repeated, trying to resurrect the name from his past.

"It's been many years, Pastor. I can't blame you if you can't remember. I think it was in either 1931 or 1932."

"Yes, I'm beginning to recall. It was at the church in Wedding, right? It was so long ago."

Knobloch flashed a broad smile at the reunion.

"Now that I've seen you again, it feels as though it were yesterday."

"I was about to be ordained as a pastor at that time," Dietrich informed him through a smile.

"Oh, you were already a pastor as far as we boys were concerned. You were *our* pastor. I doubt I will ever forget the evenings when you invited us all to your flat near the church for Confirmation lessons, which didn't seem like Confirmation lessons at all but rather life lessons. We would ask you questions about any topic. You were able to relate God to any topic we named."

"My goodness, so much has happened in my life since then. But I am still a pastor, and I wear the same kind of traditional glasses that you boys made fun of," Dietrich chuckled.

"Little did we guess that we'd meet again someday, eh?" Knobloch said, laughing. "Even less did we expect to have our reunion in the basement of a military prison."

"Some in my family warned me that I was playing with fire. But still, I'm surprised to find myself here," Dietrich said reflectively.

"Not many of the inmates here started out in life with the ambition of being here."

The smiles vanished from the faces of both men.

"Knobloch, may I ask you a very personal and confidential question?"

"Of course, Pastor."

"Is it quite normal on the first nights here for the prisoner to have serious thoughts of suicide?" He asked it as though it were the most natural question in the world.

Knobloch was startled by such a direct question. He looked at Dietrich with alarm.

"Let me ask you a follow-up question, Pastor. Does that question mean that you have been having such thoughts? I wouldn't expect such ideas in the mind of a pastor."

"Knobloch, pastors are only people, human beings, first before they're pastors. When the *Gestapo* brought me here, I felt totally lost. I considered myself as good as dead. I may have lost forever all that means anything to me. I am separated from the beautiful young woman I love and with whom I am engaged. I am prevented from carrying on my work, my ministry, my battle for the soul of the Confessing Church, also my, let's call it, my civic involvement that gives my life meaning and purpose. Without those, I have nothing, I am nothing, I have no purpose for waking up in the morning."

"I am sorry to hear that."

"I don't know how much the *Wehrmacht* knows about me. I've not been told what I am accused of. This prison makes me feel crowded by claustrophobia. I feel cut off from all that I love. I have been thinking seriously that I would be better off dead."

"Certainly not, Pastor."

"But how to do it, Knobloch? That's the problem. They've confiscated my laces with my shoes. There's no sheet on this cot with which to hang myself." Holding up the spoon provided on his food tray, he added, "You see there's no way I can sharpen it into a weapon to use against myself. I cannot think of a way to die."

"I know I would not want to be confined to this place," Knobloch agreed. "But it will probably not be forever, or even for very long. If you are being accused of a crime deserving death, they would not have assigned you to Tegel. They'd have shipped you directly to the *Gestapo* prison in the basement of their headquarters on *Prinz Albrecht Strasse*. Here you are spared the horrible sounds of the torture of others or waiting in anticipation of your own. I've been told that the torture there is terrible to endure. You may not believe it right now, but because you're here at Tegel, you may be a lucky man."

Dietrich looked at Knobloch with a mixture of desperate hopefulness that Knobloch spoke the truth and skepticism that he was a lucky man.

"Knobloch, you may not appreciate how good it is for me to hear a friendly voice." Dietrich held out to him his trembling hand. "All I have been able to hear during these last few days and nights are the distorted echoes of my own disintegrating mind going around in circles and not arriving anywhere. But even in the midst of my dark despair and tortured thoughts, my mind was beginning to show signs of being straightened out. How could I doubt that Christ will be beside me and will see me through come whatever may? How could I seriously fantasize about bringing my life to a premature end when it is God's gift for me to live fully?"

"Those thoughts sound so much more healthy."

"But you may not realize that it was a pair of eyes peering into my cell that have probably saved my life."

"A pair of eyes? How so, Pastor?"

"When I first caught sight of those two eyeballs in the wall, I couldn't know if they were friend or foe. I assumed that in a Nazi prison they were foe. But when you persisted in offering me sustenance and even risked unlocking and opening my cell door, and speaking with me in such a friendly way, I learned that the eyes were those of a friend, not foe."

"It was warmth and comfort that I was trying to communicate, especially after I discovered who you are."

"To hear such a friendly voice lent me assurance of my safety here as opposed to the torture at the *Gestapo* prison; it had the effect of chasing my despair and thoughts of suicide away. You helped me to hope again that I am not alone in this prison, and that even in this place of trial and punishment, with a Christian companion's help, I can rediscover a reason to go on living, go on striving and hoping. You have been an angel sent from God. Really. Thank you, Knobloch."

"I have regretted over the years, Pastor, that I have never taken the time to write you a note of gratitude for your devotion to us lower-class, wayward, urban youth in Wedding. You didn't give up on us when others had. Your year with us was a true turning point in my life. I'm a dozen years late, but I want to thank you now. I hope there will be some way to show my gratitude to you."

Dietrich smiled broadly at his former student and embraced him. He began to use his spoon to dig into the meager pile of cooked cabbage on the tray. After a while chewing his food, he looked up at Knobloch and said, "Perhaps there is something you can do for me, Kurt."

"What is that, Pastor?"

"I was told that I can correspond with my family every ten days. But they haven't supplied me with paper and pencil and gave no indication that they would be forthcoming. I don't want to ask you to compromise your relationship with your superiors. But I am wondering if it might be possible for you to smuggle me pencil and paper without getting into trouble?"

Knobloch showed Dietrich an enthusiastic smile. "Consider it done, Pastor. I'll have them here tomorrow at supper time."

Chapter Thirteen

I hold your picture in my hand every night and tell you lots of things, all the things that can't be put into writing, things you already know without my writing them down.

—Maria von Wedemeyer

Tegel Prison: April 1943

Dietrich's fortunes in Tegel Prison began to improve very soon, as did his spirits. Within a few days, Tegel *Kommandant* Mätz gave the order for Bonhöffer to be transferred from his holding cell in the basement to cell number 92, a regular cell on the third floor. Bonhöffer rejoiced in the move out of that depressing holding cell. He was comforted, too, that Knobloch continued to be assigned to oversee his cell. When Dietrich had arrived at Tegel he had lucked into a relatively favorable situation in which he could receive certain prohibited items from a guard. Even with the move to the third floor, his luck continued.

The move also meant that his term of solitary confinement was over. He was now allowed to join other prisoners in the exercise yard for an hour every day. He craved human company. He was also permitted to receive mail and packages—once they had been inspected for contraband, of course.

The very first day Dietrich was eligible to enjoy these new privileges, a package did arrive. Knobloch picked it up and delivered it to the prisoner.

"This prisoner sure plans to do a lot of reading," the mail inspector said as he handed Knobloch the package. "The package is barely under the maximum weight, but it consists almost entirely of books."

Knobloch rapped on the door of cell number 92. Dietrich had by now discovered that he could open the food slot from inside his cell as well. He did that now to see who was knocking on his door. When he saw who it was, he said, "Good, Knobloch, come right in."

Cell 92 was meant to be occupied only by one prisoner at a time.

His cot was furnished with a thin mattress and a more Spartan but relatively clean blanket. He had a wooden bench and stool. Knobloch saw that he must try to get him a better desk for his writing. The slop bucket stank but was empty. There was a small, barred window above the prisoner's head. If he tried to balance the stool on his cot, Dietrich would be able to see out, but he said he was resisting the temptation for the time being.

"I will wait for later so that I have something to look forward to," he explained.

Knobloch handed him the package.

Dietrich examined the postmark. "It's from my parents in Charlottenburg. There are bound to be delicious treats inside the package."

Dietrich started to take items from the package one by one and lay them on his cot as though they were meant to be displayed as at a shop.

"Look at all this, Knobloch. I feel very rich today. I want you to look them over first and choose an item or two for yourself and your family. There's plenty here so I will happily take what's left over. You're such a gift to me, Knobloch."

Knobloch looked at Dietrich's face to try to gauge his seriousness.

"Go on, Knobloch. Don't hesitate. I want you to have something from my parents."

There were six cigarettes wrapped inside a handkerchief. Knobloch shyly took two.

"Now take an additional two and enjoy them. Perhaps give a couple to your wife and enjoy your smokes together. I wish I could do that with my sweetheart."

Knobloch thanked him and took two more, thinking that four cigarettes more than sufficed.

"No, Knobloch. You must take more."

Dietrich leaned down to the cot and grabbed a small package.

"Here, take this. *Papa* or *Mütti* was thoughtful enough to include some malt extract. They know how much I used to enjoy a draught of some at the end of the day. But they don't know there's no means here in my cell for me to prepare it. So, please take it and share it with your children. I know it's very difficult to get your hands on malt these days."

The pastor snuck a furtive peek every now and then at the books on the cot. He obviously wanted to get to them.

"In a couple of months, I'm afraid, Pastor, when the weather gets warmer, all the hot air in the prison will have risen up here to the third floor," Knobloch informed him.

"That's better than the cold down in the holding cell with only that rancid blanket. Besides, I am confident that by the time the really warm weather arrives, I will no longer be here."

"You sound optimistic."

"Do you know of a reason why I shouldn't? Have you heard news of my hearing?"

"We lowly guards aren't privy to that kind of classified information. But I believe your prosecutor will be Captain Röder. Judge-Advocate Röder, actually. He's pretty fussy about the title. I have heard that he is a little eccentric and tough as nails, unfortunately. He is very thorough and will not move on to the next prisoner until he's finished with the one standing before him."

"In other words," Dietrich commented with a smile, "I shouldn't be expected to be called up before him anytime soon."

Knobloch chuckled. "If I were a betting man, that's how I would wager. I'll be in the interrogation room with you. There's very little I can do for you then. But perhaps you will feel less alone with me there. In any case, I'll see you again tomorrow."

With that, Knobloch was out the door and started to walk down the corridor to the stairs. Dietrich sat on his cot and examined the books his parents had sent. None of them were new to him. He had read them all. They remembered not to send any books he would use for research for his *Ethics* as he had instructed them.

All the more reason to have my hearing and get out of this place.

He picked up one of the books and turned to the inner flyleaf where his name was written and underlined in his father's familiar handwriting: Dietrich Bonhöffer. That was the signal they had agreed upon when the possibility of Dietrich's being imprisoned had come up. That possibility seemed merely theoretical at the time. Now Dietrich was glad the family had made a secret communication plan. When he saw his name underlined, he knew that there was a secret message from his parents inside the book.

He went immediately to the index pages at the back. It wasn't a reference he was looking for, but a word every ten or so pages, faintly underlined in pencil, starting at the end of the book. He flipped the pages and made a list of all the underlined words and then silently mouthed them.

Hans also imprisoned the same night. Christel, too. Hans taken to Sachsenhausen. Thank God, Christel has been released.

Dietrich lay on his back on the cot to rest after the excitement and effort. He thought gratefully of the kindness and faithfulness of his parents. He wiped away the tear from the corner of his eye with his knuckle as he used to as a little boy. He turned his head slightly, and it was then that he noticed the words on the wall opposite, scratched carefully in a small patient script: "Friend, in 100 years it will all be over."

Mentally, he understood the desperate feeling but nonetheless scoffed at the ridiculous sentiment. *I'll be dead in a hundred years, or probably before.* He looked back at the open window through which the bright morning sun was dancing into the cell.

As a reward for surviving his first night there, he decided to allow himself the treat of the window. Strangely apprehensive, he hesitated before lifting the stool up onto the cot and looking out. *Suppose there is nothing to see? Only the rest of the depressing prison building, perhaps a guard tower or worse, just a wall? But no, I am high up, near the roof, above the level of the wall, surely. There must be something to see.* Once on the stool, he held his breath and shut his eyes for fear of what he might not see. The window was open, and he felt the welcome fresh breeze against his face. He opened his eyes. Down below he could see the exercise yard with several prisoners chatting as they walked across the yard. How he longed to be there with them.

He looked at the vista again. He grabbed the bars and leaned as far forward as he could. Before him sprawled Berlin, the great beast. The locomotive works of Borsig were closest. Beyond Borsig were domes, blocks and the spires of churches, their roofs flaunting their red tiles in the spring. Almost lost among the smokestacks of Borsig, he noticed a nearby tower topped with a green copper dome in the Bavarian style, a Roman Catholic church. Would it ring the bells on Sunday mornings? *How I long to hear the bells. The bells in that steeple have rung before Hitler's Reich existed. They will still ring after it has fallen. They represent life before Hitler who will be blown away by the wind like the dried seeds of a dandelion.*

He closed his eyes in meditation and imagined the sweet singing of the church's choir, a Gregorian chant. He heard the words of the liturgy *"sursum corda,"* "Lift up your hearts." And there, in cell 92, he did.

June 1943

Knobloch was the first to greet Bonhöffer that morning. The pastor seemed rather gleeful in his cell.

"Good morning, Pastor. It must be the warm late spring air and sunshine that have you in an especially good mood today?"

"Yes, this indeed is the day God has made, and indeed, I rejoice in it."

Knobloch said, "I suspect also that the source of your elation might be traced back to the little envelope I delivered to you yesterday from the mailroom?" Knobloch gave him a mischievous wink.

"You would make a good detective, Knobloch. This is the first communication I have had from my dear Maria. I've read it over and over again a hundred times since I received it."

"A love letter, I gather?"

"Written and sent out in love, yes. But very reserved in content. She knows it will have been inspected by Hartung and his associates in the mailroom before it's passed on to me. She is very shy in the letter about expressing what she must know I want to hear. She wants our love to be kept private between just the two of us."

"I can understand that. I confess I was tempted, believe me, to take the letter out of the unsealed envelope and read it myself. But then I thought—"

"Thank you, Knobloch, for your consideration. Although I can tell you there's very little in the letter that a third party would find terribly fascinating."

"How is she? Is she faring well?

"Well enough, under the circumstances. She's chatty in the letter, full of energy and youth. Expressed between the lines, however, is the sentiment that she misses me."

"That must feel bittersweet. Hearing that she misses you feels reassuring, but then I am sure you must feel some sadness that it is your imprisonment here that causes her the pain of missing you."

"You've obviously been in love, Knobloch, to appreciate the bittersweetness. In the hours of emptiness in my cell, my thoughts of her grow stronger until I begin to fear that I won't be able to endure it much longer."

Knobloch nodded in understanding.

"I've been afraid that while I'm in here I would forget her face, the color of her eyes, the sweet sound of her voice. But you know, Knobloch, I think I've fallen in love a second time. The first time was in Köslin, where I fell in love with Maria herself in person. The second time was the occasion of her letter when I fell in love with the Maria in the letter."

Knobloch was sitting on the edge of Dietrich's cot. Knobloch reminisced about his wife, Marthe, and his early days in love, how they couldn't stand to be apart for more than 24 hours. Bonhöffer remained silent, listening.

"I do remember Maria's charming, youthful smile, Knobloch. She's always smiling except when she thinks of her father and brother, both killed on the eastern front. When I remember her face at those times, I want desperately to reach my arms out to her, embrace her, and kiss her for comfort—"

He stopped and chuckled self-consciously.

"Knobloch, you know, she and I have never actually done that, kissed each other I mean. Honest truth. Never. Not that I haven't wanted to. I've sensed that she was ready and willing, and I have been plenty of times as well once I realized we had actually fallen in love. But we've never had the chance to be alone. Don't you think that's rather unusual? Rather amusing, isn't it? We're certain that we want to be married, but we've never kissed."

Chapter Fourteen

There remains an experience of incomparable value...to see the great events of world history from below; from the perspective of the outcast, the suspects, the maltreated, the powerless, the oppressed, the reviled—in

short, from the perspective of those who suffer...to look with new eyes on matters great and small.

—Dietrich Bonhöffer

Tegel Prison, Berlin: June 1943

On Prisoner Bonhöffer's 61st day at Tegel, Knobloch escorted him as ordered to the waiting black, armored Mercedes in the courtyard. Reluctantly and gently, he placed the prisoner's hands in handcuffs behind his back as Dietrich was taken to the War Court building on *Witzlebenstrasse* where the prosecutor Manfred Röder awaited.

Knobloch was thoroughly nonplussed when an *SS* guard intercepted him as he attempted to join the prisoner in the back seat.

"For the prisoner only," the guard said while holding Knobloch back.

"But I have been assigned to serve as the objective witness in this man's hearing," Knobloch protested.

"Your assignment has been changed. You are to remain at your duties at Tegel. Judge Advocate Röder's orders."

Knobloch stepped back obediently but reluctantly. He looked at his former pastor, embarrassed because he had assured him that he would be with him at his hearing to provide companionship and support. Now he was being prevented from fulfilling his vow. The black limousine hurried out of the courtyard without Knobloch toward *Wirzlebenstrasse.*

Once there, Dietrich was ushered into a bare room with dark oak floors. A wooden bookcase with a few books, desk, and two wooden chairs furnished the room. A larger-than-life portrait of Hitler looked down menacingly from the wall behind the desk. The officious *SS* guard signaled for Dietrich to sit in the chair facing the bigger empty one behind the desk. He was left alone for what seemed like an hour but probably was actually only about ten minutes. This, he figured, was a strategy by the *Gestapo* to let the prisoner stew in his own anxiety. Dietrich tried to maintain an inner courage. But he was stewing in it, nonetheless, since he hadn't been given the slightest hint about the process or even what charge he was facing.

Finally, an *SS* guard opened the door, and a tall, thin, fortyish officer strode in, immaculate in his *SS* uniform. The officer placed a pile of files on the desk. Dietrich sprang to his feet immediately and gave the Nazi salute. His words seemed to bounce across the sparse room insincerely.

Röder muttered an automatic *Heil Hitler* and remained standing as he said, "Pastor Bonhöffer, so we meet again."

Dietrich was puzzled.

"We met a couple of months ago in your room in your parents' house. Major Sonderreger and I were inspecting the items on your desk, remember? We were your official escorts on your ride to Tegel Prison. I am Röder. Judge Advocate Röder. I will prosecute this case in the name of the Reich."

Röder proceeded to sit down behind the large desk and opened one of the files on the polished top. As an afterthought, he signaled for Dietrich to be seated. He pulled out a monocle from his breast pocket and leafed through some of the papers in the file, examining several of them more closely. Without looking up he said, "Normally, I would have come out to the prison for this hearing, but I thought you might enjoy an outing."

"Judge Advocate Röder, I appreciate that very much."

Röder smiled with satisfaction. "I expect your full cooperation in return. Can I expect that of you, Pastor?"

"I shall do my best."

"Good," Röder said as he looked up with the disingenuous smile still pasted on his face. "Then we shall get along famously."

Dietrich did not allow himself to be intimidated by Röder's officious manner. But he had to display enough deference to maintain the pretense that he was merely an ordinary clergyman who knew little or nothing of the larger issues.

"I need to ask first of all, Pastor, when we arrested you that evening, what were you doing within the limits of the city of Berlin, anyway?"

"Visiting my parents and sister next door. And writing a book of theology. That's what I do."

"To have several pairs of your nightclothes and underwear in the drawer of the dresser as we found them would suggest that you had been staying there with your parents for some time. You know, do you not, that you have been banned from Berlin? For you to be there was an illegal act."

"I didn't think the ban included visits with my parents, sir."

"In today's Germany, one should not think for oneself. The *Führer* does all the thinking that is necessary. But this is not why you are imprisoned."

"Oh? I have been curious about what charge I am facing."

Röder's aspect turned sterner suddenly. "I'll get there in my own good time, Pastor."

Dietrich felt like a little child who had asked his parents for an inappropriate item. "My apologies, sir, if I was getting ahead of myself."

"When the war began, when you were called up, why did you not appear?"

"Because of my service in the *Abwehr—*"

Röder interrupted him. "I'm aware that the fact of your service in the *Abwehr* might make you think you are exempt from serving the *Vaterland* at the front. Like your fiancée's father and brother, for example. Why did you not join them at the front? Why did you not accompany many of your former students of your illegal seminary as they gave life and limb for the cause of the Reich? People have been known to use their service in the *Abwehr* as a convenient place to hide."

He paused and looked directly into Dietrich's face to intimidate him and asked sternly, "Are you a coward, Pastor?"

A ridiculous question. "No, of course not, Your Honor." But he wanted to turn the tables and interrogate Röder. *How had he come to know so much about Maria's father and brother? What else did he know?*

"In fact, Pastor, why did you make matters worse for yourself by committing further treason?"

Dietrich was offended by this accusation.

"Treason? That's a charge I categorically deny, sir."

"You look confused, Pastor. I'm referring to your advising alumni of the illegal seminary at Finkenwalde to not report either. I have here in my files copies of those incriminating newsletters you sent out to show you, in case it has slipped your mind."

"Sir, with all respect, that was in 1937 when the war was still a matter of speculation. Whereas it's a reality now. A man has to have a chance to change his opinion as the times change."

"Oh, you think differently now?"

"Yes. I now think we all have a duty to come to the aid of our *Vaterland* in the time of its need. I think you'll find that the record shows that few if any of the alumni I advised took my advice. Most of them have served, and some have died. I feel I have also been doing my part. I have not avoided serving my country. I have taken some risks on its behalf. The trips I take abroad on behalf of the Confessing Church are much more dangerous now in wartime than before."

"Not as dangerous, are they, as meeting the enemy face to face in Kursk or Stalingrad?" Röder scoffed.

"The *Abwehr* provided the *Wehrmacht* with the vital military intelligence they needed to fight the Soviets there."

"Is the *Wehrmacht* supplying our forces with faulty information? Our men are being killed at Kursk by the hundreds."

"Not deliberate false information, I assure you, if that's what you're suggesting."

"Don't you feel any shame for not being there at the front to help?"

"Not at all. I feel badly for those who are being slaughtered there. But I serve my country best with my mind. I doubt many infantry company commanders would want me in their company. I'm not suited for such physical combat."

"Smarter than the rest of us, are you, Pastor?"

"Bearing arms in combat or leading a company of such men requires an intelligence of its own, a type of intelligence I simply do not possess."

"Should you not have allowed the *Wehrmacht* to make that decision? Some of my colleagues would judge that avoiding military service for any reason is tantamount to treason, which you must know is punishable by death."

Frustrated, Dietrich began to raise his voice. "But what I have been trying to say is that I have been serving the Reich faithfully."

Röder looked down at his papers skeptically.

"I am useful to the *Führer* right where I am—in the *Abwehr*. Few common men in Germany have the kinds of international connections that I do. Because I had worked with many of them in the churches before the war, I have gained their trust. I have been able to plant false information among them and learn things from such associations that are useful to my *Vaterland* at war."

"I assume this is supposed to impress me? It doesn't. Now, let's move on to something else, shall we, Pastor?"

Dietrich was beginning to show signs of fatigue. His right foot began to tremble. His face revealed disappointment when Röder indicated he had another tack for the hearing.

"Actually, I have a surprise visitor for you."

He reached back and knocked lightly in the back of the door into the corridor. Immediately, the *SS* guard entered with a delightful-looking, youthful young lady by his side.

Dietrich was absolutely flummoxed. He was caught off guard. He attempted to rise to greet the visitor. But it was as though the seat of his trousers was nailed to the chair. "Maria! God, I can't believe my eyes," he said under his breath.

"I can safely assume that the two of you know each other and need no introduction?"

Dietrich managed to get up from his seat and looked with utter glad surprise at Maria. She had a pale, very nervous look on her young face. She had never expected to be in a place or on an occasion such as this.

Finally, he answered Röder's question. "No, of course not, sir."

He approached Maria, took her hand, and sandwiched it tenderly between his two. Somehow he found the self-discipline not to do more, like kissing her, which he had an urge to do but Röder was still in the room. Besides, he had no idea what Röder was up to inviting Maria to this hearing. What a perverse tactic. Maria managed a nervous smile as she searched Bonhöffer's eyes for a clue.

Röder said, "I took the liberty of inviting *Fräulein* von Wedemeyer for this initial hearing. I am sure you don't mind, Pastor. But you look either disappointed, which would surprise me completely, or else poorly prepared for such a surprise."

"Well, yes, I admit this has caught me rather flat-footed. No one told me in advance."

Dietrich ran his fingers through his hair quickly in order to give it a more combed appearance.

"Your fiancée is a truly charming young woman, Pastor." Looking at her as though they had conspired secretly, he said, "She and I had a very pleasant visit earlier today. She tells me that your engagement has not yet been announced publicly. Can I ask why that is?"

Dietrich was still reorienting himself to the new circumstances in the room.

"Her mother has some hesitation about our prospective marriage. She thinks our age difference is too great."

"*Fräulein,* am I to understand then that the reason for your mother's doubt has nothing whatsoever to do with the fact that your fiancé is now in a Nazi prison?"

Maria answered back almost defiantly, "No, not at all. You heard already that my mother has some apprehension about the difference in our ages. She knows that Pastor Bonhöffer has done nothing to deserve imprisonment."

Dietrich looked at Maria with pride that she had answered so boldly.

"Actually," she continued equally fearlessly, "we have decided to move ahead with wedding plans as soon as my fiancé is released from this prison, which, by the way, we hope will be very soon."

Dietrich marveled at Maria's pluckiness in addressing the Judge Advocate. Röder was taken aback.

"I advise you not to get ahead of yourselves," Röder said in a tone of warning. "We have before us one of the most outspoken and intractable leaders of the Confessing Church movement who, as you know, did not shy away from critical comments about our *Führer.* He still has a lot to explain before any talk about being released is appropriate."

"Yes, but that was long ago, Judge Advocate Röder. I was still a little girl when he gave that interrupted speech on the radio. I have gone through many changes since that day and so, I know, has Pastor Bonhöffer."

"Tell me, *Fräulein,* is your husband-to-be as faithful to the Reich as you are to him?"

Maria hesitated before replying. *The question may contain a trick.*

"Of course he is. He serves our country faithfully in the *Abwehr.*"

"Then perhaps you can tell me why your fiancé aided a party of fourteen Jews to escape to Switzerland a year or so ago? Or perhaps you didn't know this, *Fräulein.*"

Telling red marks began to appear on his palm as she pressed her fingernails anxiously into it. "I do not know all that Pastor Bonhöffer does in his work for the *Abwehr.*"

"Judge Advocate, surely these questions are meant for me to answer, not your guest," Dietrich interjected.

"Then, by all means, answer them."

"I did not help any Jews *escape,*" he replied, emphasizing the word escape. "The *Abwehr* recruited them. The *Abwehr* thought they might be helpful serving as our agents in Switzerland."

Röder smiled a little too exaggeratedly in response. The smile disappeared suddenly. Without warning, he said to the *SS* guard, "It's time for you to take our guest back to the car."

At that, without missing a beat, the guard took Maria by her arm and started to escort her toward the door. She looked back at Dietrich, frightened. She was not going to allow Röder to foreclose this unique surprise opportunity to be with her fiancé. She pulled loose violently from the guard and began to run back toward Dietrich. The guard tried to catch her, but Röder waved him off. She opened wide her arms and put them around the surprised Dietrich in a spontaneous embrace. Then, before he or Röder realized what had just happened, she surrendered on her own volition to the guard and was promptly out the door.

Once she and the guard had exited the room, Röder said, "That was rather unexpected."

"Yes, I suppose it was," the overcome Dietrich replied.

"She's a feisty, fearless woman."

"Yes. That's why I love her. She's full of surprises."

"Pastor Bonhöffer, I look at you and listen to you, and think to myself, *This is the most fascinating and paradoxical prisoner I have interviewed in a very long time. And yet I find that I don't believe a word that comes out of his mouth.* Do you actually expect me to believe that the Jews you allegedly helped deliver to Switzerland were recruited to be *Abwehr* agents? Everyone knows that the Jews would never serve this country on their own free will, especially now."

Dietrich sat in silence, not knowing how to respond.

"Still, she impresses me. There's some wild animal sexuality lurking beneath that young, innocent face and bearing of hers. I'm sure that if you haven't explored it already, someday you will be the beneficiary of that."

Dietrich was offended at Röder's shameless lust for his fiancée.

"I think I will permit her to write to you," Röder said, "and you can begin writing to her every ten days from now on. And, furthermore, I will also let her visit you every four weeks or so for an hour if she so desires."

Dietrich looked up at Röder in consternation, not knowing whether to be grateful or suspicious. *What an unorthodox way to end a hearing. What a totally bizarre interview to begin with. Was this hearing meant to confuse me? Was it a set-up for the next hearing? What was the point of the Judge Advocate's jumping from subject to subject as he did? Or of including Maria in the proceedings? And then increasing my privileges?*

Yet, Dietrich was not totally surprised by the generous permission Röder granted to the couple. It had become known around the prison that he had friends and relations in high places. His maternal grandfather, Paul von Hase, was the military *Kommandant* of Berlin. As such, he was superior to even Mätz. Now *Kommandant* von Hase's nephew was a prisoner at Tegel. When the guards learned of the relationship with von Hase, they altered their demeanor with the prisoner, as did Mätz. There were prison rules to follow and enforce, but few of the prison staff wanted to risk offending the *Kommandant* of Berlin. Apparently, neither did the Judge Advocate himself.

Dietrich was on the cusp of thanking Röder for the unexpected new privileges, but Röder interrupted him by holding up the palms of his hands.

"Know that all that is on her account, not yours. She's quite a woman. I'm sure you catch my drift even if you are a pastor. Your connection to her and her patriotic family makes you look very good, indeed, in spite of all you've done against the Reich."

Röder stood up, gathered his files, and headed toward the door.

"Have a good trip back to Tegel, Pastor. The next time I see you will be there."

Röder picked up the plain black telephone receiver on the desk and shouted into it, "This is Judge Advocate Röder calling from *Witzlebenstrasse*. Corporal, let your commanding officer know my explicit order: Prisoner Bonhöffer is to spend the next night and day in strict solitary confinement. Is that understood?"

Chapter Fifteen

Working with patients gives me a great deal of genuine pleasure.... Nursing the sick was an immediate pleasure.... The first thing you learn is that the educated, wealthy breed are really an awful bunch, whereas you can't help taking to the ordinary little men and women right away.

—Maria von Wedemeyer

Tegel Prison: June 1943

One night after the hearing a frenetic Knobloch came to cell number 92, removed the cover of the slot in the door and spoke urgently through the slot. "Pastor Bonhöffer, are you awake?"

Dietrich sat up and rubbed the sleep from his eyes. "Yes. Is that you, Knobloch? What is it?"

"There's a new prisoner in the holding cell. He arrived just a few hours ago."

"And?"

"He's awfully young. You know how some prisoners react when they are first brought in?"

"Of course. How can I forget?"

"This one is in bad shape. He's scared half to death. He's literally banging his head against the wall. Three of us guards have been unable to calm him down. I thought that as a pastor you'd have some idea what to do."

The pastor got up from his cot and pulled on his baggy prison trousers. In the nighttime darkness, he followed the beam of Knobloch's flashlight down three floors to the basement holding cells.

The screaming sounded loud in the basement stairwell, but in front of the holding cell, it was almost unbearable. The young prisoner's shrieks caromed off the walls. Dietrich blinked his eyes at the lights that were always kept on, any hour of the day or night, down here. Knobloch unlocked the cell door and stood out of the way.

Dietrich entered the cell. He saw the wretched young man on his knees in one corner, his arms flailing about as two guards tried to subdue him. Blood flowed down his face from his lacerated scalp. He flung his head from side to side, trying to butt the wall. Dietrich fell on his knees beside the prisoner, who ignored him.

"The name?" the pastor shouted to Knobloch above the noise that filled the cell. "What's his name?"

Knobloch grabbed the clipboard hanging from a nail just outside the door to the cell. "Corporal Schmidt. Karl Schmidt," Knobloch yelled back.

"Karl!" the pastor shouted emphatically, trying to look the prisoner in the face. But the young man's eyes were fixed on something none of the rest of them could see. "Karl!"

"Karin!" the prisoner screamed. "Karin! Karin! Karin!"

"Karl, who is Karin?" Dietrich asked calmly.

The young prisoner repeated "Karin," but more quietly this time.

For the first time, Schmidt's eyes met Dietrich's.

"My girlfriend. She was going to be my fiancée." His voice shrunk to a mournful whisper.

"Your girlfriend?" the pastor repeated. "And where is Karin?"

"I don't know." Schmidt's body became rigid.

Knobloch read from the clipboard. "Schmidt was arrested for being AWOL. His girlfriend, this Karin, was injured in a bombing raid here in Berlin. Schmidt left his post in Italy to come to Berlin to look for her."

Dietrich stroked Schmidt's temples with his thumbs. "Karl," he said almost in a whisper, "have you found Karin?"

Schmidt stared at Dietrich, his eyes filled with tears.

He began shaking his head slowly, mournfully. "No. Her mother said she's dead."

Schmidt's body went limp. Dietrich wrapped his arms around him and allowed Schmidt's head to rest on his chest. Schmidt wept, his body totally calm now. Dietrich nodded at the other two guards to indicate that they could go now. Knobloch followed them out of the cell. He closed the door behind him, leaving Schmidt in the pastor's arms, but did not lock the door. Dietrich spent several hours with Schmidt in his cell. He spoke with him quietly, prayed with him, and let Schmidt's head rest on his chest until Schmidt fell asleep.

Later, in the early morning hours, Knobloch walked past cell number 92 and peered inside. The pastor was sound asleep on his cot.

News traveled fast in Tegel. Within just a few days, Knobloch had to pass on requests from prisoners for a pastoral visit from the pastor. Some of the staff put in their own requests for the same. Whenever a prisoner was brought in who responded negatively in any way to his imprisonment, the guards arranged for Dietrich to come and help them calm the prisoner. On the eve of a condemned man's execution, he would sit all night with the man.

When the news of the pastor's expert care for Schmidt reached *Kommandant* Mätz, he summoned him to his office. In light of all the requests for Dietrich's pastoral care and attention, Mätz requested that he fulfill the requests and thus help maintain the peace and morale at Tegel. To facilitate the process, Mätz informed the pastor that he would order his cell door to be kept unlocked so that he could slip out to respond to requests for his services without having to summon a guard to unlock the cell door.

Dietrich's joy in this new unexpected ministry was written on his face.

"I have a feeling, Pastor, that now that you have this new calling, there's little chance that you will try to escape and thus negate these privileges. Please don't make me look like a fool to my superiors."

Dietrich felt like giving the *Kommandant* a spontaneous embrace of gratitude. How unexpected, how gratifying, that this Nazi *Kommandant* should have concern for the spiritual welfare of his prisoners.

He laid yet another duty on Dietrich: Since the official prison chaplain had been transferred to minister to the troops on the front, would the pastor feel inclined to cover for the chaplain and make pastoral visits in the sickbay? Of course, Dietrich agreed without hesitation.

While they didn't mitigate the pain of his separation from Maria von Wedemeyer, these new opportunities to utilize his pastoral skills, to live out his mission, gave him a renewed sense of purpose. The man was born to be a pastor. Immediately he was filled with renewed energy. All marveled at his bottomless capacity for joy

Chapter Sixteen

The way Maria copes with everything is a miracle, and from my point of view, a blessing and example without equal. My utter inability to lend her more support is nearly unbearable. I truly hope far more for her sake than mine that this difficult time is not too protracted.

—Dietrich Bonhöffer

Charlottenburg: July 1943

My dear, dear Dietrich,

I know your parents invited *Mütti* and me to their home in Charlottenburg yesterday because in one of your letters to them, you asked them to. That doesn't take away from the genuineness of the hospitality which they extended to us all day. They were sincerely glad to host us in their home. I want to thank you for your thoughtfulness in making that request of them. I think my happiness after that visit with your parents is so firmly rooted that sorrow simply cannot reach that far, however immense it might seem.

I felt very comfortable with your parents the moment your dear mother received us at the door. Oh, I fell in love with everything about their home, so traditionally German in every way. Most of all, I loved your room. I can't think of anything I wouldn't give to have that chance to sit there again, if only to examine the inkblots on your desk pad, the desk where you wrote your books and your early letters to me. I sat for the longest time in your armchair and looked at the books on your shelf, your shoes by your bed, your favorite pictures on your wall. Several times your father came upstairs to beckon me down for dinner, but I pretended not to hear. I could not miss you and long for you more than I do, but I've done so twice as much since yesterday.

Every morning at six when we both fold our hands in prayer, we know that we can have great faith, not only in each other but far, far above and beyond that. And then you can't be sad any longer, can you?

Next Sunday, it will have been a full year since our fateful reunion at Köslin. It's really been a year, can you believe it? I find it almost incomprehensible that you should be the gentleman I met at that time, and with whom I talked so freely. My grandmother told me what she remembered about it. I blushed with embarrassment at all the silly things I said then.

I'll write again soon.

Your Maria

Tegel Prison: July 1943

Knobloch delivered the mail, and it included a letter from Maria. As much as Dietrich loved hearing from her, her letters sometimes made him feel sad. In many of them, she was brutally honest about her feelings of sadness that his imprisonment had lasted into the summer when he had given the impression that he would be released from Tegel before midsummer. That's what he honestly had thought.

He was also saddened by the initial restriction at Tegel against writing to anyone but his parents. He was so moved by her letters that he felt ashamed all the while that he couldn't respond to them or explain to her how much her letters meant to him. He did write to her, but it was either messages he communicated to her through his parents or else brief, hurried letters Knobloch offered to deliver into the post close to his home. He was hesitant to ask such favors of Knobloch too many times, and thereby increase the level of risk for him. But the restriction against writing to Maria was lifted by Röder in June. They launched into a substantial correspondence.

Several days after receiving his first letter, she replied:

Dearest Dietrich,

You wrote such a lovely letter. The very fact that I can expect another one in a matter of days puts me in an incredibly good mood. But when I read it, I became almost too happy, and I suddenly fear that I will be awakened from this dream to find that none of it is true. But my happiness is still much greater than my sadness—you really must believe this. I am sure it won't be long until we see each other again, in freedom and not at Tegel. I say that to myself and to you every morning and every night.

You say you want to hear some wedding plans. I've got more than enough of those. When you are free and in Pätzig again, you won't be able to get away without an engagement party. But we will marry soon after that. I want it to be during the summer when Pätzig looks its best. I picture that day in August in every detail: how I would meet you at the train; how I would go for walks with you and show you all my favorite places; how much you would like them all, too; and then we would make our own home here. Don't be depressed, dear Dietrich. Just think how happy we will be together later on and tell yourself that perhaps all this had to happen to realize how lovely our life will be and how grateful we must be.

Where shall we go for our honeymoon? And then after that, what? Then all that will matter is that the two of us are happy forever.

You must start choosing hymns and texts right away. I'd like *"Sollt ich meinem Gott nicht singen"* and Psalm 103. Do you think you can fit them in?

I've requested a transfer to the Augusta Hospital in Berlin. A lot of war-wounded have been brought there. Being near you in Berlin will be so much nicer, and I look forward to being able to visit your parents more often.

My dear Dietrich, if only I could relieve you of even a little of your burden. I'm with you every moment of every day, yet I feel so terribly far away. I long to be near you in reality. You know, don't you, that I am always

Your Maria

Dietrich read her scattered plans and preferences for their wedding. He was aware of how much such details were a source of pleasure for brides. He had witnessed the pleasure his sisters and their mother took in making such plans for their weddings and carrying them out to perfection.

In all honesty, however, he had only marginal interest in most of the details of the planning. There was never any doubt that Dietrich's primary focus in the wedding was theological. He replied to Maria's letter with one of his own.

My dear Maria,

Thank you for your beautiful, most welcome letter. When I think of the situation of the world, the complete darkness over our personal fate and my present imprisonment, then I believe that our future union as man and wife can only be a sign of God's grace and kindness, which calls us to faith. We would be blind if we did not see it. Jeremiah says at the moment of his people's great need, "still one shall buy homes and acres in this land" as a sign of trust in the future. This is where faith belongs. May God give it to us daily. I do not mean the faith that flees the world, but one that endures the world as it is and which loves and remains true to the world in spite of all the suffering it contains for us. Our marriage shall be a "yes" to God's earth; it shall strengthen our courage to act and accomplish something on the earth. I fear that Christians who stand with only one leg upon earth also stand with only one leg in heaven.

Most faithfully,

Your Dietrich

With each letter from Maria, he felt increasingly badly for her. She deserved a more "normal" courtship than he was able to give her, a long-distance relationship with such unbridgeable physical distance. Even if Tegel had been only a city block away from her home, the chasm between her life in freedom and his in prison was nearly irreconcilable. He tried to keep her close to him by thinking of her many times each day, utilizing the new freedom granted him to write to her, and by praying each morning and night, and many times in between, that their shared Lord would hold them both in the strong palm of his hand.

Chapter Seventeen

Tomorrow morning, I come to Tegel, and bring all the things you wanted. How I envy them for being able to go to you and be with you. It's only now as I anticipate being with you tomorrow that I realize how much it's possible to miss someone. If only I could help you in some way.

—Maria von Wedemeyer

Tegel Prison: August 1943

Maria was now allowed to visit Dietrich once every month or so, per Judge Advocate Röder's ruling. She arrived for her first monthly visit one afternoon in August.

Going through security, she was nervous. She had with her a hamper of food for her fiancé. The guard who lifted the gingham cloth covering the contents of the hamper looked up at her with a smile. He gave a sniff of appreciation for the aniseed biscuits and fresh strawberry jam. Maria reached down into the hamper and lifted out a box holding about a half-dozen eggs, which she gave to the guard. His smile became even broader, and the nervousness evaporated from Maria's face.

Knobloch, still assigned to oversee Dietrich, went immediately to the room reserved for family visits. and joined them in the windowless room where they sat across from each other at a small table. They took an awkward look at Knobloch as he took his customary place in his chair by the wall. Dietrich and Maria didn't speak to each other for a while. Knobloch presumed it was because of his presence. But even if he had not been there, they would have had difficulty speaking to each other after almost three months' separation, not counting the strained situation at the singularly peculiar hearing. Dietrich possessed little ability for small talk. And Maria, for whom chattiness came naturally, was cautious lest she say something that compromised her fiancé's well-being in the prison or harmed his prospects in his future hearing with Röder.

Their initial silence exposed a feeling of discomfort with each other. Perhaps it was the long time between visits, or the fear of saying something wrong, but they seemed almost like strangers until

Dietrich broke the silence.

"How is Mother von Wedemeyer?"

"Her health is good enough. Her eyesight is even better than before the surgery. She sends her love."

"Her regards, or her actual love?"

"She used the word 'regards.' The 'love' is my editorial alteration."

"That's what I thought. But the more important question is, do *you* still love me?"

She shyly moved her hand across the table until it took hold of his. He didn't resist. "You know I do, Pastor Bonhöffer."

That struck Dietrich as rather formal. "Maria, there's no need any longer to address me by my title. I am no longer your pastor." He took hold of her hand. "I am your fiancé who has the name Dietrich. I would like it if you used that name from now on to address me."

Maria looked a little embarrassed. "I didn't want to presume before, Pastor, I mean Dietrich." She chuckled innocently. "I'll get used to it, I suppose, calling you by such a familiar name."

"Of course, you will. We will be husband and wife soon, after all. I'm certain we will exchange other endearments as well."

Maria's face turned decidedly eager and excited. "Speaking of which, since you are now here in prison, *Mütti* has lifted her year-long prohibition against our being together. Soon she will make an announcement publicly that we are engaged. Isn't that exciting?"

Dietrich lifted up her hand in his as a gesture of victory. "No obstacles now," he said cheerfully. "Did you hear that, Knobloch?"

"That's worth a kiss, I think, Pastor," Knobloch said. "Should I turn my back so you'll be less self-conscious?"

Before he could act on Knobloch's suggestion, Maria interjected, "No obstacles except Tegel Prison and whatever that strange prosecutor decides."

"Well, yes, of course," Dietrich said. "Your guess is as good as mine in that regard. Röder does seem a little unpredictable. But my feeling is that I won't be here at Christmas."

"I found it strange that *Herr* Röder never said at that hearing what you are accused of."

The pastor had no hesitation in filling her in. "Of being 'an enemy of the state' is the way the officials of the Reich have phrased it."

Maria looked quizzical.

"That means I didn't report to the *Wehrmacht* when I was called up in 1939," he explained.

Maria was very pensive.

"Röder wouldn't accept my explanation that I chose to support this country's war effort by serving in the *Abwehr*."

"Why didn't you report to the *Wehrmacht*, Dietrich?" she asked in a changed tone of voice with more accusation in it. "That's exactly the question *Mütti* asked me when she and I argued about your proposal to me."

Dietrich was jolted by the accusatory tone.

"I'm not a coward if that's what she—or you yourself—think. There are many ways to serve one's country. Given my international contacts, I chose the way of gathering and providing the Reich with valuable military intelligence."

She remained silent, looking away from him. Dietrich was bothered by that.

"Maria, the way your father and brother served is very exemplary. But it's not the only way to serve our people. I know myself well enough to recognize that I don't have the aptitude to serve at the front the way they did. I don't want to take away from their courage or honor. But I have chosen another path."

Slowly, Maria turned her body so that she was facing him now. "I don't fully understand your reasons, Dietrich." A smile slowly came over her face. "But your explanation is enough for me for now. As long as this doesn't change your love for me, or our future together."

"Not in the least, Maria—unless it's an obstacle for your love for me."

Dietrich's inner thoughts were disturbing to him. He felt he had just dodged a relationship-altering moment with his fiancée. He deliberately had chosen not to divulge to her the entirety of what he expected would eventually be the state's charge against him. Both he and the Reich knew he had advised his students and pastors of the Confessing Church to refuse to report to the *Wehrmacht*. To the Reich, that was his more serious offense, liable to the charge of treason and its subsequent penalty at the gallows. There were also his secret anti-Nazi activities. He was well aware he was walking on thin ice. Did she realize the danger this posed to him, to them? Should he keep her ignorant of the threat to his life and their happiness, or should he unveil the whole truth to her one small part at a time?

Chapter Eighteen

It is not your love that sustains the marriage,
but from now on, it's the marriage that sustains your love.

—Dietrich Bonhöffer

Tegel Prison: September 1943

Maria made her second visit to Dietrich a little over a month after her first. She had not received an answer to her petition to be transferred to the Augusta Hospital in Berlin. Instead, Dietrich's father, Paul, hired her for secretarial and receptionist duties at his psychiatric practice. She moved into Dietrich's parents' home in Charlottenburg, where she had been made to feel so welcome on her visit there with her mother earlier in the summer.

This time Dietrich had advance notice that she would be visiting him within the next week. As Maria was escorted into the visitation room she didn't acknowledge Knobloch. Her face looked unusually annoyed. Dietrich was eclipsed by disappointment. Maria did not look as wholeheartedly glad to see him.

"Is there something wrong, Maria?" he asked immediately.

"I'm sorry if I'm not in my best mood today, Dietrich. Please don't take it personally; I've been waiting anxiously to come to see you. It's just that I see the sense of gloom everywhere I go in the city. People are disheartened by the air raids. The Allied planes are over Berlin nearly every day. People have grown tired of this war. So have I."

"Your bad experience, your witnessing the brutality at Bethel, is still fresh in your mind. That's a ponderous memory to carry around with you."

"I couldn't believe my eyes. That our own government should betray those patients who had put their trust in them for their well-being! This government behaves as if there were no law, no decency. They've been a law unto themselves since the very beginning."

"To treat mentally ill patients like that as less than human, it's shameful. It is something that's becoming a more common occurrence in Germany, I'm afraid," Dietrich added.

"The *Wehrmacht* is being defeated badly all along the eastern front. Moscow, Stalingrad, now Kursk. Yet, if anything, Hitler's cruelty is only intensifying against the Jews, the Poles, the Gypsies. I don't understand it."

"And in Bethel, against his own people," he added again. "It seems that where prayer for peace has been spoken, the Satanic forces of war and death must doubly rage since they perceive that they are about to be finished off."

"This war has become a nightmare. It's been going on so long that I have difficulty remembering what normal life was like," Maria said tearfully. "It's too late now to go back to a better and more peaceful time. People are too scared now of this government to do anything about it."

Dietrich wondered if this was the moment to risk revealing to her the intentions and strategies of the resistance, including his own role in it. "I've come to the conclusion that nothing in Germany will change, certainly not improve," he told her straightforwardly, "until something—something drastic—is done about the man who has placed himself in charge."

Maria glanced at Knobloch in the corner of the room. She looked irritated. She was so focused on her own feelings of fatigue and disappointment that she didn't appear to have heard Dietrich's last comment, nor considered the potentially seditious implications of it. She jumped to another matter.

"Oh, Dietrich. I wish that we could be alone for these visits. We never have a second of privacy."

Knobloch, who had remained unobtrusive and silent since Maria's arrival, decided to speak up. "You two must try to enjoy your visits in spite of my presence in the room. I've been ordered here. There's nothing we can do about that. You both look forward so much to these rare opportunities. Try to make the best of them in spite of me."

Dietrich gave Maria an affirming smile. "He's right, Maria. We can speak freely. Knobloch is my-most trusted friend here. We can trust him."

At that, Maria seemed to relax her whole body. She looked back at Knobloch more apologetically this time.

Dietrich reached across the table and took Maria's hand in his.

"You're right, Dietrich," she said, affectionately squeezing Dietrich's hand. "I keep taking for granted all that Corporal Knobloch has done for us. This is a part of what I don't like about myself, this irritation when things don't go exactly as I please. I'm afraid you will not like it either and you'll change your mind about me."

"What I feel for you now is far beyond what my rational mind thinks and decides."

"I get so impatient, and I complain when things for us don't go perfectly well."

"But that's natural, isn't it?"

"You always seem so grateful for what we do have and take in stride what we don't. Like our forced separation. Don't you mind it?"

"Of course, I do. I'd change the situation in a flash if I had any control over it. But I see this time of separation potentially as a period of testing by God."

"Testing? Of what?"

"I don't mean that God has put us in this dilemma so that He can see how strong we are. I don't think our God is one to initiate troubles and trials for us like that."

"Well, what *do* you mean?"

"I mean, this is a time of testing us the way fire tests metal, to purify our love and mold and shape it into something that lasts."

"I regret my emotional and religious nearsightedness sometimes, Dietrich."

"We have to try to see beyond this time of separation, Maria, and be patient and have faith that there are better times ahead for us."

"Oh, Dietrich. I felt connected to you by something mysterious, some irresistible force when I heard you from outside of my grandmother's house playing the piano. It was some force apart from the music. I had never felt anything like it before. I felt a sensation all through my body. *Mütti* and Ruth-Alice say it's just infatuation that doesn't allow one to perceive the negative in the other person. I still feel that spell of infatuation today. But I fear that sweet sensation may dissolve and disappear. I worry that there won't be any real love there when the infatuation is all gone."

Dietrich stood up and spread his arms to embrace Maria.

"Oh, dear, dear Maria. I have felt the pull of infatuation for you, too. There's nothing wrong with infatuation, is there? An important part of that infatuation is desire, a desire that must be sanctified and satiated within the bonds of matrimony. The love of a man for a woman, or a woman for a man, has to begin somewhere."

"But how long can it carry a couple? Without consummation and physical bonding, is infatuation enough? I have read that scientists think that infatuation lasts 18 months at most. That's such a short length of time."

"Maria, we will be married soon. The sooner the better. Up until now, or perhaps until that fine day of our wedding, it's our infatuation and," he paused, "let's be quite frank about it, Maria—our physical attraction to each other, our sexual desire, if you will, for each other that brings us together and will lead us to the altar. Your sister and mother are right. In infatuation, we see only the heaven of our own happiness. But when we're married, things will change. In a good way, I mean. It will be the vow of marriage that sustains and strengthens the love between us. Ask your mother. Ask my parents. Ask any couple that has been married for any period of time."

He was thinking of his parents' long but imperfect marriage. They've discovered many imperfections in each other and experienced some disappointments that might have threatened their love for each other. But they would agree, he knew, that their youngest son was right. "Love is like the tides. There are periods of low tide but wait long enough and you'll experience high tides as well. It's their marriage vows that have helped them time and time again persevere during the low tides and tolerate, and even embrace, those imperfections and disappointments until they enjoy the high tides again."

"At least it's better living with your parents now. At Pätzig I was restless and lonely and irritated at my mother over the littlest things. It was too quiet. I was almost glad that the fall weather outside was gloomy. I seem to have lost my capacity for enjoying anything."

"Lovesickness, they call it, don't they? Or might it be sexual frustration?"

"I'll have to consider that. It was a totally new sensation for me. But, on the train ride back to Pätzig from my last visit, every fragment of my being was clinging to you. My thoughts were racing about you and how you held me so close. I wished so desperately that I could take your place here in prison. I don't like to see you this way. I see you in your old worn prison clothes. Your hair is thinner every time I come to see you."

Dietrich felt relieved at their newfound honesty and intimacy.

"But," she continued, "when I got off the train, I was so teary. With every step away from the train station, the more I felt my heart pulled back to Tegel. I could hardly stand being at home. I'm so overjoyed to begin life anew in your parents' house."

Dietrich pulled her closer to him than he ever had before. She did not resist or give the slightest indication that she wasn't enjoying it.

"I miss you so when you leave, Maria. I feel so lost. But as every day without you passes, I take comfort that I am another 24 hours nearer to seeing you again."

"You see what I mean? You always see the good in a bad situation."

"Or I *choose* to see the good."

"I hope that when we are married, I'll absorb some of that quality from you."

"It's seldom absolutely quiet in here. There's the racket of other inmates. Guards shouting, Metal doors clanging shut."

"How do you stand it?"

"There are moments in the day, though, when things get quiet, or I don't hear the noise. I love the resulting solitude. It seems that the quieter it is around me, the more clearly I feel the connection to you, Maria."

He pulled her body even closer to his until there was no space between them.

"It's as though in the solitude, the soul develops a sense of the presence of a loved one, which I hardly knew in my busy everyday life outside this prison. So though I miss you badly and am frustrated, I cannot say that I feel lonely or abandoned for one moment here. Therefore, you must not think of me being unhappy in here."

Maria had begun to sniffle. Dietrich handed her a handkerchief from his pocket.

"What are happiness and unhappiness, anyway?" he asked. "Our happiness depends so little on our surroundings and circumstances, only on what is inside a person. I am grateful every day that I know you are thinking of me wherever you are. That makes me happy."

He hadn't relaxed his embrace. He tenderly kissed the tears at her eyes and on her cheeks. She giggled endearingly.

"We have our letters to each other to fill the in-between times before my visits," she said.

"Ah yes, the letters. I rejoice in every word you write, every detail, which allows me to share your daily life. In my bolder daydreams I picture our life together. I read each letter a hundred times, and a hundred times again the next day."

"Your letters, Dietrich, are my daily nighttime reading. I wouldn't survive it without them."

They became silent for a while. Finally, Dietrich asked, "What else are you reading? Still your favorite, Rilke?"

"I've started reading some theology because I know how much theology means to you. I want to find answers to my questions."

"Have you found some?"

"Not really, I'm afraid. Just more questions."

"Then the theologians who wrote those books have done their job well."

"The only theologian I've been reading lately is you."

"There are some better ones to read. Try Karl Barth. But, tell me, which book of mine, if any, do you find the most helpful?"

"I'm afraid some of your books are over my head. But I like *The Cost of Discipleship—Nachfolge*—the most because it's what we studied together in my confirmation instruction. But I can't read it for long because my heart begins to yearn for the author himself rather than his erudite words."

Reluctantly, Knobloch interrupted the visit. "I'm afraid, friends, that it's time. I am sorry, Maria, but the rules say that the visit is over. You will need to leave."

Only then did Dietrich kiss her gently on her lips and release her slowly from his embrace.

Chapter Nineteen

I often worry and wonder whether I really do you any good by seeing you in Tegel.... When we sit there making conversation, which is really only superficial, even though we know of a hundred, indeed, a thousand things we want and need to say, and given that we feel like crying, I simply can't imagine how such a jumble of emotions can help you in the very least.

—Maria von Wedemeyer

Tegel Prison: October 7, 1943

Maria was still working in Doctor Bonhöffer's office in Charlottenburg. She felt totally affirmed by Dietrich's parents and genuinely fortunate to enjoy their gracious company every evening after work. They seemed like personages from another era, a simpler time in Germany's history. Dietrich's father insisted that it hadn't really been simpler. He chuckled as he told of taking the trolley to the office in the 1920s. In the mornings he would get off the trolley some five or six stops before the one closest to his office in order to buy meat for dinner at the butcher.

"You bought the meat in the morning? How would you keep it cold all day at the office?"

"You had to buy it in the morning because you might not be able to afford a cut of meat by the afternoon. With the rampant inflation during the post-Great War years, it wasn't at all out of the realm of possibility that the price for a kilo of beef would go up by 500 percent in less than a day."

Dietrich's youngest sister, Suse, added at the conclusion of her father's story, "At least there was beef at the butcher's to buy. Today there's none available because it has been requisitioned by the *Führer* to feed his troops."

"Every decade has its own problems, I guess," Dr. Bonhöffer assented.

Dietrich was such a rational, even-keeled person. She came to see where he had inherited his emotional solidity that she so admired and coveted. So little seemed to rattle him.

On the other hand, Maria could often felt so self-conscious that she could be thrown off her emotional path by the smallest setback. She didn't always mention these setbacks in her letters to Dietrich, much less during her visits with him at Tegel. She didn't want to reveal to him what she considered her emotional weaknesses and the foolish juvenile fears and worries that she hadn't yet outgrown in her late teens.

She wondered as well whether she was too dependent on Dietrich's even-keeled nature to rescue her from life's dangers. Was she simply content to allow him to cope with the difficult things, not only for himself but for her, too? Did she need to grow up some more and find her own strategies for overcoming life's setbacks? It was such a perilous time. Everyone in Germany was suspicious of everybody else. It didn't feel as though the German people were one people supporting one another. They were on the precipice of defeat now for the first time in several decades.

Every day there was news about one section or other of the city having been destroyed or at least impacted seriously by Allied bombs. Like others, Maria could feel the distant thunder of the bombs reverberating. Some days the rumbling got louder and closer to Charlottenburg, causing her to dread not so much her own death as the threat to her future with Dietrich. She didn't say anything about her fears when around Dietrich's parents. But some days she was terribly apprehensive that their plans for married life together would be altered irreparably by the events of this seemingly endless war. She had been burdened by such misgivings for some time.

She tried to silence such thoughts as she rode the train again to visit Dietrich. She almost didn't go. She didn't want him to see her under a dark cloud of negative thoughts. But the closer the train was to Tegel, the more agitated she became. *This is a mistake.*

She went humorlessly through the security process at the prison. The guards seemed less jovial than usual as well. While she was very glad to be there where her true love was imprisoned, she was disappointed that she couldn't escape the shadow of the cloud before being led to the visitation room.

When she arrived in the visitation room, Dietrich and Knobloch were chatting amiably. They raised their eyes to acknowledge her.

Dietrich rose from his chair and gave her his customary self-conscious peck on her cheek. *How desperately she wished that he would take her wholeheartedly in his arms and give her a long, passionate kiss,* she thought. But now that she had been living with his parents for several months and observing them and how dispassionately they related to each other as a married couple, she understood much better why he didn't. There wasn't much physical contact between his parents, at least not in front of her.

Dietrich guided her over to the small table at which they sat on these visits. Just like the last time, they didn't exchange many words after they'd sat down. They customarily expressed their mutual relief at being together after an absence of a month or so. Maria was afraid to say anything for fear that her voice would betray the despondency that she hadn't been able to leave outside the prison. It occurred to her that perhaps he was trying to hide something from her, too—a sadness, a concern or fear—and thought better of launching into a conversation.

He took hold of her hand as if to assure her that his silence was not an indication of any change in his love for her. At least, that's what she wanted to believe. He smiled at her shyly but still didn't utter a word.

She and Dietrich continued their silent visit for a while longer. A month has passed since the last visit, but so little seemed to have changed. *It shouldn't be this way,* she thought. The whole time she wondered if there was something seriously amiss between them. She imagined that he might have been wondering the same thing.

Finally, the silence was broken and her tension relieved. She could breathe more easily again.

"We don't have much to say today, I guess," he offered.

"No, I guess not," she replied.

"Sometimes I just love the silence," he added. "I love people, but the time when the prison is silent at night is what I wait all day for."

"I'm sorry if you are uncomfortable with the silence, Maria. It seems that it's only the old, like my parents, who can be comfortable sitting silently with each other."

"If I know you love me, then I can grow comfortable with it. When it's only the two of them, your parents' home is wonderfully quiet."

Dietrich chuckled at her remark. "Yes, at least until Ursula comes over to visit. Chatty is an understatement to describe my dear older sister's demeanor."

Maria remembered the evening at Ursula and Rüdy's home the night Dietrich was arrested. That night she was glad for Ursula's chattiness. It helped relieve Maria's terrible confusion and anxiety.

"I'm learning to enjoy it more. I enjoy this silence right now, in fact."

After a while, Dietrich commented, "Silence is a holy moment, don't you think? Silence can bring people together."

"It's difficult for me to be silent alone, however," she responded. "The silence leaves too much empty space for my anxious thoughts to rise up and fill my heart."

Maria had truly accommodated to the silence between them once she knew that it wasn't because of Dietrich's discomfort being with her, or that it meant a change of heart in him.

Suddenly, without warning, the prison floor began to vibrate. The walls began shaking. Within seconds, a sonorous hum filled the visitation room and grew into a furious roar.

Dietrich looked at Knobloch. "Bombers, Knobloch? In broad daylight?"

Knobloch shot up, grabbed his metal portable chair from the corner, and carried it hurriedly to a vacant spot underneath the narrow rectangular barred window, which was set almost two meters from the floor. He stepped on the chair. He stretched his tall body in order to look out through the window.

"Yes. Damn! About five of them. Martin B-26s, I would guess. American."

Maria looked fearfully into Dietrich's face. It was unusual to see anxiety and fear on his. He stood up and took Maria into his arms protectively.

The door to the room opened suddenly and violently. Two guards ran in holding rifles.

"Knobloch, take the inmate to one of the vacant holding cells in the basement where it is safer," one shouted above the roar. "We'll take his guest to the exit out of the building. *Schnell,* Knobloch. There's not a second to waste."

Just then, the neighboring cell block that was the identical twin of the one they were in burst into a raging blaze. Flames shot out through the windows of the cells. The two guards hurried their pace.

"Knobloch, the prisoner to the basement! Now!"

One guard took a rough hold of Maria's arm above her elbow and started leading her none-too-gently toward the door out of the room. "I am sorry, *Fräulein.* Your visit must end. It's an emergency."

"Go, Maria! Go right now!" Dietrich ordered.

At that, Knobloch and Dietrich ran toward the door leading back into the cell block.

When the guards and Maria were out the door into the stairway, she almost lost her footing as the building rocked at the blow of a bomb nearby. The mighty impact forced some bricks to fall from the corridor ceiling, almost striking them as she and the guard passed.

"Bend low!" the guard shouted to her. "Hands over your head."

She stopped and looked back up to the door leading to the visitation room at the top of the stairs. Knobloch and Dietrich stood there, trying to see down through the storm of dust and plaster and smoke from the neighboring cell block. Contrary to their orders, they had detoured from their rushed journey down to the basement in order to check on Maria.

"Maria! Maria!" It was Dietrich's voice. "Can you hear me? Have you been hit? Answer me if you can."

She aimed her voice upward toward the top of the staircase.

"Yes, Dietrich," she was able to answer. "I can hear you. I think I am well. I have not been hit."

"*Fräulein,* no dawdling. We must hurry!" the guard shouted.

She looked back to the door and yelled, hoping Dietrich and Knobloch were still there. "I can't leave you here while the prison is being bombed, Dietrich! I'm coming back up."

Immediately, Dietrich shouted back. "No, no, Maria! You must leave with the guards and escape the building!"

"No, I can't leave you here alone even if we die together."

The guard intervened by grabbing her arm with his hand once again. "*Fräulein!* There's no time to waste. You must exit the building for your safety. I insist. Please follow orders."

She didn't hear Dietrich's voice any longer from the maelstrom of dust and rubble above. Only silence. He and Knobloch must have obeyed reason and gone down to the basement. Reluctantly, she did as ordered and descended the staircase with the guards.

Though she hadn't been hit, when she got to the little train station outside the prison grounds, her body collapsed from exhaustion and shock on the hard, wooden bench for waiting passengers, She was shaking almost uncontrollably. The palms of her hands were wet with sweat. Her heart beat frantically in her breast, and her mouth was desert dry. Her face was covered with grime and dust. She was still too panicked to consider what had just happened.

Dietrich's neighboring cell block was still ablaze. Dietrich's own cell block, though, was not on fire. Dust was settling around the building, and black smoke surrounding it, but it still stood four stories tall as it had when Maria had entered an hour or so previously. *Had Dietrich survived?* She looked back at the partially destroyed prison and wondered if she would ever see or hear Dietrich again.

The train to Berlin came surprisingly soon. As Maria stepped into the coach, other passengers stared at her sooty face as though she were an alien of some kind. She nodded her head toward the destruction outside each window as she passed it as if to explain her dishevelled appearance.

She found a vacant seat beside an old farm wife. "It's a dirty shame what the enemy is doing to our poor country," she commented as she handed Maria a handkerchief from her purse to wipe her face. Maria made no response.

It became evident that Tegel had not been the Americans' sole target that afternoon. Scattered among the houses and warehouses along the railroad tracks were other buildings that had suffered even worse damage. Black smoke belched out of shattered windows. Forlorn-looking residents of the apartment blocks stood outside the ruined buildings and huddled in little groups for support and seeking answers. Others were despondently examining the piles of rubble and twisted metal for any possessions of theirs that they might retrieve and perhaps use as they begin new lives as survivors—if there was new life to begin.

As the train moved toward Berlin Maria began to shed most of the immediate effects of the bombing at the prison. Her heart was numb rather than racing as before. Her utter exhaustion rendered her absolutely still and listless in her seat.

How was Dietrich? Was he safe? Was he still alive?

The closer the train came to the center of Berlin, the more frequent were the demolished buildings, many of them apartment blocks that had been either entirely or partially destroyed by bombs. Maria wasn't certain any longer that she could refer to them as "enemy" bombs. Who was the "enemy" anymore?

Witnessing the scenes of loss and destruction, the pace of her heart picked up again. Adrenaline started to break through the dam and flood her bloodstream. *How extensive had this bombing raid been? Had the bombs hit Charlottenburg? Were Dietrich's dear parents victims of it?*

She was overcome by raw horror once she stepped off the train at the station in Charlottenburg. The lot adjacent to the station was no longer a plaza where farmers could come into town to sell their produce and craftspeople their creations. It was now an open crater as deep as any quarry in the countryside. The wide-open mouth of the pit seemed to scream a silent, broken protest of pain and sorrow to the heavens.

A few houses on the streets leading to *Marienburgerstrasse* had been struck by bombs. They stood ruined as silent evidence of the madness of this war, and of the collateral punishment inflicted on innocent citizens for the *Führer's* arrogant wager that he could usher in a thousand-year Reich by conquering the nations of Europe and destroying Russia.

Suddenly, the fear she felt at the bombed prison returned with a wicked vengeance. She was overcome by it. She couldn't think clearly. She couldn't make sense of what she was seeing.

She ran like a scared child to *Marienburgerstrasse* and stopped in her tracks. Another house across the street from Dietrich's parents had been struck, becoming a gutted twin of the one that had been hit in 1942.

She alternated between shock at the extent of the damage to the neighbor's home and relief that the bombs had left Dietrich's parents and their daughter and son-in-law's home completely untouched. She intended to walk across the street to her temporary home but couldn't move. It was as though the soles of her shoes were attached by an invisible substance to the sidewalk. Her knees were trembling frightfully. Her brain was sending the message to her legs to take a step toward home, but the legs either didn't receive the message or chose to disobey it. She felt utterly defeated. She lowered herself hopelessly to the sidewalk and sat forlornly on the concrete, weeping, her bruised hands covering her face in fear and shame.

This war had come home.

She had a sudden urge to run away, to where she didn't know, just somewhere, anywhere away from the destruction around her all over the city. Maybe back to Pätzig, so far away from everything that the Allies would not think to bomb the area. But not to Pätzig, so distant from Dietrich in Tegel that she would die of the shame for having abandoned him. The storm of bombing had been raging here earlier today, even in safe, comfortable Charlottenburg. There was no place that was truly safe any longer. But she wanted, she needed, to run.

But instead she remained seated there on the cold concrete like a fool, feeling like a coward, weeping from fear: for Dietrich's safety at Tegel, for Dietrich's parents' safety in Charlottenburg, for her own safety, too. The bomber could return to *Marienburgerstrasse* at any time, even tonight. Where could she escape it? Was this infernal war doomed to be an eternal one?

An automobile passed on the street. She pulled her hands away from her face. Whoever was in the car must not see her like this, at the end of her rope. To her relief, the car passed without stopping.

But, from somewhere—perhaps it was a fleeting thought or vision of Dietrich in the turmoil of the prison today—she discovered within her a new determination to persevere, to pull herself together, to conquer her fear.

Pronouncing the word "persevere" silently to herself made her think of one of Dietrich's sermons she had heard years ago. "To persevere, translated literally," he had said, "means remaining underneath, not throwing off the load that burdens us. People of faith must bear it, not collapse underneath the load, but bear it, remain underneath it, to find that Christ is there, too, underneath his cross, and gently assuring us that we don't bear our load alone. And thus, we gain hope and grow stronger underneath our own load and persevere."

She sat on the hard concrete, less pathetically now, contemplating the words of that sermon in a way she had not when she had first heard it years ago. It was as though magically she was hovering above her defeated body, burdened by fear as never before, and seeing herself collapsed on the sidewalk. She was deeply ashamed by what she saw. But she was discovering a new resolve. She would not allow herself to collapse underneath her load. She would bear it. She stood and wiped the fragments of detritus from her skirt, readjusted her clothing, and stepped out into the street to cross to Dietrich's parents' house.

Chapter Twenty

Be brave for my sake, dearest Maria, even if this letter is your only token of my love this Christmas-tide. We shall ponder the incomprehensibility of our lot, why, over and above the darkness already enshrouding humanity, we should be subjected to the bitter anguish of a separation whose purposes are difficult to understand.

−Dietrich Bonhöffer

December 22, 1943

The season of Advent felt long. Maria applied for a visitor pass for November just a few days after she had arrived home from the bomb ravaged Tegel in October. But precisely because of the fury and consistency of the bombing, the mail was undependable. Either her request for the pass never arrived at the prison or else it had arrived, but the pass itself had been delayed in the mail, or misplaced or destroyed in the chaos. She had no choice but to wait.

In the meantime, Maria worked with the village children on the annual Nativity play. She taught the children about the angel's visitation to a young virgin and the promise of a child who will be the world's savior. "This is the holy child whom we will welcome on Christmas Eve with songs and carols," she told them. The Nativity play was usually a highlight of the season for Maria, but this year it left her feeling empty.

She heard the Old Testament prophet Isaiah's brave and noble promises of one fine day on earth when wars will cease, and tears will be wiped away from the eyes of the mournful and suffering by God himself. But the ancient holy words that year sounded like the rote narration of someone else's dream. It's a nice sentiment, to be sure, she thought, but hardly likely to become true as the war around them continued to rage on. But she knew that in the midst of all the turmoil and bad news, however, Dietrich clung fervently to Isaiah's promise.

The visitor pass finally did arrive, in a mangled envelope. The date written on the pass was November 13, a whole month before its arrival. Maria decided to go and celebrate Advent and Christmas with Dietrich on December 22. It would have been over two long, tortuous months since her previous visit that was disrupted by the bombing raid.

She would need help this time when she arrived at the prison. She wrote ahead to Knobloch to solicit his assistance, even though she didn't describe the help she needed.

He was there waiting for her at the entrance to the prison as requested. He greeted her kindly and commented on how impatient Dietrich had been to see her.

In her right hand, Maria held a spruce tree almost a meter taller than her. It came from the grounds of Dietrich's brother-in-law Hans's home in Sacrow. She had joined Dietrich's parents there to retreat from the almost nightly bombing raids in and near the city. Christel had offered their home as a sanctuary since it was off the beaten track and thus far untouched by Allied bombs.

Maria intended the tree to serve as a *Tannenbaum* in Dietrich's cell. The guards at prison security chuckled as they saw Knobloch carrying it and wished them both a *Fröhliche Weihnachten* and allowed them to continue into the prison with the *Tannenbaum* uninspected.

Maria and Knobloch looked at each other in surprise. The guard did let them upstairs into the inmates' area, not to the visitation room as usual. Maria had never been allowed to visit Dietrich in his cell instead of the visitation room. *A relaxation of the rules for Christmas,* she figured. *Or else the guards were so distracted by the sight of her with the tree that they lost track of things.*

Knobloch struggled with the tree as they ascended the three flights of stairs to Dietrich's floor. There was a freight elevator normally used by the prison staff for cargo, but the bombing raid had rendered it unusable. Knobloch interrupted his progress up the stairs to rest his tired arms. He let the base of the trunk of the tree down onto the floor.

"Good Lord," he said. "How did you manage to carry this tree all the way from the pastor's parents' home to the station?"

"I had no choice. If I wanted to share Christmas with Dietrich, then I had to beat the odds and get the tree to the train."

"You've probably not heard the good news—I mean, the *potentially* good news—from the pastor yet."

"His letters, no matter what they contain, are always good news to me."

"Yes, of course, *Fräulein*. But I shared the news with him only two days ago. I doubt he's had a chance to write to you about it yet. Or else he posted the letter and it may arrive in Charlottenburg while you are here."

"Well, are you going to share the news with me?"

"I really should allow the pastor to have the joy of sharing them with you himself."

"But you brought up the subject of the news on your own initiative. You've succeeded in tantalizing me and making me helplessly curious. I can't possibly wait now until we get upstairs."

"Well, since you must know, Judge Advocate Röder's notes from his research for the pastor's hearings and his notes from the first hearing were lost or destroyed in the bombing raid that occurred when you were last here."

"What? All of them, lost or destroyed? *Gott in Himmel.* How can his prosecution of Dietrich's case possibly continue without the notes? Does that mean that Dietrich will have to be released and all charges against him dropped?"

"Well, we mustn't get our hopes up too high. Let's wait to discuss this with the pastor."

Dietrich let out a hearty laugh when he saw the tree. He took it from Knobloch's hands and tried to take it into his cell. He was able to bring in the bottom of the tree. After several attempts to fit the whole tree through the small door, however, he had to admit defeat. He was unable to stand the tree in an upright position.

She had asked the Von Donhányi's servant Martin to cut the tree to the height she had estimated to be slightly lower than the height of the ceiling in the visitation room. She had had no way of knowing that the height in the cells was a good meter lower than the visitation room.

Knobloch took his customary place in the corner of the cramped cell, and Dietrich and Maria sat down opposite each other at Dietrich's desk, which he quickly moved out from its position against the wall directly underneath the small window. Dietrich was still holding the Christmas tree in his right hand as he sat.

Knobloch took the tree from Dietrich's hands as if it were the baton passed from one runner in a race to the next.

"Pastor, when I get back, I will requisition a saw and cut off a hundred centimeters or so from the bottom of the tree."

Maria left her free hand waiting on the desk for Dietrich to take it. He looked irritated, however.

"I need to chide you for being up and about between here and Berlin. You know that not all of the tracks are operational out of Berlin since they've been damaged by bombs. The Allies could very well bomb the track your train is on when you get on it to return to Berlin."

But he couldn't maintain the irritable look for very long. Within a moment, a smile spread across his face. He might indeed have been concerned for her safety, but he knew that for love one must take risks, at least reasonable ones.

"Poor Karl was a victim of the bombing raid last month when you were here. He had already lost Karin, his fiancée to be. It's all very sad. That is another 20-year-old sacrificed at the altar of the bellicose Reich. *Hitler must be made to pay for his sins.*

Maria, of course, didn't know who Karl and Karin were. But she sensed Dietrich's grief and anger, which for her was sufficient. *I'll never grow accustomed to the waste of young lives in Hitler's megalomaniacal war.*

Suddenly she could see out of the corner of her eye that Knobloch was starting to lay the tree on its side on the floor.

"No, no, please don't do that, Kurt," she said immediately. "You've seen that I've made some old-fashioned ornaments out of various objects—pinecones, thistles, eggshells. They're rather fragile. I'm afraid they'll get damaged if you lay it down on its side."

"It's my turn to hold the tree, Knobloch," Dietrich said, and took the tree from a physically relieved Knobloch. Dietrich continued to converse with Maria while cradling the tree with his one arm. She heartily wished that it was her, and not the tree, he was embracing and holding so tenderly.

She took out a package wrapped in a white handkerchief from her bag.

He looked at her quizzically.

"Go ahead, it's for you, for Christmas," she encouraged him.

She watched with tearing eyes as he opened the handkerchief to discover a wristwatch.

"It was my father's watch," she told him. "He was wearing it when he was killed. There's the slight crack on the glass but I know it still works. It's been running since we received it from the front. I wind it every second day or so."

Dietrich's eyes teared up as well.

"This is not just any watch. I know how much your father means to you. You don't want to keep it for yourself to remember him by?"

"No, it would make me happier if I knew you had it. It's the only thing of father's that we got back from the front."

Dietrich sat in reverent silence. Finally, he said, "That makes it extra special. I don't know how to thank you."

She smiled and said, "Just hurry up and get out of here and marry me."

They both laughed. Maria had forgotten how good it felt to laugh, especially in unison. It acted on her like a love potion.

"Does your mother know you have given it to me?" Dietrich asked.

"Don't spoil the good mood, Dietrich. Yes, she knows. She agrees. Enough said."

She didn't tell him about the ugly scene her request for the watch had caused. *Mütti* hadn't received even so much as her late husband's wedding band. She wept as she gave the watch to her daughter, slipping in an accusation of Maria's dishonoring her father's memory. But in the end, she did agree.

Dietrich slipped the watch onto his wrist.

"Look at that," he said, holding up the watch on his wrist. "A perfect fit." He returned the handkerchief to her.

"Of course. What did you expect?" Maria said, dabbing her eyes with the handkerchief. "You are so much like him in every way, don't you recall? He's the kind of man I want for a husband."

"I had hoped to be home by Christmas," Dietrich announced. "The second hearing was scheduled for December 17, but it was postponed, so here I still am."

"Postponed because the Judge Advocate no longer has the files and notes he needs?"

"I presume so. They never tell the prisoner the reasons. But I see you've heard about the loss of the notes."

"Yes, Knobloch informed me. Isn't that a miracle, Dietrich? Out of that horrible event, there may be a turn of luck in your favor?"

"Doesn't God always work that way, creating light out of darkness, hope out of despair?"

"But the hearing was only postponed, not canceled? How can Röder proceed without the notes?" Maria asked.

"We'll have to await a greater miracle, I'm afraid. Röder has recruited two expert documentarians to take the few slips of paper that were discovered in the ruins of the bombing and try to reconstruct all the files in their entirety."

"He cannot be serious about that, can he? How can they replicate all the files and notes?"

"I suppose expert documentarians have their ways. I'm sure that Röder himself has a lot of the information stored in his memory."

"And what he misremembers, no one will be able to refute."

"You're beginning to catch on to how the Nazis wage the game of warfare, my dear. I'm afraid there will still be a hearing no matter what notes can be reconstructed or fashioned, accurate or not and what Röder can or cannot remember accurately."

"Oh, Dietrich, that's some time into the distant future. Let's not allow this to distract from today, our first Christmas together. Let's change the subject."

"Gladly, my dear."

Maria noted that this was the second time in this conversation that he had called her his "dear" instead of using her Christian name. "I like it when you call me dear; it comes from your heart."

The rest of the visit passed by like a fraction of a minute. They shared their childhood memories of Christmas. He smiled wistfully, his eyes tearing as he related how his family gathered together around a sumptuous dinner table on Christmas Eve with the roasted goose and potato dumplings and apple and sausage stuffing; and how partway through dinner his father would quietly rise from the table without speaking or otherwise drawing attention to himself and exit to the neighboring room. When everyone had eaten their fill, his mother would ask about the whereabouts of Father. No one seemed to know, even years later when the oldest children knew perfectly well where he was. Just then, the doors into the parlor would slide open and reveal a tall *Tannenbaum* beautifully decorated, and piles of wrapped presents underneath the tree.

"Right now, I long to be a little child again," she said in a deliciously moving bittersweet tone, "sitting on my father's knee in the soft candlelight and gazing in wonder at the dancing flames of the fire in the fireplace, anticipating in the depths of my being what surprises this night held in store for us. Dietrich, isn't it true that feeling such joy in every inch of our body and soul is the most important, precious thing about Christmas?"

"Yes. Maybe that is what the Lord meant when he said unless we can feel such delight in our depths the way children do, we won't recognize the Kingdom of God."

"Oh, to feel that way again, when troubles are nonexistent, the war is a distant memory, and our separation is over."

"Maria, I understand. But don't you think we can be together even when separated? I have this watch now, which you gave me. You will be all around me here in Tegel, my Maria. It's so hard to be apart when we are in love, but we're never really apart in our heart and soul, are we?"

"I will be sad away from you, Dietrich. I can't deny that. But I have your parents near me, and Ursula and Rüdy next door. But when I think of you here, deprived of all that, the sadness and fear are too much to bear sometimes."

"I have my good friend, Knobloch, here. And, remember that Christ visits prisons and will not pass me by. I will not be alone."

Chapter Twenty-One

I can no longer condemn or hate a man for whom I pray, no matter how much trouble he causes me.

—Dietrich Bonhöffer

Tegel Prison: January 13, 1944

As soon as Maria arrived at Tegel that day, Dietrich could tell that she had been weeping.

"Something happened, Maria dear? Some trouble on the trip here?

"No, nothing new." she replied while tenderly petting his unshaved cheeks with her hands.

"It's just that I'm tired of it all. The war. The bombs. The deep pits in the streets. The suffering and death. Coming here to see you."

Dietrich took a step back from her as though he had just been slapped in the face. He remained silent to allow her to explain.

She suddenly clasped her hand over her mouth and looked in horror at him. "Oh, no, no, Dietrich! I didn't say very well what I really mean. I mean that I have to visit you *here* in *prison*, not that I have to visit you."

Dietrich smiled indulgently at her misstatement. "I understand. This is not the best environment in which to cultivate our love for each other."

"I wish for once we could be alone," she said as she turned her head toward Knobloch seated in the corner, "without supervision, no matter how friendly and trustworthy."

Dietrich responded instantly. "Maria, haven't we been through this before? Soon we will have many years to visit alone."

"Not soon enough. Have you heard any news about your hearing and when we can expect you again at Pätzig?"

"No, Maria, unfortunately, no word has been delivered from Röder's office—unless you, Knobloch, have heard something through the grapevine?"

Knobloch replied in the negative.

"I hate Röder!" Maria exclaimed.

"Just be patient, my dear Maria. Hating him will do no good. It certainly won't get me out of Tegel one moment sooner."

"But don't you hate him? He may get you executed."

"I don't hate him personally. The *Gestapo*, maybe. Röder is only their agent in this matter."

"Then, don't you detest them?"

"On principle, yes, I detest what they stand for and their insane philosophy and cruel practices. But I don't hate each individual in the *Gestapo.*"

"Is it enough to hate them only on principle?"

"I've had to ask that question of myself concerning the *Führer* himself. To hate what he says and does and stands for and leave it at that. Or—"

He cut his sentence short. "But more hate in my heart will do absolutely nothing to their hearts, only injure my own."

"How can that be?"

"Remember that we stand under the Lordship of the One who prayed from the cross that God forgive those nailing him to it. He died on that cross for you and me—and also for those whom we call

our enemies and who call us theirs. When I see a *Gestapo* agent, I try to see a fellow child of God. That's how I survive in here."

"Just don't ask me to pray that God bless them or Röder either. I almost hate you for not having more anger at them. Sometimes it seems as though Jesus is not familiar with the real world. Lately, it's become a den of vicious evildoers who get away with evil things without consequences."

The room became silent. Only Maria's frustration and anger hung in the air. Dietrich took her gently by the hand and led her to one of the two chairs at the table.

"Oh, Dietrich. Right now I don't know what to think. You confuse me. Love confuses me. The very thing that attracted me to you in the first place was your reasonableness, your sturdy commitment to your values. Now, frankly, it drives me crazy. How can you be so reasonable toward your deadly opponents? I think you are being overly charitable toward them. All because you have committed yourself to be remade in the shape of Jesus? I don't understand it. I should hate you for this—yet I still love you, probably even more, even though I don't share your reasonableness and charity. It frustrates me to no end."

"Certainly, we don't need to be identical in every way for our love to grow and flourish, do we, Maria? I don't love you any less now than before."

"I'm frustrated, too, because I never know which Dietrich I will see when I come here. The gentlemanly Dietrich with whom I had such enjoyable times before he was arrested by the *Gestapo?* The sweet Dietrich who inhabits the letters he sends to me? Or will it be the puzzling Dietrich of these visits who is still a mystery to me?"

"I have often thought that way about you."

"You have?"

"Yes. I wonder if we were blessed with even 50 years or more as married husband and wife, whether we would ever really understand each other completely. Marriage will change us, I know. But won't I always remain Dietrich and you Maria? Even in marriage, don't the two persons always remain at bottom two solitudes, two mysteries, to each other? Isn't there a hidden part of you I will never know or comprehend as hard as I may try? Doesn't even the deepest love remain forever—out of reach?"

"That's a rather pessimistic view of marriage a full year after we've become officially engaged, isn't it?"

"Not pessimistic for me. It means I will never get bored with you or our marriage. There will always be some new dimension of you that is mysterious to me, that I have never encountered in you before. More of you to love, and more of me for you to love."

"Dietrich, that is the most I have ever heard you talk about your love for me, I think."

"You haven't doubted my love, have you?"

"No, it's just that often you are so reticent to talk about your feelings."

"Reticent? Some others have said that about me. I am, I suppose."

"Ruth-Alice is one of those. She's concerned that you are so reticent that you will fail to communicate some things to me."

"It's just that I spend so much time in solitude now for weeks on end, Maria. Perhaps Ruth-Alice doesn't see that or understand my environment. I apologize if I seem overly reserved at times with you. I find it difficult to be sociable again after so much time to myself."

"I talk to you every day on my walks. Then I can tell you anything in my life. Only Father has been like that."

"Knobloch and I are able to share a lot of ourselves with each other. But Kurt can't be seen by the authorities to pay special attention to me."

"I must learn to understand your being reserved. It's what you are and I should accept it. It's just that when we can be together, the time goes by so quickly, and before you know it, I have to leave."

"Yes, that frustrates me, also. It is so hard when you leave. But now I can look at your father's watch, and it's almost as if you were here with me."

He squeezed her hand tenderly.

"I usually weep to myself on the train back to Charlottenburg," she said and began to whimper a little as she spoke. "Other passengers look at me strangely. I think either they feel sorry for me for being so openly sad, or else they hate me for having someone I care for in this prison."

Dietrich was about to respond, but Maria raised a finger and placed it over his lips. "Shhh. I have a confession to make to you. *Mütti* insisted that I tell you." She looked away from him.

"I danced one evening—with another man. It was a New Year's party at the von Kleists'. One of my grandmother's nephews was there on leave. He'd been serving in Italy. You know how bad the fighting has been there."

"Yes, so I have heard."

"He took part in the defense against the Allied advance from Salerno. He looked so tired and sad—and so I danced with him when he asked me."

"Why shouldn't you? After all, he's a relative."

"I didn't think I was doing anything bad. But *Mütti* reminded me that I am engaged now, and that if I assume a serious responsibility like engagement, I must bear it. So she says I must confess to you. I hope you're not angry or jealous."

"Maria, how could I be angry? I think that was quite natural and a very generous gesture on your part. It wasn't as though you were ignoring me while you got up and danced. Remember that I am the one in prison, not you."

"Oh," she exclaimed, as she smiled reassuringly at him. "I'm so relieved to hear you say that."

"Maria, your coming to visit just before Christmas made my Christmas. The gift of your father's watch. The tree from Hans and Christel's homestead. It made me think of them as well as the *Christkind*, especially Hans in prison. You haven't told me about your Christmas."

"I've held off telling you because I don't want you to think of me as a sad, ungrateful woman. It was one of the saddest Christmases in my whole life. We sang Christmas carols after dinner as always and heard the Nativity story again, just as we have every year. That was Father's privilege every December 24 to read aloud to the rest of us. Ruth-Alice did so this year. I couldn't hold back my tears as I listened. Oh, Dietrich, I love my sister, but I missed him so. And I noticed the empty space at the table where Max used to sit. I had to get up quietly and leave the house. The night was starry and cold, the way an artist would paint it. I took a long walk and realized how much I missed you. I thought of you all alone in your cell. It was very difficult to celebrate the birth of the *Christkind* when I was so lonely for Father, Max, and you."

Dietrich wrapped his arms around Maria, and they embraced in a more passionate and uninhibited way than ever before. Their bodies pressed tightly together, his hands stroking her from her lower back to the back of her neck. If she had any objection, she gave no indication.

"Whenever I go out to walk on a chilly and dark night," she intimated, "I find I always think of you, my darling Dietrich. I find the mysterious darkness can open my heart in ways that nothing else can and release forces that are unfathomable but good and consoling."

"Especially on that one particularly holy night when it seems the veil between heaven and earth is lifted. Angel choirs singing in the dark nighttime."

"In spite of all that I have said to you today, I assure you that I am sad but not despairing."

"I think those words describe the state of my soul as well."

"My dear Dietrich, let's vow to be perfectly honest with each other always no matter how much the truth hurts. Can we promise this? I make such a solemn promise to you right this moment. I want so badly to be close to you, to share our secrets with each other. Oh, Dietrich, I'm so grateful to have you."

"Isn't this like a new beginning for us? It's the start of a whole new year. We can put so much of 1943 behind us and move forward. Let's make 1944 the best year ever for you and me and Germany. I think I can promise that this was the final year for our *Führer* to abuse Europe as his private playground."

Maria was so emotionally overcome by their intimate embrace that she didn't inquire any further about what he might have meant by such a bold promise.

Pätzig: January 20, 1944

My dear diary, my truest friend, my confessor to whom I can divulge everything that happens to me, every reaction I have and every thought that occurs to me, uncensored, in its barest truth, without fear or self- consciousness.

This last visit to dear Dietrich at Tegel was most difficult. I risked sharing deep thoughts that I was fearful of his hearing lest he think of me as a malcontent and ingrate.

As you know better than anyone, dear diary, I come back often from these prison visits in a depressed mood near despair. I don't know what I can do or say to lift up his spirits. I come home on the train feeling totally useless to him in spite of his protestations otherwise.

But yesterday's visit was not wasted time or effort. He embraced me while I was tearfully relating my unhappiness at Christmas with neither Father or Max or Dietrich near me.

I experienced such a reassurance within his strong arms, such happiness that he would brave caressing me so intimately even though Knobloch was there to see it. He has never embraced me in such an unambiguously romantic way. I've never felt happier or so loved.

There in his arms, I felt the strength of his back. When my body pressed against his, I thought I would totally lose control. I felt a strange but welcome surge of love rush through me. Or was it lust? It seemed so unfair that we couldn't just carry on as couples do in more normal circumstances; that I couldn't take his hand and we could make love. And then we would walk hand in hand out through the prison door and the big gates at the roadside, the two of us, and go forward, on and on; and they would never come after Dietrich to bring him back.

Chapter Twenty-Two

It's awful, the sound of the Berlin bombs clearly audible, and I can't go there. I wish I were in Berlin; there at least I'd know what's happening and can be closer to you. As it is, it's dreadful knowing that you are in Tegel on your own. May God protect and preserve you for my sake.

—Maria von Wedemeyer

Berlin: February 4, 1944

The bombing raid sirens were screaming their urgent warnings of danger all over Berlin. But Maria was not there to hear them. She had gone back to Pätzig from her previous visit at Tegel. She had promised Dietrich that she would try to come again on his birthday. Dietrich's mother, Paula Bonhöffer, telephoned the von Wedemeyer household that morning. *Mütti* answered the telephone and conversed with *Frau* Bonhöffer for an unusually long time.

After her mother had finally placed the receiver back on the cradle, Maria asked her, "Who was that on the telephone, *Mütti?*"

"That was Dietrich's mother advising you not to travel to Berlin today nor continue to see Dietrich at Tegel. The air raid early warning sirens are going off all over the city."

"Air raid sirens in the daylight? Bombing raids only happen at night." Maria realized the error of her statement even before she had finished it. The Allies had become certain that the Germans didn't have sufficient anti-aircraft weapons any longer to counter their bombers, so they had brazenly begun raiding in daylight, and hardly ever at nighttime. It struck her also that the air raid at Tegel during her last visit there had occurred in the daylight.

"Because *Frau* Bonhöffer says there could be imminent air raids at any time and the railway will not be safe today."

This news caused a jolt of panic to course through Maria. Not because she was particularly fearful of an air raid, having survived the one at Tegel. She knew the sirens were going off all the time and the citizenry of Berlin was complaining regularly because often they turned out to be false alarms. It was likely, she thought, or at the very least possible, that this warning was the same and the trains would be running on schedule as usual. No, the panic she felt was that now that *Mütti* knew from Dietrich's mother's well-intentioned telephone message that there might be the danger of a raid, her mother would now do her utmost to try to dissuade Maria from going to visit Dietrich on his birthday as she had promised. It wouldn't have been beyond her mother to turn herself into a physical barrier between Maria and the door that Maria would have to use with some measure of physical force to remove and get past her mother. Maria didn't want to engage in anything that could escalate into a physical confrontation.

"*Mütti*. I know what you're thinking," she said insubmissively. "But I will risk the danger and do as I promised Dietrich I would do— come and visit him on his 38th birthday. Don't even begin to think that you can talk me out of it," Maria warned her.

"But, Maria dear, what if there is a bombing raid?"

"If there is one, there is one. If there isn't, there isn't. I know that the threat of a bombing raid would hardly stop you from taking a train to go see your imprisoned husband if he were still alive. Am I right?"

Mütti merely shrugged her shoulders in surrender. She surprised Maria and put her arms around her in an embrace and tearfully said, "Mia, dear, I've already lost more in this war than a mother or wife should be asked to lose. Just keep your eyes open for danger and if the train conductor shouts out instructions to the passengers, obey them. Enjoy your visit and then come back in one piece."

Surprised and relieved at how relatively easy it had been, Maria took her suitcase and carried it to the train station in town. She waited a quarter of an hour and then boarded the train for Berlin when it arrived. "We can't guarantee successful passage into Berlin, I'm afraid," the conductor informed each passenger as they stepped aboard the train. "We've been advised of air raids. Just so you know. You go at your own risk."

Several hours later, as the train approached the outskirts of Berlin, one could see clouds of black smoke rising above the horizon. Along the tracks were family homes in various stages of destruction, windows blown out, roofs removed forcibly, their remnants lying helplessly on the ground around the house. Sometimes it looked like one house had been lifted up and dropped down on another, Fire trucks of various colors stood on the streets, and black-and-yellow-jacketed fire personnel investigated the smoldering ruins of homes and stores for survivors. It was difficult to imagine how and where one would start to rebuild or even pick up the pieces of the shattered human lives that were accustomed to living here.

"This is precisely what Göring and his Luftwaffe left in their wake in London and Warsaw," one middle-aged passenger said to no one in particular with bitterness. "What goes around comes around."

The train, however, was stalwart in its progress toward central Berlin, although more slowly than normal. The rails were surprisingly clear of the fallen debris. Buildings near the *Bahnhof* were partially impacted by the bombs. As the train neared the tunnel entrance into the station, the conductor shouted, "Ladies and gentlemen, please do not panic. Form an orderly line, single file, to deboard the train. Then follow me in a line directly downstairs to the air raid shelter in the lower quarters of the station. For the sake of everyone's safety, do not take a detour to the café or gift shop. Toilets can be found near the air raid shelter."

Imagining that an Allied bomb could come piercing at an unannounced moment through the roof of the station while the passengers were walking put a fright into Maria. She labored hard to remain calm. The lights in the corridor leading to the stairs to the basement had gone out, leaving the passengers in darkness.

"Put your hands on the shoulders of the person in front of you in line and follow him or her accordingly," the conductor instructed. Maria placed her palms on the shoulder of the little woman in front of her. She could feel the woman's diminutive body trembling in fear. She looked back to see whose hands were on her shoulder.

"You're still so young, just a girl. All of life ahead of you," she said to Maria over her shoulder. "You shouldn't have to be endangered like this. I am old and have lived my life. My children are grown and leading their own lives." She began to sob as she spoke. "If I am killed in a bombing raid, it is no loss, but you, so young—"

Together with the other passengers from the north, they arrived successfully in a half-lit dingy room with a line of wooden benches lined up against the walls. The passengers were instructed by the conductor to choose a bench and find a place to sit. The walls had faded paint and might have been the original walls when the station was built decades ago. Maria placed her arms around the older woman whose shoulders led her safely to this shelter. She put up no resistance. She continued to tremble as though her body were affected by the cold.

"Hello, *Frau*, my name is Maria von Wedemeyer from Pätzig in Pomerania." Nervously, she replied, "I am Inge Müller. I've been a Berliner all my life. How do you do? I've never been as scared in my own city as I am now."

Maria wasn't convinced that her attempt at friendliness was helping the woman cope with her fear. In fact, all it was doing was heightening Maria's own sense of imagined danger that she thought she had forced out of her mind. She remained silent and left her fellow passenger alone.

Maria noticed that her own knees were shaking slightly when they began to hear the muffled sound of distant persistent gunfire, probably German anti-aircraft guns. Other women shrieked. Maria covered her ears with her hands so that she wouldn't hear either the gunfire or the shrieks of fear. She needed to be an isolated island now, impervious to the faces and reactions of the others, lest they give birth within her to fears and a sense of impending dread.

She looked toward the squat figure of the train conductor who was watching over the group that could spill over into uncontrolled chaos in a second. He patiently answered the questions of the passengers, saying repeatedly that he couldn't see what was happening outside the station and had had no radio contact with other railway staff who were on the ground. "These raids only last a brief time, I assure you." His voice sounded authoritative. "It's not passenger terminals that they target. It's the freight terminals farther out that they want to destroy. I'm certain that we'll get a coast clear message soon. Just be patient."

The conductor walked with a slight limp, his leg injured during the Great War, perhaps? He was surely accustomed to the chaotic sounds of warfare. Just then, the whole room rocked at the booming sound of what Maria could only imagine was a bomb dropped close to the passenger station. The lights on the ceiling flickered for several seconds, failed completely for a few more, and finally gathered the strength to turn on and stay back on. Maria wanted to believe the conductor's reassurances, but the vibration of the room from the bomb set her back into a more fearful state. She pictured Dietrich in his cell and prayed fervently that the raid was not affecting Tegel, and that he was safe.

Her imagination took her back to a divine service one morning many years ago at Finkenwalde. The text for Dietrich's sermon was from Mark when Jesus and his band of disciples were crossing the Sea of Galilee in a fishing boat and a wild and furious storm suddenly arose. The wind started howling furiously and blowing the waves of the lake into the boat. Even as experienced fishermen and seafarers the disciples were beside themselves with terror.

"In fearful times," Dietrich had said in his sermon, "we must choose between faith and despair. We must convert our fears into prayers. The frantic disciples searched all over for their Master and found him sound asleep in the hold. They voiced their fears and their anger at Jesus as a prayer: 'Teacher, do you not care that we perish?' Then Mark writes that immediately, Jesus awoke and said to the wild sea and wind, 'Peace, be still!' And the wind ceased, and there was a great calm."

Somehow Maria still remembered that Sunday sermon from her girlhood. As an adult woman now, she knew that prayer wasn't magic, and that by converting her fear of the bombs into a prayer, the Allies wouldn't automatically decide to cease fire. But she knew she would feel less alone amid all these strangers if she did utter a prayer.

"Look to Christ beside you when you are afraid, think of Christ, keep him before your eyes, call upon Christ and pray to him, believe that he is with you now, helping you...." Dietrich had said by way of conclusion of that memorable sermon. "Then fear will grow pale and fade away, our strong and living Savior will make the evil inside us recoil and make fear and anxiety themselves tremble and put them to flight."

The conductor broke into the anxious silence of the passengers. "Friends, I have good news. I'm told the Allies have had their fill of bombing our terminal. The coast is clear. Rise carefully, please. Form the same single line as when we came down here, take hold of the shoulders of the person in front of you, and follow me up the stairs to the grand hall where you should be able to make your connections to your final destination, or exit the station if central Berlin is your final destination. May you be granted a safe remainder of the day. *Heil Hitler!*"

One by one, the passengers rose to their feet like bowling pins that had been knocked down. Maria was suspicious and unsure whether she ought to take the conductor's word as gospel truth that the raid had ended. The war had this effect on her, inspiring suspicion of official pronouncements rather than grateful trust in their stated intentions to serve and protect the public.

She observed two intrepid-looking men rise and join the queue up the stairs and place their hands on the shoulders of the person in front of them. She rose up and joined the line as well. Out of the cough-inducing dusty basement, the passengers emerged into an airy, open space with ticket booths on each side where Maria headed to buy a transfer for the train to Tegel. Surprisingly, there was little evidence in the grand hall of a recent air raid. The benches for waiting passengers were in their proper places, only devoid of any passengers. The snack bar and other shops looked strangely unmolested considering the violence of the explosions they had felt down in the bomb shelter.

The train to Tegel departed on time. Some relieved extroverted passengers continued to babble about the bombing raid and their experience in the basement shelter. It was as though the whole experience had been merely a distraction from their mundane wartime lives. There seemed to be no apprehension among them of a possible warning implied in this unusual daytime air raid. They were obviously oblivious to the prospect that the opponent might have grabbed the upper hand in the conflict. Were the people in denial that all the propaganda broadcast by their trusted leaders to the contrary, it was actually now quite possible, if not likely, that Germany could be defeated?

Maria felt that her life recently was one disappointment after another. She was not the least bit surprised that no sooner had her train to Tegel left Berlin central station when the conductor announced that the train had to return to central Berlin. The Allied bombs had succeeded in damaging the track. She wouldn't get to keep her promise to Dietrich to help him celebrate his 38th birthday after all. She felt she had let him down again, a thought she recognized almost immediately as irrational. Had she succeeded in going to Tegel, wouldn't Dietrich have reminded her sternly of how foolish she had been venturing so far away from Pätzig? That, after having been warned by his mother of quite possible even likely air raids along the way. She had made a gallant if somewhat risky effort to get to him, hadn't she? Could he have expected any more of her than that?

But she acknowledged to herself that it was her own high expectations of herself that she hadn't met. She couldn't understand why she expected so much more of herself than was reasonable.

At the same time, however, she surprised herself by how quickly she got past her disappointment and accepted the fact that to go see Dietrich on his birthday was absolutely impossible despite her best efforts. It appeared that it was simply not to be. She recognized that this had not been how she was accustomed to accepting disappointment before.

Chapter Twenty-Three

God allows himself to be edged out of the world and onto the cross. God is weak and powerless in the world, and that is exactly the way, the only way, in which he can be with us and help us.

—Dietrich Bonhöffer

February 1944

Several days after Maria's missed visit, two letters from Dietrich arrived at Pätzig. In one he informed her that poor Knobloch had lost his home in one of the bombing raids that had destroyed another wing of Tegel Prison. "God be praised, K's wife, Marthe, and their two young daughters were unhurt but, like so many others in Germany now, the family had to find a way to begin again from the ground up."

Dietrich intimated in his letter that he had also written to her mother to ask if she could make room in the house in the case of this emergency for four more refugees of the war to provide an environment for their necessary rest and recovery. Dietrich told her how helpful Knobloch had been to him including how such a godsend he had been, smuggling Dietrich's love letters to Maria out of the prison and hers to him into the prison. Dietrich had wisely not included his name but referred to him only as "K" in his letter to her mother so that the mailroom censors remained in the dark about the matter.

When Maria arrived home, her mother gave her Dietrich's other letter and told Maria about receiving Dietrich's letter requesting shelter for Knobloch. *Frau* von Wedemeyer told her daughter that she decided to respectfully decline to take in the refugees displaced by the bombing in case the prison authorities' suspicions were aroused. She didn't want them to suspect her of any wrongdoing

So typical of her mother, being ruled by what others might think. Typical of the whole German people in general right now, in fact.

Dietrich wrote that he had spent the entire night before her expected birthday visit with frightened patients in sickbay who were traumatized by the bombs. He made only a brief, passing reference to her absence on his birthday. He acknowledged the relentless presence of the bombing and quipped that perhaps the Nazis were helping to celebrate his birthday with their big fireworks display.

In Knobloch's absence, another guard delivered to Dietrich's cell a package of books from his parents. In the package he found a kind, warm birthday greeting and their tangible apologies for not being able to travel to Tegel to bring the books personally.

When Knobloch returned to work, he and Dietrich spent the better part of his first day sitting side by side on Dietrich's cot. Dietrich commiserated with him about his loss, and gave thanks with him for Marthe and his daughters' safety. They were hiding in a neighbor's basement shelter. Dietrich said very little in response to his sad story. He had learned in prison that words of comfort are often little more than ineffectual gibberish. A sturdy hand on the shoulder speaks so much more eloquently. Knobloch requested that Dietrich pray to the Almighty Father for strength and fortitude in rebuilding their home and lives.

"I'll do better than that for you, Knobloch," Dietrich told him. "Only a suffering, crucified God can help us in these times. I will pray to that suffering God for you and the family, and for all who have no hope other than God's abiding presence with them in the midst of suffering."

As Knobloch left, Dietrich ripped open the package and looked inside the flyleaf of each book to see if his name had been underlined. Sure enough, it had been. He began examining the index pages hungrily for the coded message: "Hans taken to Charité Hospital in Berlin with a self-inflicted virus. Has learned from Rõder that your hearing and his will occur simultaneously. State intends to present the same evidence in both trials. Self-inflicted illness in the hope of delaying the trials until after Valkyrie. Canaris has been relieved of his duties in the Navy but sends word that July 20 is still on target and expected to succeed."

July 20 cannot come soon enough. May God grant it success for the sake of Germany and the world.

Except for the one that arrived a few days after his birthday, letters were not arriving from Maria as often as before. He knew that the postal system had been thrown into chaos by the bombing raids. Maria had been busy filling in for a colleague who needed time off work to give birth to a baby. News of this newcomer's arrival into the world filled Maria with exciting dreams of her and Dietrich's life together after prison and the day they would bring babies into the world themselves.

Just as Dietrich was thinking about this, a guard came to cell 92 to deliver an envelope. Dietrich looked at the writing on the envelope. It was not in Maria's handwriting, but he opened it nonetheless. Indeed, it was not from Maria, but from Ruth von Wedemeyer instead. He was disappointed, but her letter brought his tired mind to attention.

My dear Dietrich. God be with you. Thank you for your kind letter. I am sorry I cannot accommodate your request to provide a place of respite for the small family who has suffered the loss of their home in the bombing raid. It is so kind of you to be concerned about them.

You know by now that Maria attempted to visit you on your birthday. I had expressed my disapproval before she left Pätzig. Let me assure you, not because I didn't think you deserved her attention on your birthday, but because of your mother's having warned us of air raid sirens in Berlin. Thanks be to God, Maria arrived back home safely after enduring an air raid in the shelter in the basement of the Berlin Bahnhof.

Dietrich, I must alert you that Maria is unhappy, I think very, very unhappy. She is anxious and frustrated to the point of feeling ill. Ruth-Alice is doing a wonderful job of nursing Maria back to health and strength. I believe her worsened condition has to do with the recent attempt to visit at Tegel.

Dietrich paused reading at that point. He was not surprised that Maria was unhappy. He could see the unhappiness in her during the last couple of visits. He pulled off his spectacles, wiped the lenses on his sleeve, and replaced them on his nose This was a ritual he performed unthinkingly whenever he was confronted by information that he felt powerless to change or a situation before which he was totally helpless.

The letter continued:

And not just the most recent visit, for each one seems to upset her more. I know you probably disagree with me. But, frankly, I am afraid that trying to maintain her relationship with you over the miles and in the prison is too much of a strain on her. Put yourself in her place: a young girl visiting a fiancé in prison, a man she has hardly had the chance to get to know under normal circumstances. I assure you that I know none of this is your fault. I have been corresponding with your mother and father. You are a member of a remarkable family, Dietrich. I have no doubt of your suitability for Maria, once the war is over, as we all pray that it will be soon. In the meantime, I wonder if it is generous of you to insist on Maria's loyalty. It may be a while before she has the strength to write to you. Her spirit may be willing, but right now, her flesh is weak.

BOOK THREE

Who am I? They often tell me
I stepped from my cell's confinement
Calmly, cheerfully, firmly,
Like a Squire from his country house.

Who am I? They often tell me
I used to speak to my warders
freely and friendly and clearly,
as though it were mine to command.

Who am I? They also tell me
I bore the days of misfortune
equably, smilingly, proudly,
like one accustomed to win.

Am I then really that which other men tell of?
Or am I only what I myself know of myself?
Restless and longing and sick, like a bird in a cage,
Struggling for breath, as though hands were compressing
My throat, yearning for colors, for flowers, for the voices of birds,
thirsting for words of kindness, for neighborliness,
tossing in expectation of great events,
powerlessly trembling for friends at an infinite distance,
weary and empty at praying, at thinking, at making,
faint, and ready to say farewell to it all.

Who am I? This or the Other?
Am I one person today and tomorrow another?
Am I both at once? A hypocrite before others,
And before myself a contemptible woebegone weakling?
Or is something within me like a beaten army
Fleeing in disorder from victory already achieved?

Who am I? They mock me, these lonely question of mine
Whoever I am, Thou Knowest, O God, I am thine.

—Dietrich Bonhöffer

Chapter Twenty-Four

I'm terribly sad. Just imagine, my old school at Altenberg is closing down. The organization for the evacuation of children to the country, or something of the kind, is moving in and taking over after the summer holiday. It's enough to make one weep. The school has existed for 250 years. And now it might be destroyed, utterly destroyed like everything else in his blasted war.

—Maria von Wedemeyer

Tegel Prison: July 1944

Once the page on the 1944 calendar turned to July, those in Tegel who knew and cared about Dietrich were concerned. Knobloch had more dealings with Dietrich than anyone else in Tegel, so he was the most profoundly troubled by the changes in Dietrich's outlook and demeanor. Dietrich had descended into as deep a pit of despondency as Knobloch had seen since his first nights of confinement when he openly considered suicide. The most recent visits with his beloved Maria hadn't flowed smoothly. In fact, because she had been caught in an air raid en route, she didn't arrive as expected on the pastor's 38th birthday.

After that, he received a letter from Maria's mother. It was after he read it that Knobloch and *Kommandant* Mätz first detected his emotional turn for the worse. He was more remote from his fellow inmates and more disconsolate whenever he mentioned Maria. Knobloch didn't jump to the conclusion that either Maria or Dietrich loved the other any less. Rather, he discerned that something unforeseen had inserted itself between them like a grey cloud that darkened his outlook.

It was during this doleful period that Dietrich uncharacteristically refused a request for prayer from another prisoner. He always responded to such a request gladly no matter how exhausted he might be.

It happened down in sickbay, which Dietrich tenaciously considered his parish for whose souls he felt particularly responsible.

One warm day in June, one of the patients announced out loud that he had heard from a good source that hundreds of boatloads of Allied troops had landed on the beaches of Normandy. Furthermore, hundreds of British and American planes had infiltrated the air space over the central European continent with only token German resistance and had dropped thousands of paratroopers behind the Nazi lines.

"Jesus Christ! We're done for!" shouted one curmudgeonly patient in a corner bed who was known as a particularly loyal Nazi. "We've still got some time to square things with the damned Jews for all they've done to us over the centuries, assuming the Almighty preserves the life of our *Führer* long enough." He turned to Dietrich as his chaplain. "Will you pray for us and for the *Führer,* Pastor Bonhöffer?"

Dietrich, who had been standing near the window, suddenly turned rigid, and stood speechless, his face as red as a fresh beet. "I'll not pray for you, you whining piece of Nazi shit, or for your mad *Führer, "* he pronounced as he stomped angrily out of the sickbay.

A day or two before Dietrich had confided to Knobloch about Maria's sickness, which her mother's letter had informed him. "She deserves better, Knobloch," he began. "I'm overwhelmed by the thought of how difficult I have made things for her. I have expected nothing of her but her perseverance in the face of the obstacles to our love. But I have not made allowances for her despair about our future. She is having fainting spells. She has erratic moods. She has lost her appetite for the things she used to enjoy. She says she doubts the value of her visits to me here. Her mother insists that none of it is my fault, but I know she is just being charitable. Maria would have been better off never meeting me."

My dear Maria,

Thank you for your recent letter. No, it didn't depress me at all, as you feared, and none of what you confided surprised or dismayed me. It was all more or less what I have observed and thought for a while. I knew that we couldn't speak to each other honestly in the way we do unless we loved each other very much. What does dismay me is that you should love me at all when we're able to see each other so little, dearest, most beloved

Maria,

I've sometimes been afraid that you said yes to me out of pity. I now know it wasn't that, and that you felt as I did.

So, it sometimes torments you to think of me? My dearest, dearest Maria, isn't it enough for you to know that you've made me glad and happy? More so than I ever hoped for in all my life. Apparently, you're beginning to doubt your love for me and that I love you as you are, that I want you somehow to be different from who you are? The one thing I do not want is that you should be or become unhappy because you feel the lack of something that I am failing to provide you. Please know that I am quite convinced by experience that I cannot go on without you. We belong to each other and will remain together.

It's your little "yes" of January 1943 that I cling to whenever I have to wait for a letter from you for any length of time.

So now you say you won't be coming again to Tegel for some length of time. Dearest Maria, if you find it too tiring and emotionally taxing to come here, it goes without saying that you are right not to do so.

We don't know, given the extraneous factors, how often we shall see each other again in this life, the times being what they are. Maria, we simply must not lose patience. God's will, and the need for our subjection to it are quite beyond dispute. But every day, rest assured that I love you very much and hold you very dear and always will.

Yours, Dietrich

Dietrich shared with Knobloch the contents of his letter of reassurance to Maria. Yet, it didn't lift him from the pit of depression into which he had plunged. For the next few days, he remained alone in his cell. He became forgetful. At least twice a day he asked him to confirm the day's date even though he had provided him with a wall calendar.

He was singularly fixated on the 20th day of July, for reasons he didn't divulge to Knobloch, who only came to comprehend that fixation after the events of that watershed day became known.

On June 30, Tegel Prison was thrown into a flurry when General Paul von Hase, the military *Kommandant* of Berlin, made an unannounced appearance to visit his nephew in cell 92. For over five hours in Dietrich's cell, the two of them finished off four bottles of *Sekt* champagne. His uncle's sudden bold appearance just at that moment in time indicated to Dietrich that the Valkyrie coup, in which his brother-in-law Hans, as well as his uncle, had been integral, was still scheduled for July 20. He wanted to shout at the top of his lungs, "Fellow prisoners, be ye of good cheer. Soon Hitler will be dead and life can begin again for all of us!"

The Valkyrie conspirators led by Colonel Claus von Stauffenberg were risking decisive action. The war had dragged on too long, they felt. Jews were being rounded up and murdered with a vengeance. On the eastern front particularly, the barbarism of the *SS* had been given free rein. It was as if the devil and his hordes had crawled out of hell and roamed the earth.

Initially, the devout Roman Catholic von Stauffenberg had been reluctant to participate in a violent coup against a superior. But the events of recent years helped to convince him that now was the time to act in much the same, courageous way Dietrich had when he joined the *Abwehr* and the conspiracy four years earlier. "It is hopeless to look for salvation from the Allies," von Stauffenberg told others involved in the July 20 plot. "It is time now for something to be done by us. He who has the courage to act must know that he will probably go down in German history as a traitor. But if he fails to act, he will be a traitor in his own conscience before God."

And so on July 11, von Stauffenberg visited Hitler at his Alpine retreat, Berchtesgaden. He carried a bomb in his suitcase. But when he noticed that Himmler was absent from the meeting, he telephoned General Helmut Stieff in Berlin, who ordered the assassination attempt be postponed for over a week in order to have Himmler and others of the inner circle present. "My God," said von Stauffenberg, "shouldn't we do it now? All the arrangements for the transfer of power have been made, and people are waiting and hoping for word."

Eight days later, Hitler ordered von Stauffenberg to appear at Hitler's East Prussian headquarters, the Wolf's Lair, to give an oral report. Once again, von Stauffenberg arrived with the bomb in a briefcase. Again, Himmler was absent. Von Stauffenberg was ordered by Stieff to hold off the bombing attempt. Von Stauffenberg returned to Berlin.

He was commanded by Hitler to return to Wolf's Lair to address a 1 p.m. meeting the next day, July 20. At von Stauffenberg's request, the driver stopped at a small Catholic chapel where he entered for prayer.

Afterward, von Stauffenberg rendezvoused on the grounds with the officer, whose task it would be to inform the Berlin conspirators after the bomb had gone off. All that was left was for von Stauffenberg to set the bomb, place it near the *Führer*, and slip out of the room before it exploded. Von Stauffenberg used the nearest men's room as a place to activate the time bomb. He entered the meeting room, took a seat near Hitler, and placed the briefcase under the table about six feet from Hitler. Von Stauffenberg didn't notice, however, the huge plinth that served to support the massive oaken table.

He excused himself from the meeting to visit the restroom and proceeded to slip out of the room with barely three minutes to spare before the scheduled explosion of the bomb. Surreptitiously, he walked out of the building to a distance of about three hundred meters. Suddenly, von Stauffenberg heard an ear-splitting explosion inside the building and saw bluish-yellow flames shoot out the windows.

He mistakenly concluded that his mission had been successful and that all the members of the evil inner circle were killed. That failure led to a series of reprisals against hundreds, if not thousands, of both conspirators and others with minimal, if any, involvement in the conspiracy.

When they inspected inside, they found the huge desk in smithereens. The room smelled of burned flesh and hair. The ceiling had plummeted down to the floor. Several men lay dead, but none of the dead were ones whom von Stauffenberg called "evil incarnate." Hitler was up and around, albeit cartoonishly mussed, his hair on end. The huge plinth had shielded him from the blast.

"It was Providence that spared me," Hitler announced triumphantly. "This is a vindication of my life's work. I must continue it."

Chapter Twenty-Five

In me there is darkness. But, God, with You there is light; I am lonely, but You do not leave me; I am feeble in heart, but with You there is help; I am restless, but with You there is peace. In me there is bitterness, but with You there is patience; I do not understand Your ways.
But You know the way for me.

—Dietrich Bonhöffer

Tegel Prison: July 21, 1944

Word spread quickly among the staff of Tegel Prison that yet another coup against the *Führer* had been attempted and failed. Knobloch wondered if that was possibly why the pastor had been so anxious in the days leading up to July 20.

The radio in the sickbay blared. It was one of the very few spaces in Tegel where inmates had unlimited access to the radio; it kept the sick inmates contented. Sometimes when no one was looking, Dietrich would twist the dial to the BBC, which was strictly forbidden anywhere in the Reich. On most days, before he left sickbay to return to his cell, he would turn the dial back to the original German station.

This morning, not a single word of English could be heard. Everything was in German. No one could mistake the strident voice of the *Führer* who spoke confidently on the radio.

"If I speak to you today, I do so for two special reasons. In the first place, so that you may hear my voice and know that I myself am sound and uninjured; and in the second place so that you may also hear the particulars of a crime without peer in German history. An extremely small clique of ambitious, conscienceless, stupid, and criminal officers had forged a plot to eliminate me and my staff of officers in command of the *Wehrmacht*. The bomb, which was planted by Colonel von Stauffenberg, burst two meters from me. I myself am unhurt, but several of my colleagues were injured, one of them fatally. The clique of usurpers is an extremely small band of criminal elements who are now being mercilessly hunted and eliminated. A time of accounting will be given as we National

Socialists are wont to give. It has once more been granted me to escape a fate that holds no terrors for me personally, but which could have brought down terror upon the heads of the German people. I see in this another sign from Providence that I must and therefore will continue my work as before."

Dietrich made only the slightest effort to disguise his repulsion at hearing Hitler's glee at his miraculous survival of yet another plot against his life; he was devastated in its failure. The pastor was seldom irritable or on the verge of exploding in anger, but the survival of the *Führer* yet again had plummeted him into deeper despair and defeat.

The curmudgeonly Nazi-sympathizer patient shouted, "You heard our invincible *Führer* in his own words. Recompense is coming with a vengeance for these cowardly fools. *Heil Hitler!"*

The stubborn patient's words made the situation worse. The pastor could not hold back his frustration. "Perhaps, *friend,"* he said sarcastically with ironic emphasis, "they set the bomb because Hitler *deserves* to die for all the damage he has brought to Germany, and the inhuman destruction to the Jews and all of Europe."

Knobloch said to him privately, "Pastor, beware. If word of this slips out of sickbay, as I am almost certain it will, and if the authorities hear of it, they will surely damn you to death."

"Maybe so, Knobloch. I'm not sure I care a rat's ass today what happens to me. You are looking at a man who is as good as a dead man already."

Knobloch took him by the arm and guided him out of sickbay before any more damage could be done.

"Knobloch, yesterday's verse from Psalm 20 was very interesting and timely. 'Some put their trust in chariots and others in horses, but we rely on the sure word of the Lord our God,'" Dietrich said, bitterly. "Knobloch, the tanks, guns, and howitzers of the Nazis will sure as hell be stilled forever by the sharp sword of God's eternal word. Mark my words."

By the end of the day, Knobloch was a hundred percent positive that Bonhöffer had played an intimate role in the von Stauffenberg plot to assassinate Hitler and overthrow the Nazi regime. The authorities moved quickly during the week after the assassination attempt. Admiral Canaris, who had been removed from his post as an admiral in the navy already, was arrested and quickly put on trial as a key leader of the resistance. In spite of his serious illness, von Dohnányi was crudely transported from the Charité Hospital to the more punitive conditions at the Sachsenhausen Concentration Camp. The pastor's uncle Paul von Hase was sentenced to death by a notoriously zealous Nazi judge and executed at Plötzensee prison.

Letters from Maria were more and more infrequent, leaving Dietrich in a morass of uncertainty about the constancy of her love for him and the prospects of their future.

About a week after the failed coup, his sister Suse, three years his junior, rode on her bicycle from Charlottenburg to visit her brother at Tegel to see how he was doing. She had arrived not knowing whether he was still an inmate there. Once through the security detail at the entrance, she walked her bicycle along the gravel path to the chain-link fence by the enclosure of the exercise yard where Dietrich and Knobloch were walking to enjoy the warm sun. It was as though she had timed her visit to correspond with her brother's time in the exercise yard. She bent over and pretended to examine the front tire of her bicycle. She pulled down the kickstand and removed the air pump from its brackets on the frame. She unscrewed the tire's valve and intentionally inserted the pump head incorrectly so that air hissed from the tire. She glanced up and saw the familiar form of her brother and Knobloch approaching the chain-link fence.

"Suse, is that you?" Dietrich asked with surprise. "This is a most pleasant surprise! By bicycle all the way? This is Knobloch."

Suse looked at Knobloch warily.

"He was a part of my parish in Wedding ten or more years ago. He's my best friend here at Tegel. You can say anything in front of him."

"I hear things and, then again, I don't hear everything," Knobloch amended. "But if you have something special or delicate to communicate with your brother, I'd advise you do it now because, in a moment, I'll be out the gate to help you fix your flat tire."

"Dear brother, I see you are still here," Suse remarked.

"For the time being, God be thanked. I don't think it will be for much longer, however. They'll be ransacking all of Germany for evidence of who else was involved in the July 20 plot. Eventually, they'll find something."

Knobloch moved slowly toward the gate to open it. Suse glanced nervously in his direction.

"It's all right," Dietrich assured her. "He knows. Or at least guesses."

"Perhaps it will be all right. Maybe they won't find anything connecting you to the plot."

"Let's not fool ourselves, Suse. It isn't likely I'll survive the war."

"That's exactly what Maria fears. She wrote me a very despondent letter. I'll be meeting her right after this visit. She and I have become good friends."

"She hasn't written to me in many weeks."

"That's because she doesn't know what to say. She's confused about the future."

"Tell her that I know she still loves me. I will write to her again. I must be honest with her about the increased possibility of my death. I know she won't like me writing about it. But I want to assure her that I can better face the possibility of my death if she—if all of you— allow me to accept it and not try to avoid the topic. Death doesn't seem to me such an alien thing. Just the other side of life, not so fearful if it's accepted."

"But brother, you mustn't give up."

"My fate is out of my hands."

Maria waited as prearranged on one of the hard benches that had been provided for waiting passengers on the tiny wooden rectangle of a station in the Bunhof valley. The train glided along the edge of the platform, barely pausing for Suse to jump from the last step onto the wooden platform and grab her bicycle from inside the train.

She cut to the chase immediately. "I need to talk to you here, Maria."

"Here? On this platform?"

"Yes. There'll be another train in two hours; that's enough time for me to tell you what I need to say and to eat something with you here." Suse fanned her face with her bonnet and made a sign for Maria to sit down beside her.

"I'll get right to the point, Maria. Dietrich says there's a very good chance that he won't survive the war. He's hanging on by his fingertips, I could tell."

Maria's eyes welled with tears. She covered her mouth with her hand and rested her head on Suse's shoulder.

"I want to tell you also about my sister Christel and her husband, Hans. Do you remember they were arrested on the same evening as Dietrich? Dietrich doesn't know it yet, but the reason Hans's and Dietrich's trials have been delayed is that Hans wanted it that way. He thought that if they could just delay what is probable and ride out the war in prison without coming to trial, they might survive by outliving the regime. If they came to trial the plot and their part in it might be discovered."

"The plot?" Maria asked. "I'm confused. What plot?"

"Why, the plot to kill the *Führer*. The one that failed yesterday."

"Are you telling me that Dietrich knew about that plot in advance?"

"Maria, he's known about the most recent one and all the other failed plots before that—not only knew about them but helped plan them."

"*Mein Gott!* He never said a word about them to me. We had promised to be honest with each other always in all things!"

"And he would be very upset with me if he knew I have just told you. The less you know, the safer you are."

"He knew about such plots? And actually helped to plan them?" Maria asked as though she hadn't heard Suse correctly before.

"Yes, Maria, he was in the *Abwehr,* as he said. But at the same time, he and some others were plotting to kill Hitler."

"Like Hans, buttering his bread on both sides?"

"Yes, exactly."

Maria shut her eyes. "I am envisioning my father, resplendent in his *Wehrmacht* uniform, leaving home to fight the Russians. A loyal German, a patriot. But I recall also how much he distrusted Hitler and hated what Germany was becoming. But Dietrich plotting to *murder* the *Führer?* That's taking the distrust to a whole other level. I do not know what to think or how to react or even what I feel about it." She proceeded to weep some more and wondered, *Can I possibly marry someone who was essentially a traitor?*

"Maria, the military officers involved in the plot were just like your dear father: patriotic Germans who couldn't bear to see what has been done in the name of such patriotism. Even now, Dietrich feels they waited too late. Dietrich could no longer live with what he'd learned about the Nazis. He could no longer refuse to act."

Maria turned to look at Suse with confounded eyes.

"Maria, your father was a courageous man." Suse put her arms around Maria who looked so lost. "I take nothing away from his courage and sacrifice. But perhaps Dietrich's is a better kind of courage and sacrifice. Maria, do you know how many Jews this *Führer* has killed in the name of the *Vaterland* with the unwitting help of brave soldiers like your father and brother and so many others? It must be in the millions by now."

Maria didn't respond. She continued to weigh Suse's words, but her mind was focused only on her immediate resentment of Dietrich's having kept her in the dark about his real work.

"You're feeling betrayed by my brother, Maria?"

"Yes, can you blame me? He misled me to believe that his activity with the *Abwehr* was honest work."

Maria stepped back and no longer clung to Suse.

"Maria, just listen to yourself. Can any of us be sure what is honest work any longer? Hasn't this war, and this *Führer,* turned so many values we held dear upside down? If Dietrich and Hans and our brother Klaus had just done military intelligence for the Reich, would that have been honest work?"

Maria couldn't answer. She wasn't accustomed to thinking in this way.

"Isn't it a little naïve to think that working to undergird the Reich is honest, responsible work while working to further the resistance is dishonorable, Maria?"

"Admittedly," Maria conceded, "I had assumed so in an unexamined way. Your calling me naïve makes me feel like a little girl being admonished by my wiser, more worldly wise peer."

"Maria, I apologize for my stern tone. It's time you reexamined your assumptions, don't you think?"

"Maybe it's time I took another step in growing up."

"Are you willing to love Dietrich only as long as he works to further the aims of a corrupt and morally bankrupt Reich, but distance yourself from him if you discover that he has been secretly working to undermine the evil Reich? That's the way it appears to me."

Suse paused for emphasis.

"I'm sure it feels like a betrayal to discover that your fiancé has told you only a part of the truth, that he chose to withhold from you the information about his role in the resistance. But, Maria, can you see how withholding from you the whole truth was not to mislead you, but to protect you?"

"Oh, Suse, I'm so confused. This is still all so new to me. But, yes, I'm beginning to look at it differently than before."

"Then you can see that Dietrich's keeping from you the secret of working for the resistance is an act of love rather than the duplicity of a lover?"

"Oh, Suse. Have I been wrong about this all along? To be disillusioned by Dietrich's participation in the plots rather than proud? To have been afraid to see him myself today and sending you to see him in my stead?"

Suse remained strategically silent to allow Maria to make sense of her revelations.

"Perhaps only Hans and Dietrich and the other conspirators had the courage to put an iron bar in the spokes of Hitler's wheel, as Dietrich would name it. I've only been thinking of myself and my dream of a married life with Dietrich. Poor Dietrich. All alone with his disappointment," Maria said through her tears.

"When Hans decided to take drastic action to try to get their trials delayed, do you know what he asked Christel to do? To obtain a culture of diphtheria bacilli from our father's hospital. She did as requested and smuggled the culture into the prison in a batch of sweets. Hans ate the sweets and bacilli and became very ill. So the trial was postponed until Hans is well enough to participate. Do you see, Maria? In such times as these, a wife is called on to do unusually brave things for her husband.

So are fiancées, don't you think? In the wake of this new information about him, I'm sure you've had thoughts about ending the relationship."

Sniffling, Maria could not speak. Instead, she nodded her head reluctantly.

"Dear Maria, can you delay your decision just a few more months until the war is brought to a close? Put off any drastic action that both you and Dietrich would consider tragic?"

Maria looked at Suse intensely as she listened and considered her words.

"Dear Maria, this hellish war will come to an end. If by some miracle Dietrich survives, the two of you will be free to marry. Just wait a few more months. People in the know like Christel assure me that's all it will take for the Allies to infiltrate Germany and bring this war to a close."

The train from Tegel to Berlin was approaching. Maria embraced and thanked Suse. The color had returned to Maria's pale cheeks.

"Suse, you have done more than you know. Don't misinterpret my confusion. Give me some time to get used to what I've heard today. I assure you that I love Dietrich more than anyone living. He's an inseparable part of me, and I am going to be with him until the end—if, whenever, and however that may come."

Chapter Twenty-Six

Dietrich and I have not heard from each other for ages. What on earth is happening? I know my illness has stolen my energy and enthusiasm and the bombing has, too. But at the same time, I wonder if my soul knows something I don't admit to myself consciously, and so I am reluctant to write to or visit Dietrich. After the failure of the plot, there has been such a furious rash of random arrests. Dietrich doesn't say it in so few words, but he must be feeling the noose tightening around his own neck because I feel it for him as if it were strung around my own.

—Maria von Wedemeyer

August 1944

On the train ride back to Charlottenburg after her conversation with Suse, Maria relapsed back into her confusion. Her mind couldn't digest all the new information Suse had communicated to her. She was besieged by questions. *How could Dietrich plot to assassinate the Führer? He is such a gentle man. He is a man of faith. He was a pacifist when we first met. How could he condone this violence?*

The *Führer* certainly held no special place of affection in her heart. But she had always held firmly to what she had been taught since she was a little girl, that it is the duty of the country's citizens to remain loyal to its leaders. How else did society function? She prayed that she would yet be able to reconcile Dietrich's apparent treason with her childhood heritage.

She was further disoriented by the fact that when she arrived at Marienburgerallee, Dietrich's parents' home was empty of all its inhabitants. In all her emotional turmoil, she had forgotten that they had gone to stay temporarily with their daughter Christel in Sacrow to be away from the more frequent bombing raids in Charlottenburg. Maria telephoned them and arranged for their family driver to come to fetch her to Sacrow.

During the drive to Christel's, her mind turned to Dietrich's disappointment that the plot that he and Hans and the resistance had planned so long and meticulously had failed. How more tightly must he feel the noose around his neck? She didn't know how to respond or how to muster all the strength she would need to return to Tegel as soon as possible to be with him and comfort him.

Christel and Dietrich's parents welcomed her with open arms when she arrived. Christel, though, was shaken to the core.

"The news has not been good, either for Hans or Dietrich," she told Maria.

"The failure of the plot last month?"

"That, of course, but more than that. Much worse."

"Worse?"

"The *Gestapo* has discovered the *Chronicle of Shame.*"

"What new thing is this that I have not been told about?"

"Hans didn't tell me about it for the longest time either. I'm certain Dietrich kept knowledge of it from you, too, for the same reason—to protect you."

"I'm learning that there is a lot that Dietrich has not told me, presumably 'to protect me.' But, tell me, what is the *Chronicle of Shame?*"

"Ever since the Nazis prepared to invade Poland in 1939, Hans has kept a record of the atrocities perpetrated by the *Wehrmacht, SS, Gestapo,* and particularly the *Einsatzgruppen* that followed in their wake. Hans spared me the details of those atrocities in Poland, and especially against the Jews. Hans entitled the record the *Chronicle of Shame.* He hid it in the safe at the library at the military base at Zossen. He was certain it would never be discovered there."

"In wartime, never say never, I've learned."

"Correct. In the massive manhunt after the failed coup of July 20, it seems someone broke under torture and revealed the existence of the *Chronicle of Shame* and its location. After that, it didn't take the *Gestapo* more than a few days to discover it and bring it to Himmler."

"They can trace the origin to Hans?"

"Surely! It's a nail in his coffin. But the *Chronicle* implicates Dietrich as well. He uncovered many of the atrocities by way of his contacts throughout Europe and reported them to Hans for the *Chronicle.*"

Suddenly, the room started spinning, and Maria had to hold on to the arms of the sofa to prevent herself from falling to the floor. The vertigo she had been suffering in recent weeks returned with a new twist. Now she no longer was just imagining and fearing that Dietrich's life was in mortal danger. She *knew* it.

Tegel Prison: August 23, 1944

Maria, disconsolate, sat waiting by herself in the visitation room. The windows to the outside were without glass. The various air raids had blown them out, and the prison administration had deemed it futile to replace the glass since it was likely that another bombing raid could occur on any day.

Knobloch knocked gently on the door and entered. *"Fräulein* Maria, how good to see you here after your period of illness."

"Yes, I've been ill," she said with fatigue in her voice. "Ill from worry and concern. Ill on the doorstep of utter despair. I didn't want Dietrich to see me like that."

"In any case, he will be very pleased and relieved to see you today."

Almost on cue, Dietrich entered the visitation room. His face exhibited his surprise at Maria's presence but also pleasure and gratitude.

"Maria dear! What a surprise! You are well enough to travel here! God be thanked! You can't know how glad and grateful I am!"

"Dietrich dear, how sorry I am that I have not come for so long."

"When you are sick, it is understandable that you were not able to come. I bear no resentment whatsoever. Just immense gratitude right now."

"You forgive me?"

"There is nothing to forgive, dear Maria. Please know that."

"Sometimes forgiveness is difficult to accept. Like now."

"Now, entirely on your own volition, you've made the big decision to come and visit me. And move to Charlottenburg to help my parents. I can't even begin to tell you how happy I am. I had just begun to reconcile myself to the likelihood that you would be recalled to the Red Cross and that we wouldn't see each other for ages."

"Given what happened on July 20, I wasn't sure they would allow me in to visit you."

"It is a godsend to me that they did. But we can't be sure they will allow it for very much longer."

"Once Himmler has read the *Chronicle of Shame,* he'll undoubtedly see to it that these visits stop."

Dietrich's face turned as white as blown snow. "You've learned that they have located the Zossen files?"

"Yes, I heard it from Christel. She despairs of Hans's and your lives."

Dietrich was speechless.

Maria quickly reassured him. "I'm proud of you and Hans for the *Chronicle.* A rare piece of truth in the morass of official lies."

"We had hoped that the *Chronicle* would convince the German people and the Allied leaders of Hitler's brutality and savagery."

"It's the assassination plots that I have more trouble understanding," Maria continued. "When I met you, Dietrich, you were contemplating going to India to study with Gandhi, the disciple extraordinaire of nonviolence. Now you're a participant in a plot involving murder. How do you explain it?"

"That's what my book *Ethics* is intended to do once I finish it."

"I can't wait for a book. I need more than theological words on a page. I need answers directly from you!"

"I understand you do. I just fear that this changes your love for me."

"No, it just makes me despair that we will ever be able to fulfill our dream of being married and having children."

"Maria, after everything I saw and witnessed in Europe and heard about from trustworthy friends, I could no longer sit by and not take responsible action."

"Violence is a responsible action by a follower of the Prince of Peace?"

"We follow Jesus Christ in the real world where evil is in bitter warfare against the Kingdom of Christ."

"Yes, but isn't participating in violence taking up the ways of evil?"

"Not necessarily. By itself, violence is neutral."

"I don't follow, Dietrich. You're just splitting academic hairs."

"Maria, the reasons for my actions are theologically based. I pray that you will understand and agree with me."

"It's important to me that I gain some understanding of your motives."

"God is the Ultimate. God established the state to use the sword to establish and maintain justice for its people. The state is not excluded from accountability for its use of the sword to the One who established it. The state must not use violence to injure or harm its people arbitrarily."

Maria was silent.

"You witnessed such arbitrary use of violence by Hitler's state as they used force to remove the mentally ill patients and eliminate the Jewish patients and staff at Bethel."

"That was awful."

"Maria, there are hundreds of other instances of such misuse of violent brute force by our government all over Europe. The *Führer* and his government cannot escape accountability to God."

"You and the others in the resistance have proclaimed yourselves as the agents of God's accountability? That's rather arrogant of all of you, isn't it?"

"It will certainly be seen that way, I'm afraid, by Judge-Advocate Röder and Himmler and Hitler himself."

"But you call your participation in the assassination plots '*responsible* action'?" Maria was looking even more perplexed.

Dietrich hesitated to continue with his explanation as though he were introducing Maria to a whole new realm of reasoning, and not sure it would be productive.

"God established the Church as His representative in the world to keep the state in check. For years after Hitler came to power, the *Reichskirche* closed its eyes to how Hitler was abusing his power. I tried to awaken the Confessing Church to these abuses and to call it to counter and speak out against the state's methods. But it also refused to be responsible and do so."

Maria's voice softened its tone, and her face revealed a faint ray of understanding.

"I remember your efforts and tireless dedication."

"Then Hans and his accomplices in the resistance seemed to offer the sole avenue for responsible action, to work to rid Germany of a government that is injuring citizens unjustly based only on race and ethnic origin and leading the country to inevitable defeat. Inaction in the face of such evil is evil itself, I think. Rightly or wrongly, I judged joining the resistance to be the will of God for me for this time. I acted and put myself in God's hands. I will let God judge if I have been right or wrong."

"And now that judgment shall be soon," Maria said tearfully.

"I don't fear either the death that may be approaching quickly or the judgment. The One who will judge me is the same One who accepted me as his forever in my baptism and has reassured me of it many times since."

"Oh Dietrich, I fear your death. I would be left bereft. My dreams would be shattered. There would be nothing left. Nothing." She broke down and wept uncontrollably in his arms.

"There will still be you, Maria von Wedemeyer. Unique child of God. Gifted mathematician. Faithful Servant of God. The one who will be loved by me from all eternity. The one who I hope will love me through eternity."

Maria was so overcome she could hardly speak. "Oh Dietrich, I'm so frightened to think about it."

"More than I fear my own death, I fear the death of others like my parents, Hans, and you, Maria. Please know that, Maria. It is important to me that you do. Why are we so afraid when we think about death? Death is not wild and terrible if only we can be still and hold fast to God's Word. Death is not bitter if we have not become bitter ourselves. Death is grace, the greatest gift of grace that God gives to people who trust him. Death in Christ is mild, that death is sweet and gentle; it beckons to us with heavenly power, if only we realize that it is the gateway to the way we were intended to live with God and one another. Just think, Maria dear. What is hidden from us now will be revealed in its fullness."

Chapter Twenty-Seven

When Christ calls a man, he bids him come and die.

—Dietrich Bonhöffer

September 1944

August 23, 1944, was to be the last time Maria von Wedemeyer and Pastor Bonhöffer were together on this side of eternity. They both sensed it. They held their embrace for a long time at the end of the visit. Maria especially was reluctant to let go of him. Dietrich continued his embrace. Eventually, he loosened his arms around her. He would have loved to continue but came to the conclusion that the longer they clung to each other, the more difficult it would be for both of them to part and pick up the strands of their lives without the other.

Parting was indeed difficult. Dietrich laid down a sheet on the floor and knelt. He gestured for her to do so as well. He spoke a tender prayer that the Father continue to hold each of them firmly in the palm of his hand, come what may. He added a clause that all those who face danger or death for their efforts to bring the government's atrocities to an end might be granted a heavenly blessing. He asked that where he had sinned, he might find God's gracious mercy and forgiveness.

Before he closed, he squeezed Maria's hand and paused to compose himself. Then he gave thanks to their God for the gift of each other's love. He had more to say, but his voice gave out, and he trembled as he leaned over to kiss the tears from his fiancée's cheek.

As Dietrich and Knobloch returned to cell number 92, Dietrich remarked, "My days here at Tegel are numbered. The *Gestapo* is going to want me under their strict observation and supervision in their own prison. Knobloch, you have been a godsend to me during my 18 months here. I don't know what I can do to thank you for all that you have done for me and for Maria."

Knobloch listened in silence as they walked down the corridor. Once they had stepped into the cell, he closed the door behind them and in a half-whisper spoke conspiratorially to Dietrich.

"Perhaps there is at least one more thing that I can do for you, Pastor, while you are still here in the *Wehrmacht's* custody."

"What do you have in mind, dear Kurt?"

"The *Gestapo* prison is no place for you, Pastor. You've heard how brutal their torture is. You are already paying a dear price for your participation in the assassination plots. I would hate to think of your suffering any further pain or punishment from those brutes when there might be a way to avoid it."

"A way to avoid it? At this late juncture?"

"I've been contemplating a plot of resistance of my own, Pastor, that just may succeed in getting you out of Tegel."

"I'm pretty well resigned to paying the price for my actions against the state, Kurt. I don't want to shirk what I have coming to me. But I have to admit that I am always open to your ideas."

"I think I have a way to help you to escape not just Tegel but Germany altogether."

"Escape? Knobloch, you would be putting your own life and Marthe's in jeopardy."

Since Knobloch had met the pastor's youngest sibling Suse most recently, he contacted her surreptitiously to serve as a conduit between him and the rest of his family. He requested that whoever in the family might be able to procure a mechanic's uniform in the pastor's size do so and deliver it, with food coupons and cash, under the cover of night to his home, which he was rebuilding, five kilometers east of the prison. Knobloch would smuggle the uniform into Tegel by wearing it underneath his work overalls. The pastor would put on the uniform in the sickbay where he would be noticed by fewer, if any, guards. At the end of the workday, he would simply walk through the gates beside Knobloch. They would go to the garden house and hide there. The biggest hurdle would be whether he could remain hidden and leave the country secretly without being caught.

The next weekend, however, something transpired that caused Pastor Bonhöffer to put aside the escape plot altogether. On Saturday, September 30, Dietrich's brother Klaus noticed a car parked near his home. Klaus was certain he recognized the vehicle as a *Gestapo* car. He drove to his sister Ursula and her husband Rüdiger's home in Charlottenburg.

Knobloch arrived at their home at almost the same time as Klaus to discuss the details of the plan to fly Dietrich on a false passport to Sweden. But Ursula and Rüdiger explained to him that the *Gestapo* would most likely be arriving at any moment to arrest at least Klaus, if not Rüdiger as well. The escape attempt must be called off. Klaus was indeed taken away from the Schleichers' home to the *Gestapo* prison the next day, and when Knobloch informed Dietrich, he did indeed decline to go through with the escape because of the risk to the rest of the family, Maria, and her family, too.

"Knobloch, I am most grateful for all you are trying to do for my safety and survival. But my conscience prevents me from proceeding with the plan. If I were to escape Tegel and leave Germany, the potential power of my witness for peace will be blunted, neutralized. God's way, as we have seen it in Jesus' suffering and death, is for one who dares to rebel against the Nazi horror to pay the price, even if it's the ultimate price. I must complete what I have started."

Exactly one week later, October 8, 1944, Dietrich was seized by the *Gestapo* and taken secretly from Tegel to *Prinz Albrecht Strasse.*

Chapter Twenty-Eight

*There are many indications, I'm afraid, that I am going through an
emotional crisis. My relations have noticed with growing alarm how
desperate I look. I have begun to have fainting fits. Not even the snug and
secure surrounding at Bundorf are able to banish the realization that my
chances of being reunited with you are steadily dwindling, and there are
plenty of people around me who question the wisdom of our relationship
under these circumstances.*

—Maria von Wedemeyer

***Gestapo* Prison, Berlin**
November 1944

For more than a month, Dietrich had awakened each
morning in the prison in the basement of the headquarters of
the *Gestapo* on *Prinz Albrecht Strasse,* truly a place as void of
mercy and hope as there was on the face of the earth.

The cells were underground. They measured about one
meter by about two meters at most, with no light from the
outside. Perpetual night, in other words.

When he was first interrogated, Dietrich was threatened
with torture. He was told that the fate of his parents, his other
family members, and his fiancée hung on the truth of his
confession. If he was tortured in any way in the interrogation
process, his noble and pure soul betrayed no sign of it. The
building, which doubled as the headquarters of the *Gestapo*
and its most notorious prison, was the target of numerous
Allied bombing raids. Dietrich remained calm and stalwart
through them and was a source of reassurance for many of the
other inmates.

By way of the secret code he and his family used to
communicate with one another, Dietrich learned that his
brother-in-law Hans had endured much hardship since he had
been brought to the *Gestapo* prison from Sachsenhausen. His
health had deteriorated greatly so that he was a mere shadow

of his former self. During one extended Allied bombing raid, he suffered a stroke that rendered him partially paralyzed and blind. Still, he was accorded no mercy by the *Gestapo* who knew that he was one of the conspiracy leaders.

Maria's cousin Fabian von Schlabrenndorff was also confined in the *Gestapo* prison on suspicion of having played an active part in one of the other unsuccessful assassination attempts on Hitler. On several mornings Dietrich and he were able to have words with each other in the bathroom even though the prisoners are not allowed to speak to one another. Dietrich tried to encourage Fabian by remarking to him one day, "Pain is a holy angel who shows treasures to me, which otherwise remain forever hidden. Through the experience of pain, men have become greater than through all the joys of the world. It must be so, and I tell this to myself in my present situation over and over again. Franz, I feel the pain of my longing for Maria so very acutely. But the pain needs to be overcome every time. There is an even holier angel than the one of pain, that is the one of joy in God."

Schlabrenndorff and many other inmates found Dietrich to be good-tempered, always showing the same respect and courtesy toward everybody. In a short time, he won over his warders who were not always kindly disposed toward the inmates. He always did his best to cheer up and comfort his fellow prisoners. He never tired of repeating to them that "the only fight which is lost is the one which we give up." He remained hopeful that he might yet be set free without trial if some influential person had the courage and opportunity to intercede on his behalf.

As bad and primitive as conditions in the *Gestapo* prison were, Dietrich recognized that they could have been far worse. He had been told by Schlabrenndorff and several others who had it worse when they first arrived a little before him. Dietrich theorized that the slight improvement in the conditions in the prison and the treatment of the inmates indicated that the war was about to have run its course.

Himmler, after all, wasn't unintelligent. He must have seen that for all intents and purposes, the war was lost. He put out his own peace feelers secretly to the Allies to make a separate peace. He considered the inmates as bargaining chips in any negotiations for clemency for himself.

Hitler didn't seem to be in any hurry to be rid of the resistance members. He might have thought that the *Gestapo* could still wring some information out of one or two members of the resistance about others in the plots.

Dietrich learned from Schlabrenndorff that Maria was still in the home of his parents. Apparently, she had come to the *Gestapo* prison numerous times to try to visit him but each time her request was refused. Dietrich was immensely grateful for her faithfulness and for persevering in her requests to visit. Just knowing that she had tried gave him more strength and determination to endure than she could know.

The *Gestapo* had also not allowed his parents to visit him in prison for weeks. He and the other remaining conspirators were pariahs to the *Gestapo* as were those connected to them even if they had not done anything to violate Nazi law. They were guilty by association in the minds of the *Gestapo*.

Dietrich was pleasantly surprised when the *Kommandant* approached him after breakfast one December morning and informed him that he was allowed one Christmas letter to either his parents or Maria. He sat down immediately and wrote his fiancée, not knowing if he'd ever get the chance again.

19 December 1944

My dearest Maria. I am so glad to be permitted to write you a Christmas letter and to be able, through you, to convey my love to my parents and brothers and sisters, to thank you all. It is very quiet here now. But I have found often that the quieter my surroundings, the more vividly I sense my deep connection with you all. So, I haven't for a moment felt lonely or forlorn. You are my constant companion. Your prayers, the memory of our last embrace, our recent prayers raised up to God, your kind thoughts of me from a distance, all are invested with real existence, I have no doubt. I am thankful every single day that I have you—all of you—and that makes me happy and gives me strength.

I am distressed only by hearing from your fine cousin Fabian that you had made the arduous trek to this prison but were not allowed to come in to visit with me. How I long to see your beauty with my own eyes.

We've now been waiting for each other for almost two years, dearest Maria. Don't lose heart. I am glad that you are with my parents. Give my fondest love to our mother and the whole family whom I hold dear. Here are another few verses that have occurred to me in recent nights. They are my Christmas greeting to you, my parents, and my brothers and sisters. In great love and gratitude to you.

I embrace you,
Your Dietrich

Powers of Good

With every power for good to stay and guide me,
Comforted and inspired beyond all fear,
I'll live these days with you in thought beside me
And pass, with you, into the coming year.

The old year still torments our hearts, unhastening;
The long days of sorrow still endure;
Father grant to the souls thou hast been chastening
That Thou hast promised, the healing and the cure.

Should it be ours to drain the cup of grieving
Even to the dregs of pain, at thy command,
We will not falter, thankfully receiving
All that is given by thy loving hand.

But should it be Thy will once more to release us
To life's enjoyment and its good sunshine,
That which we've learned from sorrow shall increase us,
and all our life be dedicated to thine.

Today, let candles shed their radiant greetings;
Lo, on our darkness are they not thy light
Leading us, haply, to our longed-for meeting?
Thou canst illumine even our darkest night.

When now the silence deepens for our hearkening,
Grant we may hear thy children's voices raise
From all the unseen world around us darkening
Their universal paean, in thy praise

While all the powers of good aid and attend us,
Boldly we'll face the future, come what may.
At even and at morn God will befriend us,
And oh, most surely on each newborn day.

Chapter Twenty-Nine

My dear Maria, let us never lose faith in what befalls us; all of it is bestowed on us by good and kindly hands. I shall be thinking of you a great deal on the anniversary of your father's death. Father is with God. He is only a step or two ahead of us.

—Dietrich Bonhöffer

12 January 1945

Dear *Frau* Bonhöffer,

It is a new year, but still the years-old war persists. I fervently pray and hope, as I am sure that you and your husband do, as well, that 1945 may mark the end of this terrible global conflict in which very little good has been achieved. I am glad that my Maria was able to be of help to you during the weeks and months of relentless bombing by the Allies. Thank you for releasing her back to us here in Pomerania.

You lost your first son Walter in the Great War. Now your sons Klaus and Dietrich are prisoners of the state, as is your daughter Ursula's husband Rüdiger and Christel's husband Hans. They and you are in my prayers every morning and every night before I fall asleep.

Please pray for us here in Pomerania, too. The Soviet Army has surrounded and occupied the region of Pätzig and I fear the day they discover that my husband Hans and son Max fought them on the eastern front in 1942 they will seek revenge on our family.

Maria, of course, is a beautiful young woman of almost twenty-one, desirable to the Russian soldiers who display very few inclinations towards self-discipline in their attitude and behavior toward women like her.

Partly for that reason, I have sent Maria westward over the Oder and Elbe rivers in a covered wagon toward hoped-for safety in the sectors of Germany currently occupied by English and American troops. In the wagon with her, Maria also has a neighbor, *Frau* Döpke and her two little children, and *Fräulein* Rath who has a high temperature. But Maria is an experienced and well-trained nurse who is capable of caring for the sick and young. Their destination is the village of Celle in the west where *Frau* Döpke has relatives. I just hope and pray that whoever of our German troops remain on the route leave Maria and the inhabitants of the wagon in peace. If they are anywhere nearly as badly damaged from the bombing as some of the other roads in Germany, some of the ones Maria plans to take towards Celle may have been rendered nearly impassable. Please pray for Maria and her passengers.

You need to know that despite the fact that Maria has not heard from Dietrich since Christmas and she is sick with worry, her inspiration for this perilous errand to the west is her fiancé who has risked so much in his efforts to resist our *Führer*. She considers this necessary mission of mercy to be her tribute to his courage and love for the helpless.

We may soon receive orders for the general evacuation to the west. In the meanwhile, we are secretly making preparations in advance. I hope to be able to save lives and prevent panic from setting in here.

Once she has seen everyone settled in at Celle, Maria will try to make her way back to you and resume her desperate search for Dietrich, but it will take some time for her to travel there.

Please accept my heartfelt thanks for all the maternal and paternal love you have bestowed upon my daughter.

Yours,

Ruth von Wedemeyer

Two days after this letter was postmarked, much of Pätzig and its surrounding area were caught in the crossfire between Russian forces from the east and a ragged battalion of the

German *Wehrmacht* that had arrived in Pätzig only days earlier to try to hold back the invading Russians. The *Wehrmacht* battalion looked much depleted and consisted largely of older men who previously had been rejected due to age or pre-existing injury or frailty. Scattered among the older men were boys barely old enough to have graduated from the middle levels of school.

The first volley of machine gun fire erupted from the Russian side. The Germans made a poor and ineffective response with the old inferior rifles with which they had been supplied. The lone piece of German artillery let loose its firepower in the direction of the enemy. Suddenly, the von Wedemeyer farmhouse was ablaze, not from Russian artillery fire, but the proverbial "friendly fire" from the *Wehrmacht*.

The war had come to tiny, peaceful Pätzig. *Frau* von Wedemeyer had evacuated earlier some twenty kilometers westward to a bomb shelter provided in the larger city of Rostock.

There were tense moments when Maria wasn't sure of the safety of the traveling party from Pätzig, but their trek in the covered wagon across the Oder and Elbe rivers was successful. At one crossroads British soldiers gruffly ordered everybody out of the wagon and inspected it for escaping *Wehrmacht* soldiers. When Maria stepped off the wagon and gathered the children tenderly in her outstretched arms as a mother hen does her chicks, she felt terribly weak in her knees. She was afraid she would faint from fear even though she knew they had nothing to hide. She had no previous experience with the Brits, but she had seen enough of war to know that rules could be changed without a moment's notice. Once the Brits were satisfied, however, that they weren't transporting stowaway *Wehrmacht* soldiers, they allowed Maria and her passengers to board the wagon again and signaled for them to resume their journey westward. Maria felt the muscles below her stomach relax.

Maria bade everyone a tearful farewell in Celle, abandoned the wagon, and continued the journey by train to

Berlin. Surprisingly, even with the fierce combat on the ground between the Russians and the remaining stump of the *Wehrmacht*, a few railway lines to the capital city were still functional. As relieved as she was about having delivered her passengers safely, she was disturbed after hearing from *Frau* Döpke's relatives in Celle that the news had reported ferocious fighting in Pomerania, but no detailed news about survivors or fatalities. The train trip to Berlin was tenser and more anxiety-provoking to Maria than the wagon journey as her thoughts focused on her mother: *Has Mütti survived the warfare in Pomerania? Is she safe? Why wasn't I there to support her? But I had a mission to fulfill and couldn't be in Pomerania, too. Damn this infernal war!*

When Maria arrived in Berlin after several changes of route necessitated by torn-up tracks, she found everything in a state of turmoil. Familiar signposts had been destroyed, and it was difficult to find one's way around. She managed to locate *Prinz Albrecht Strasse*. But the *Gestapo* headquarters was a partially demolished skeleton, and Maria wasn't confident initially that she was even entering the correct building. She was unable to get information from the closed-mouthed *SS* and *Gestapo* functionaries about Dietrich's whereabouts.

She did learn from Dietrich's sister Ursula that her husband, Rüdiger, also an inmate now in the *Gestapo* prison, had heard through the inmate grapevine that Dietrich was among those who were assigned to be transported to the Flossenbürg Concentration Camp in the Palatine Forest in Bavaria. With nothing else to go on, Maria set out southward with a case of warm men's clothing to find Dietrich. Her journey was delayed because of the limited number of trains able to reach Nüremberg. She cobbled together a lengthy itinerary by way of Munich, passing not far from Dachau. Arriving in Munich late at night, she had difficulty securing a hotel room. The following morning, refreshed and with renewed determination, she caught an express train to Nüremberg and charmed the conductor to prevail upon the engineer to make an unscheduled stop at the town of Weiden. She stepped off the train at the miniscule station and walked the final seven kilometers to Flossenbürg through the rain, carrying the heavy case of clothing.

She burst into tears when she was turned away unsympathetically without any further information than that there was no Dietrich Bonhöffer there. She took the circuitous, exhausting trip by train back to Berlin, which was in even worse disarray than when she left it five days earlier. She hoped that people there would have better information, but if the officials at the *Gestapo* headquarters on *Prinz Albrecht Strasse* had any, they were not about to share it with her or anybody else.

5 February 1945

Maria returned to the Bonhöffer home in Charlottenburg, distracted and unable to focus on even the simplest household tasks. Dietrich's parents understood her anxiety, both for Dietrich and her mother. God alone knew Dietrich's condition or even if he was still at Flossenbürg; The *Gestapo* could have easily had decided to transfer him elsewhere to await his trial.

Berlin and neighboring municipalities were bombed relentlessly by the American Eighth Army. Much of central Berlin was a confusing maze of fallen stone, cement, and shattered asphalt. Nonetheless, the People's Court was spared serious damage. The notorious Judge Freisler still had time and opportunity to sentence alleged conspirators to death, among them Dietrich's brother Klaus and his sister's husband, Rüdy Schleicher.

In a letter that arrived in the mail miraculously from her cousin Fabian, also imprisoned at *Prinz Albrecht Strasse*, Maria learned news of Dietrich's new location. After the dust from the American bombing settled and the coast was clear temporarily, the prisoners were divided into two groups. Dietrich was assigned to report to the van that would transport him and over fifteen others to Buchenwald Concentration camp near Weimar. Maria judged the information shared by Fabian to be more dependable and trustworthy than the confusing tidbits that she was able to wring from the *SS* and *Gestapo* officials. Fabian didn't mention a single word in his letter about Dietrich's being transferred to Flossenbürg as she had been led to believe by the *SS* and *Gestapo*.

Berlin: May 1945

Karl and Paula Bonhöffer waited expectantly but with some trepidation for the arrival of the Allies and the Soviets in Berlin and the final indignities of the war. They were plagued by an almost paralyzing sense of uncertainty about the whereabouts of their sons Klaus and Dietrich and sons-in-law Rüdiger and Hans. The last they had heard was that Hans was at Sachsenhausen Concentration Camp not far from Berlin, while Klaus, Dietrich, and Rüdy were still confined to the *Gestapo* prison on *Prinz Albrecht Strasse.*

Paula's grief was augmented by watching Maria beside herself in her own deep sorrow. It seemed she had an intuition that Dietrich's end on this earth would not be a good one. But she could not rest until she made yet one more effort to locate him.

February, March, and April came and went without any success or progress. Then she heard a rumor that Flossenbürg had been liberated by the Americans advancing from the south and the prisoners, including Dietrich, set free in München. Actually set free! Near the end of June, not knowing for certain that the tracks were still intact, she boarded a train for Bavaria eagerly in the hope of seeing him at-large on the streets of München.

Chapter Thirty

All disciples of Christ have their own cross waiting for them.
Each disciple must endure our allotted suffering and rejection.
But each of us has a different share;
some God deems worthy of the highest form of suffering
and gives then the grace of martyrdom.

—Dietrich Bonhöffer

Munich: June 1945

The telephone rang in Maria's modest hotel room in München. Her week-long search for news of Dietrich felt increasingly futile. She was beginning to think that in her desperation to find him she had latched on naïvely to the rumor she had heard from a total stranger that the Flossenbürg camp had been liberated. That had led her to believe and hope that Dietrich might possibly be in the city somewhere. She knew that he had contacts there from both his work for the Confessing Church and his military intelligence work for the *Abwehr*. She was kicking herself now for never having asked him for the names of those contacts, though by the nature of intelligence work he probably wouldn't have revealed them to her anyhow.

She was ready to collapse in bed and fall asleep, exhausted by the difficult travel, the delays, and her constant awareness of the danger that Allied bombers could strike the train at any moment. The Allies had long ago abandoned their policy of avoiding civilian targets.

But the caller on the telephone might be somebody in München who had news for her. By a miracle of miracles, the caller could even be Dietrich himself! Despite her utter fatigue, she sprang out of bed and picked up the receiver eagerly.

"Hello, Maria dear? It's Paula here in Charlottenburg."

"Oh, hello, *Mütti*" She had begun calling Paula *Mütti* since, in recent years, she had felt closer to Dietrich's mother than her own. "I have had no success in getting leads to Dietrich's whereabouts."

"No, Maria dear, you won't get any."

"How do you know? I'll keep searching until I get a lead."

"I'm so sorry. What I mean is, we have heard news."

"News? Of Dietrich? Is he back in Berlin or Charlottenburg? Has he been spared?"

"No, dear Maria, I'm afraid that it's bad news."

Maria was silent at the other end of the telephone line.

"Oh, Maria dear. This is so difficult. I cannot find a kind way to say this so I'll be blunt, I'm afraid. Dietrich has met his end."

Again, Paula's telephone receiver turned silent as though Maria was no longer there. After a few moments of silence, Paula could hear muted sniffling.

"This is heartbreaking for you, I know. I know how much you loved Dietrich."

Maria's sniffling turned to doleful weeping. "I love him profoundly. He's the only man I have ever loved." Her weeping intensified. "I've never loved any person as much as I love him, not even my father."

Paula began to weep quietly as well, even as she tried to collect herself and give Maria time to absorb the sad news.

"How did you hear the news?" Maria asked between bitter sobs.

"We had the radio tuned to the BBC last evening. We happened to hear the most extraordinary program. It was as if the program was intended personally for us."

"*Mütti,* I don't understand. What kind of program did you hear?"

"It was a memorial service from Trinity Church in Brompton, near London. A service for Klaus and Dietrich."

"A memorial service? For Klaus and Dietrich? Memorialized in Britain? I hope the day will come when such a service is held in Germany."

"Dietrich's old friend and colleague, the Bishop George Bell of Chichester, presided and preached a beautiful homily at the service. Dietrich's former student at Finkenwalde, Franz Hildebrandt— remember him?—also paid a moving personal tribute."

Maria was overcome with a panoply of feelings: surprise, anger, gratitude, immeasurable sadness. But she tried hard to listen to Paula. This was the first news she had heard of Dietrich in months, even if it was not the news she wanted to hear. *Mütti* sounded so dispassionate, but then again, she had had about 12 hours to absorb it and regain some emotional equilibrium. Besides, it was the Bonhöffer way.

Emotional detachment. Maria knew that she loved her sons deeply, and now she has lost not just Walter, but also Klaus and Dietrich.

"*Mütti, y*ou have lost so much as a mother. It's a lot to bear. I don't think I could bear it."

"Dear Dietrich would tell me that Christ bears the load with us. I believe so, too."

"I remember Franz from my times of worshiping at Finkenwalde as a girl with my grandmother," Maria said. "Franz was of Jewish extraction. I know how desperate Dietrich was to keep that a secret from the *Gestapo*. Bless Franz for speaking at Dietrich's memorial service."

"Father telephoned Franz this morning and asked about Dietrich's final days."

"And?"

"Franz said he hadn't heard from Dietrich since last year. But a fellow prisoner of Dietrich's, Captain Payne Best, a British intelligence officer, has been released and returned home to Britain. Franz has talked with him and learned that Dietrich was among those who were hanged at Flossenbürg."

"Oh, my God. Hanged? My dear, sweet, gentle Dietrich? It cannot be!"

Maria's weeping became almost uncontrollable.

Finally, she gained enough control to be able to ask, "When did it happen, *Mütti*?"

"On April 7, I believe."

"Oh, my poor Dietrich," Maria said sadly. "His sweet voice is no more to be heard. Germany is poorer without him."

"We're all more impoverished now," Paula responded through her tears,

"April 7? Over two months ago. It's no wonder I couldn't get any information about him. I feel as though after April 7, somehow my spirit knew, and felt the sadness wash over me. But Dietrich always told me not to abandon hope. I have no regrets about my attempts to find him since April 7."

"And you shouldn't have any, my dear. It's what I would have done had Karl had been missing. It's what Ursula did when Rüdy was in Buchenwald and Flossenbürg. You both did the right thing. It's what true love does."

Now the search was over. Maria was desperately unhappy with the result but relieved all the same that she had received some kind of answer to the mystery. A heavy burden was lifted off her shoulders. She tried to squelch the feeling of anger rising up in her heart that Dietrich had involved himself in anti-Nazi activities, which he knew could lead to a fatal conclusion like this. But she accepted his reasons. She was immensely proud of his courage.

Losing him was such a hard blow. The dashing of their dream of marriage seemed so cruel. *How am I to go on without him? Without the hope of finding him alive? Without searching for him all over Germany? What's next? Which way am I to turn?* Her whole body trembled.

There was still much more she wanted to know. *How did Dietrich face his death? Despite his certain human fear of the gallows, did he leave this bitter world in peace?* She received Franz Hildebrandt's telephone number in London from *Mütti* and resolved to call him. She knew how much Dietrich loved him. Dietrich would want her to call Franz to share their mutual sorrow and find consolation in each other.

Chapter Thirty-One

Come now, Death, highest feast on the way to everlasting freedom,
death. Lay waste the burdens of chains and walls,
which confine our earthly bodies and blinded souls,
that we see at last what here we could not see.
Freedom, we sought you long in discipline, action and suffering.
Dying, we recognize you now in the face of God.

—Dietrich Bonhöffer

July 1945

Franz told Maria that the last person to converse with Dietrich just before April 7 was British Captain Payne Best. He had been brought to the Buchenwald camp on February 21, just a few days before Dietrich arrived there with over a dozen or so others from the *Gestapo* prison. Best was detained as a foreign prisoner of war in cell number 11, not within the bounds of the main camp itself, which held Jews, Jehovah's Witnesses, Gypsies, homosexuals, and others whom the Nazis had not yet had opportunity to exterminate. In the meantime, they were used as slave labor.

The building in which Best, Dietrich, and other *Gestapo* prisoners were warehoused was built as an air raid shelter for the higher officials of the camp staff. Ironically, the *Gestapo* prisoners were assigned to the strongest, safest structure of the camp. Hitler wanted desperately to preserve these "enemies of the state" as long as possible for interrogation purposes. Hitler counted on Dietrich and some of his fellow conspirators to break under the infernal conditions and inhuman interrogation methods at Buchenwald and reveal the names of other guilty parties.

Among those interrogation methods was the notorious Witch of Buchenwald. Ilse Koch, the sadistic wife of Buchenwald's *Kommandant*, was an oversized red-headed woman. She was given free rein over the entire camp. She would ride through the camp on her horse carrying her ridiculous riding crop in imitation of her *Führer*. She would force the slave laborers in the camp to have sex with her. Most horrifying, she collected lampshades, book covers, and gloves made from the stretched skins of tattooed camp prisoners. Buchenwald was one of the many Nazi centers of death but it was not merely a place where prisoners were executed. It was a God-forsaken place where death was sordidly celebrated and worshiped. The heads of some prisoners were shrunken by some process the Nazi scientists had devised and were taken home by guards to present to their families as gifts, or by the officers to their mistresses.

For most of the two months that Dietrich was detained at Buchenwald, he shared a cell with General Friedrich von Rabenau. The general, an early defector from the Nazi cause, was at least 20-some years Dietrich's senior but no two prisoners forced to be roommates got along more pleasantly and made better use of their time. They spent hours discussing theology. Rabenau had received a degree in theology at the University of Berlin after his days as a general were over. In his conversations with Rabenau, Dietrich spoke passionately of "theology from the bottom up" instead of the usual "top-down" variety. "We most clearly find Christ in the lives of those who are oppressed and sidelined," Dietrich said. "Today in Germany, that's among the Jews in the gas chambers of places like Auschwitz. They are today's Christ nailed to the cross."

Rabenau and Dietrich whiled away many hours talking theology and playing chess on a small chess set Best gave them. The other *Gestapo* prisoners admired Dietrich for his unfaltering sweetness and humility. He diffused an atmosphere of happiness and joy in every small event of the inmates' lives. He was blessed with deep gratitude for the mere fact that he was still alive.

Best and several other prisoners approached Dietrich quietly one afternoon. They told Dietrich that they were certain that if the prisoners all banded together, they could manage to escape Buchenwald.

On Easter morning they all heard the rumble of gun and cannon fire across the Werra River nearby. The Nazi guards were terrified that this was the long-feared sound of American troops advancing from the west. One of the more humane overseers of the guards, Sippach, was determined to flee the camp before the Americans discovered it. By now, the guards had relaxed their discipline and left the prisoners undisturbed for the most part, for fear that they would wreak revenge on the Nazis once the Americans arrived.

Best particularly was convinced that Sippach could be persuaded to aid the prisoners' escape and flee with them. Best and the others were enthusiastic about their realistic prospects for freedom. Dietrich was less enraptured by the idea. He thought they should hold on and wait it out, sheltering from the elements at Buchenwald until the Americans arrived, which they surely would, Dietrich assured them, within days.

On the afternoon of April 2, Sippach ordered the prisoners to go to the air raid building to pack their belongings and prepare to evacuate the camp, quite possibly on foot since petrol for the transport vans was next to impossible to get at this stage of the war.

They did not evacuate on foot after all. The *Führer* himself still took a special interest in the particular group of prisoners in which Best and Dietrich were included. Hitler knew that the Allies were approaching Berlin rapidly, particularly the Soviets from the east. Despite Göbbels's fervent denials on the radio, Germany was close to defeat and Hitler wanted desperately to make sure that the twenty or so inmates at Buchenwald who were conspirators against him had trials, even if they were mere formalities, and have their death sentence carried out "properly" before his own demise. Therefore, he ordered a full-size lorry to be driven to Buchenwald to transport the prisoners, including Dietrich, to Flossenbürg Camp in Bavaria, far off the routes taken by the Allies to Berlin.

The process of transporting the prisoners was a comedy of errors. The sixteen men were ordered to board the lorry with whatever luggage of theirs still remained. Dietrich carried with him several books, one a volume of daily Bible readings collated by the Moravian Brethren. There was barely room for eight prisoners in the back of the lorry; in addition to human beings and some luggage, there was a huge pile of firewood. Since petrol was almost non-existent now in Germany, the lorry's engine was powered by wood. But they were crowded into it somehow.

Once all had boarded, the guards gave the driver the go-ahead signal. With much effort, and a deep, painful-sounding grinding noise, the vehicle lurched forward. At about one hundred or so meters, however, it came to a sudden stop. The wood-fueled engine continued to idle, and within a few minutes, the lorry was filled with fumes, prompting one of the prisoners to exclaim, "My God, this is a death van. We are being exterminated by gas!"

The lorry had to stop every hour for the flues to be cleaned and the wood in the engine restocked. The lorry progressed at the rate of fifteen or so kilometers an hour. They had no light or heat, and nothing to eat or drink. Dietrich, no longer a smoker himself, had saved his rations of tobacco. He insisted on contributing his scanty supply for the common good of his compatriots, hoping that the nicotine would distract them from the cold and hunger.

The time came when nature asserted its call. Several of the prisoners insisted to the guards that they needed to relieve themselves. The three guards argued among themselves about the request. One finally rose and opened the rear doors of the lorry so that the prisoners could step off and do what they needed to do.

It was daylight and a new morning. The prisoners were not at all sure where they were headed, and the guards were either ignorant of the destination—not uncommon in those last chaotic days of the war—or would not divulge the information. A couple of the prisoners reckoned that they were on the road to the Flossenbürg camp because that camp was supplied with the means for trial and execution.

At one point, someone recognized the village of Weiden. The guards, who had been with this group of prisoners since Buchenwald, got out of the lorry and came back with two loaves of bread and a large *würst*, which they gave to Dietrich to divide up and distribute to the group. Best remarked that Dietrich was serving a new and unique kind of Eucharist.

It is painfully ironic that less than a short month later, Maria would step off the train to Nüremberg at the station of this very same little village in order to look for Dietrich. After months apart, Dietrich and his love had been so close to each other, yet so very far.

The driver proceeded to the police station in Weiden but was told that they could not accommodate all the prisoners on the lorry. They would have to continue the hellish journey. When the lorry finally scaled the big hill to the camps near Flossenbürg, guards came out of the gatehouse and ordered, by name, three prisoners to deboard and come with them into the camp. Dietrich and the other prisoners waved farewell to their compatriots, sensing an ambiguous omen.

The driver received orders from somewhere through an extremely staticky radio to continue the journey south until they came to some place that could house the remaining prisoners.

The prisoners looked at one another in puzzlement, shrugging their shoulders. Lest they jinx their luck, none dared to say out loud their growing hope that since apparently there was room for only three inmates at Flossenbürg, the rest would not end up there and might be spared a trial and sentencing.

It was now Wednesday, April 4. There were fourteen of them left on the lorry destined to arrive who knew where. As long as it wasn't Flossenbürg, they agreed that wherever was fine with them.

The ancient lorry continued clanking along until it stopped at a humble roadside farm. The farmer's wife emerged carrying several loaves of newly baked rye bread and a jug of fresh milk. It was the best bread any of the prisoners had tasted for years with no hint of mold on it.

"I have been so engrossed in the war that I had forgotten that with its natural beauty and charming farm villages," said Dietrich as he savored the bread. "Germany is still a place where God sustains life in the present; that it is not just a memory from before the war."

The lorry continued its journey. At dusk, it arrived at a large city on a river that Dietrich recognized from its medieval architecture as Regensburg. The lorry doors opened, and the prisoners were ordered brusquely into the jail attached to the courthouse. Inside, some of them recognized individuals already incarcerated there, including the surviving relatives of poor, murdered von Stauffenberg and the jurist and early opponent of Hitler, Fritz Gördeler. They were assigned five inmates per cell. Von Rabenau and several others chose to share a cell with Dietrich.

These four men were Dietrich's final companions on earth.

On Thursday morning, April 3, the doors of the cells opened, and the prisoners washed at the one sink that still had running water. There were great reunions, introductions, and exchanges of information in the crowded corridor.

In his usual thoughtful and sensitive way, Dietrich took *Frau* Gördeler aside gently and told her about the last weeks of her husband's life as he had observed them at Buchenwald. She was in tears, but valued this eyewitness account of her husband's courage in his last moments.

Ever the optimist, Dietrich believed that he had now escaped the worst danger, enjoying renewed hope that he would survive. *Maybe Maria and I will still have our wedding after all.*

The lorry was loaded again with the fourteen prisoners and a new pile of firewood for the engine. The lorry made its way along the Danube until, after just a few short kilometers, it skidded on the muddy road and stalled. One of the prisoners was an engineer and volunteered to examine the engine. He confirmed that the steering apparatus was irreparably broken. The driver stopped two pedestrians passing the lorry to requisition them to order a replacement vehicle in Regensburg.

The guards let the prisoners out of the lorry by the river to stretch their legs and wash. At around midday, a replacement bus appeared from Regensburg, its windows intact. Ten new men with automatic pistols took over supervision of the transport but the prisoners felt it was such a pleasant luxury to drive through the valley in the more comfortable vehicle, they were tempted to imagine that they were on a tour bus on holiday.

By early afternoon they arrived in the village of Schönberg, which was inundated with refugees fleeing the Russians in the east. The prisoners were ordered to disembark outside a school where some of the other resistance leaders were already confined. They were led to a large classroom on the first floor, which was to serve as their temporary communal cell. The room was furnished with proper beds covered with prettily colored, handcrafted blankets.

Dietrich sat for a long time at an open window, sunning himself as though he didn't have a concern in the world. He noticed that some of the other prisoners were showing signs of depression and spent time listening to each of them. The inmate in the bed next to his was Russian POW Kokorin, who was Molotov's nephew. Kokorin was an avowed atheist, but that evening he and Dietrich spent several hours discussing the essentials of Christianity and Dietrich learning Russian.

The next morning, the atmosphere in the school-prison was lively. The prisoners recorded their attendance for history's sake by writing their names and the date over their beds. After months of sleeping on a plank, it was heavenly to be able to sleep in a real bed. Some compassionate villagers came by the school with a great dish of steaming potatoes, and on the next day, Saturday, they appeared again with potato salad.

To a man, the prisoners were certain that there would be no more trials, given the general confusion in the country.

On Friday, April 4, however, unbeknown to the prisoners housed in the school, Hitler gathered his lieutenants in a room in the still-intact Chancellery in Berlin and made a decision about the "special prisoners." Hitler gave the order for the trials to resume at Flossenbürg, with the explicit direction that, above all, prisoners Canaris, Oster, von Dohnányi, and Bonhöffer were not to survive.

Gestapo Criminal Commissar Sonderegger, one of the two officers to arrest Dietrich in his parents' home in Charlottenburg almost two years prior to the day, was ordered to travel overnight to Flossenbürg to act as prosecutor in the trial of Dietrich and von Dohnányi specifically. Before arriving there, Sonderegger stopped at Sachsenhausen Camp and presided over a hasty court-martial in which he condemned von Dohnányi, lying half-conscious already on a stretcher, to immediate death. Sonderegger arrived at Flossenbürg in the early afternoon of Saturday, April 5, and immediately set to work to arrange for a special court-martial in the next few days.

Unaware of this, the prisoners in the classroom continued to be hopeful. There was an out-of-tune, dusty, grand piano in the classroom. It was Sunday, and Dietrich played some pieces of music on the piano. Several were hymns that sounded familiar to the prisoners who joined Dietrich in humming along. He ended his impromptu concert with a beautiful piece by Mozart, which Best, at least, recognized as the emotionally haunting Piano Concerto No. 21. As he played the keys expertly and soulfully, Dietrich thought longingly of Maria. Tears flowed down his cheek, and he was unable to continue. The other prisoners had never seen him weep before.

After Dietrich collected himself, several of the prisoners approached him. "Today is Sunday, Pastor. Might you conduct a worship service for us?"

"Our time is at hand, I know. But most of you are Roman Catholics. I am a Lutheran pastor, and I would be performing a Protestant, specifically a Lutheran, service. Wouldn't that pose a problem for you?"

The prisoners looked at each other, gauging their responses.

"Besides, friends, there is young Kokorin to consider. I don't want to ambush him with a Christian service he might feel obligated to attend."

Kokorin replied swiftly. "Pastor, since you took time to try to explain Christianity to me, a total neophyte, I want to take the time to join you and my fellow inmates in this worship."

"Are you sure, Kokorin?"

"Yes, Pastor, if you and the others permit me."

Dietrich surveyed the circle of earnest faces surrounding him. Several of them nodded in almost plaintive agreement. Seeing their eagerness to worship together at this grave time, he agreed to their solemn request. Sensing now that his hours in this life were diminishing, Dietrich performed the functions of a pastor the way he had begun his adult life in Berlin.

As he began the service, he said, "Brothers, the worship of the Lord Jesus Christ is an act of resistance against a political and military leader who has overreached and claimed for himself powers reserved for God."

He knew that not many of his fellow Christians were accustomed to thinking of worship in this way. But he also understood that the congregation of condemned prisoners had experiential and existential knowledge of what he was saying.

He read the Gospel lesson from Luke and pointed out how often Luke employs songs in the first several chapters of his gospel. "Mary sings when she is greeted by her cousin Elizabeth. Zechariah sings when his son John is born. The angels over the field sing of peace and goodwill when they share with the shepherds their 'good news of great joy.' Why songs?" he asked. "Because these songs are acts of *resistance* against the status quo. Let us now join our voices in singing *'Ein Fester Burg ist Unser Gott,'* and let us sing it boldly and fervently in this prison and under the threat of death whose power we will defy with praise of God." After the hymn, he expounded on the Old Testament text for the day from Isaiah. "With his wounds, we are healed." He closed by quoting the new Testament epistle for the day in I Peter. "Blessed be the God and Father of our Lord Jesus Christ. By his great mercy, we have been born to a living hope through the resurrection of Jesus Christ from the dead."

He had barely finished the quotation when the door to the room opened suddenly and two *Gestapo* called out, "Prisoner Bonhöffer, come with us." The other prisoners knew what those words signified.

So did Dietrich.

He went into the corner of the large room where he had deposited his few earthly things and dug out a book. It was a volume by Plutarch that his parents had given to him for his birthday, on their very last visit with him in Tegel Prison. He inscribed his name and home address inside the front and back covers to leave a clue for posterity about his having been in the makeshift prison in the school. He pulled Best over to him. "If and when you survive and make it back to England, please go visit Bishop George Bell in Chichester and describe what became of me." Best caressed Dietrich's hand. "God willing, I will do as you request."

Dietrich bowed his head solemnly in thanks. He surrendered to the two waiting deputized civilians, who led him outside into the transport that would finally deliver him to Flossenbürg. The other Buchenwald prisoners followed on foot as a group as far as the guards would allow them and bade Dietrich a tearful farewell.

News of Dietrich's pending execution was disseminated as widely as possible throughout the prison and concentration camp system that still remained. Once he saw the notice, the camp doctor at Dachau contacted his corresponding colleague at Flossenbürg, Dr. H. Fischer-Hüllstrung. The Flossenbürg doctor was among the very last human beings to observe Dietrich before his death.

On the morning after he was transported from Schönberg to Flossenbürg, Monday, April 9, bright and early at 6 a.m., having been sentenced to death by Sonderegger the afternoon before, Admiral Canaris and General Oster were led one by one out into the courtyard and hung at the gallows, which had been constructed in the center of it.

Through a partially open door leading into the room where Dietrich waited his turn in the courtyard, the doctor saw him remove his prison garb as ordered. Naked, the pastor knelt on the concrete floor and prayed fervently.

"I was certain," said Dr. Hüllstrung later, "that God heard his prayer." As he was led by the arm to the courtyard, Dietrich's face was void of any bitterness. He asked the guard if he could stop at the foot of the gallows and pray, which he did once more. The guard stood nearby and waited. He was sure he heard the name Maria spoken in the prisoner's short but intense prayer.

To add insult to injury, Prosecutor Sonderegger strutted into the courtyard and stood beside Dietrich silently at the foot of the gallows.

"Prisoner Bonhöffer," Sonderegger said almost in a whisper, "you have been an enemy of the state for many years, a deadly threat to our *Führer*. You are now receiving the punishment your actions deserve." Then raising his voice so that others in the courtyard could hear, he added, "You have reached the end."

Dietrich turned and looked Sonderegger directly in the face. "For you, perhaps, the end; but for me, the *beginning*."

Then Dietrich ascended the five or so steps to the noose awaiting him and submitted as a victor.

Chapter Thirty-Two

I can still see us sitting on the floor of Maria's other friends, engaged in animated discussions and debates. Maria's was a scintillating, fascinating personality that attracted men of solid intellect, so she was usually surrounded by two or three serious rivals for her favor (sometimes hopeful, sometimes despairing) of whom Paul Schniewind was always one.

—Maria's friend Ursula Wolff, 1948

June 1945

Even though Maria now knew that Dietrich was dead, she was still unsatisfied. She wanted to know more. Her tireless pursuit of Dietrich in his last weeks and months was replaced by a hunt for his final resting place. After a series of telephone calls to the *Gestapo,* she knit together the insubstantial scraps of information she had gathered, like pieces of a puzzle.

According to Dr. Hüllstrung, the crematorium at Flossenbürg was out of order at that time, so the bodies of the men executed that day, including Dietrich's, were heaped unceremoniously in random piles in the courtyard, and the corpses abandoned near the cellblock. In this, too, Pastor Dietrich Bonhöffer had the honor to be joined to millions of other victims of the Thousand Year Reich

With the Americans approaching rapidly, the staff of the camp was ordered to evacuate immediately and retreat deeper into Germany.

When the American troops entered the walls of the abandoned camp, they discovered the crude pile of corpses and relocated them respectfully into a mass grave.

Maria was embittered at the *SS* that her fiancé's remains and those of several of his fellow conspirators had been hurriedly abandoned without a proper burial. Her bitterness drove her to silent tears. *Dietrich ought to be honored and treated as a national hero for working to eliminate Hitler, who caused nothing but chaos, terror, and death.*

Fortunately, the war ended shortly and, suddenly free to come out into the open, a group of supporters of the resistance petitioned the victorious allied officials to permit the erection of a memorial marker at the mass grave. The marker listed the names of the members of the resistance whose remains were presumed to be buried there, among them Hans Oster, Wilhelm Canaris, and, on the top of the list inscribed on the marker, Pfarrer Dietrich Bonhöffer. Maria was pleased with the building of the memorial. However, she did not get the opportunity to visit the site and see the memorial until 1948.

In the first years after the war, Maria experienced a prolonged and painful sense of disorientation. She found Berlin and its environs a place of darkness. Around every corner she was confronted by the ruins of sites and buildings from the days of the early success of the Nazis, as well as locations such as *Prinz Albrecht Strasse,* reminders of Dietrich's suffering and pain. Immediately after the end of hostilities, she embraced both Karl and Paula, thanked them for all they had done for her and their son, and left Berlin.

She traveled west and north to be reunited with her mother, who now was also homeless. Fortunately, Ruth had obeyed the order to evacuate Pätzig before the Russians arrived, and she was spared in the bombing of her family home.

Ruth was taken in by her eldest daughter Ruth-Alice von Bismarck in Hamburg, where Ruth-Alice and her husband, Klaus, had settled. Klaus had assumed a position in journalism. *Mütti's* original intention had been to share a household with Maria's beloved grandmother, who had tried to escape westward from the invading Red Army. Unfortunately, her escape attempt failed. She died in Köslin in October 1945 at the age of 78 years. Maria lamented that she hadn't seen her dear grandmother since the previous year.

Maria was grateful to be with her mother again, but she had difficulty adapting to the hectic urban life of Hamburg. She felt that her presence in the household of her older sister and her husband was an imposition. Within months, the differences between her lifestyle and theirs, as well as her mother's, became apparent. Maria began to appreciate how much her relationship with Dietrich had changed her, deepened her, expanded her horizons, and made her more assertive. She realized that she needed to find her own place to live.

Though Maria was happy for her sister, seeing Ruth-Alice in a satisfying marriage with Klaus was extremely difficult. Each new day, each tender kiss between the couple, each evening husband and wife shared together contentedly on the sofa, was a vivid and sad reminder to Maria of what she and Dietrich had hoped for but was now out of reach.

For many weeks during the fall of 1945, exhausted by the war and from her search for Dietrich, Maria was unable to focus on her future. *What's the point? It all seems too empty and flavorless without the love of my life by my side.* She knew that Dietrich would have urged her to relish the excitement of moving forward to a new chapter in her life, but she could not force herself to feel excitement about anything. All she felt was an unbearable loneliness and longing for Dietrich.

To create some emotional distance from her grief, loneliness, and profound longing for Dietrich, her mind wandered in the direction of mathematics. She resolved to follow her childhood ambition of becoming a mathematician. She never forgot how Dietrich had encouraged her to follow her dream in mathematics, in spite of the lack of her family's support for a woman studying such a male-oriented discipline.

One morning, without really thinking about it, she placed an envelope containing her application to the University of Göttingen in her purse and walked down the street in Hamburg. She paused as she approached the post office. She spied a trash receptacle across the street. Her mind raced chaotically back and forth. *Apply to the university or throw the application in the trash?* Suddenly, within her, she heard the voice of Dietrich beckoning her irresistibly in the direction of the post office. She opened the door and handed the envelope to the postal clerk.

She was accepted to study mathematics at the University of Göttingen and found comfort and encouragement that it was a place that she and Dietrich had in common. Dietrich's twin sister, Sabine, and her husband, Gerhard Leibholz, had made Göttingen their home until Gerhard's Jewishness made teaching at the university impossible and Dietrich convinced them to flee to England.

At Göttingen, though she met some interesting male students who came from nearby male or coeducational colleges for weekly dances, Maria's heart still belonged to Dietrich wholeheartedly, and she was unprepared to give it to anyone else. Several years into her time there, however, she met a handsome young German law student named Paul Schniewind. A welcome distraction from her intense studies, she enjoyed the company of a male once again. Maria described Paul as an earnest gentleman seriously devoted to his law studies.

When Maria met Paul, she had already applied for a scholarship to continue her own studies of mathematics for a year at Bryn Mawr College near Philadelphia in the United States. This was a unique and potentially exciting opportunity for her. She remembered how thrilled Dietrich had been in his first sojourn to Union Seminary in New York in 1930 and 1931, and how impressed he had been with the United States and the American people, even though he experienced theological studies in America as rather superficial and shallow. Again, the opportunity to taste life in the United States represented another experience she could share with Dietrich.

The couple decided that Paul would remain at Göttingen for the year that Maria was at Bryn Mawr. She would return to Germany after the year, and they would resume their relationship where they had left off when she departed.

Maria had a difficult time fitting in at Bryn Mawr, especially socially. She was well-liked by her classmates in the all-female college but, at the same time, was kept at arm's length by them as a rarity—a German woman with wartime life experience. Three or so years after the conclusion of World War II, for many of her classmates, daughters of Eastern socialites, the war was a distant concept, an increasingly irrelevant fact of European history. Unless they had a brother or boyfriend who had served in the military, they had very little personal connection to the war. Maria's own experiences isolated her from her peers and intensified her loneliness.

When she returned to Germany in 1949, even though she and Paul had difficulty readjusting, Paul wanted to settle down and get married. His proposal threw Maria into an existential dilemma. Maria still grieved for Dietrich. She thought of him daily, sometimes just momentarily, but on others very deeply and longingly. Contemplating the intimacy of marriage with a man other than Dietrich filled her with guilt and anxiety.

She consulted a Lutheran pastor about her feelings but was told that it was no sin or act of infidelity to marry someone she also loved when Dietrich was deceased. *Do I love Paul? Or do I merely admire a fine gentleman, and is that enough for marriage?* In addition, she felt peer pressure in letters from her Bryn Mawr classmates who were overjoyed that she had such a handsome and promising man, from her own country, as a potential spouse. Ruth-Alice, too, encouraged marriage. Would it be likely, she asked Maria, for many other opportunities to come along for a 26-year-old spinster? After much soul-searching, Maria said yes.

Ironically, the mathematics faculty extended an invitation for Maria to return to Bryn Mawr to study for a master's degree in mathematics along with a substantial financial fellowship. The faculty was that impressed with her promising potential in mathematics.

Soon after their engagement, Maria and Paul were confronted by another fork in the road: to live and study apart for several more years. Paul was most generous with his encouragement for her to accept the invitation from Bryn Mawr. Maria was flattered by the confidence that the faculty had in her. At the same, Paul's enthusiastic encouragement for her to return to the United States confused Maria. *Is Paul dissatisfied with me? Why is he so eager to have me go? Have I failed him some way as a fiancée?*

While she pondered those difficult questions, she also wondered about more nagging, profound worries: *Is Paul jealous of Dietrich? Have I talked too much about him and our times together? Have I inserted Dietrich between my husband and me? Is Dietrich and his memory hovering over our relationship?*

Maria didn't talk about her doubts and worries with Paul. She wrote to Bryn Mawr to accept the invitation and offer. Instead of exulting in her joy and pride, however, she relapsed into a bout of depression. Despite the affirmation she received for her accomplishments in mathematics, she walked the halls of Bryn Mawr feeling like a woman who had failed in her marriage.

Paul completed his law studies at Göttingen and traveled to Bryn Mawr to be with his new wife. Unfortunately, his German law degree was no help in finding employment in his field in the United States. Instead, he took a teller's job at a local bank. Maria attended classes and researched and wrote papers for her degree. They formed their first home in beautiful, leafy Haverford. They earned a little extra money together by babysitting the infants and toddlers of Maria's classmates.

Before receiving her master's degree, Maria became pregnant. Paul seemed to resent her focus on the pending arrival of their firstborn, and was not shy about expressing his unhappiness in working as merely a teller when he had been trained as a lawyer.

Their son Christopher was born in late 1950, the first American citizen in the Schniewind family. Shortly thereafter, Maria was granted her master's degree. Secretly, without saying a word about it to Paul, Maria wished ardently that Dietrich could have been in the auditorium to witness her receiving her advanced degree in mathematics. She received the parchment from the university president's hand with tears flowing down her cheeks, though neither the president nor her classmates knew the real reason why.

The Schniewinds joined an Episcopal church in Haverford, and Maria particularly found a spiritual home there. A second son, Paul, Jr., was born in 1954. Maria was hired as a statistician with the American Pulley Company in Philadelphia. But after two years she saw a better opportunity to further her professional education and career with the Remington Rand Univac computer company where she was introduced to data processing.

In 1955, her mother-in-law fell gravely ill in Halle, Germany. With the toddler Christopher and the infant Paul, Jr. in tow, she went to Halle, but arrived only in time for the funeral. When they returned to the United States, Maria could not disguise her resentment that Paul had declined to go to Halle to bury his own mother. *So very unlike Dietrich.* She and Paul decided that their marriage and the complication of a second child had become too much of a strain. They divorced—a decision Maria did not take lightly. It, too, went against

all she had been taught in her childhood and youth. Paul returned to Germany and found work as a lawyer while Maria remained in the Philadelphia area as a single parent of the two young boys.

Epilogue

I have grown to become more than 'Dietrich Bonhöffer's fiancée.'

—Maria von Wedemeyer

As the boys grew up, it became apparent to Maria that they needed a male role model, a father figure. In 1959, Maria met a fine man, Barton Weller, at her Episcopal church. Barton was an inventor and head of a company that manufactured electronic components. After a brief courtship in which Maria was not as terribly racked with guilt or hesitant with doubt as the first time, Maria and Barton were married and moved to Easton, Connecticut, where his factory was located. Maria settled into the life of a suburban American homemaker and mother.

Feeling somewhat intellectually challenged, she used her spare time to dig into Dietrich's *magnum opus, Ethics*. The unfinished manuscript had been completed by his friend and former student Eberhard Bethge in 1949. Knowing that Dietrich had been working on the manuscript off and on during the two years of their engagement, she had found it too challenging emotionally to read the early German editions. The English edition was published and released in 1955. Maria saw it at a bookstore in New Haven, grabbed a copy immediately, and put it in a place of honor on their bookshelf in their home in Easton. She finally found time to begin reading it almost five years after its American release.

Maria recalled that Dietrich had told her that she would find his explanation of his reasons for joining the July 20, 1944 conspiracy to assassinate Hitler within *Ethics*. While Maria found the theology in the book dense, she struggled through it and indeed discovered dimensions of his theological reasoning about responsible Christian action in the world she had not understood before. She was immensely proud that in the late 1950s and 1960s America was discovering Dietrich Bonhöffer. His theology was quoted and discussed in theology schools and parish churches alike. Maria was ready to share Dietrich proudly with a curious public.

Bart had two daughters from a previous marriage, and Maria

reveled in being a mother and stepmother and ran the Sunday School at the local Episcopal church. But she missed her professional life and wanted to return to it, much against Bart's wishes. Thus, her second marriage failed, too. Maria was the first to acknowledge that she simply took on too much of the burden of the family's happiness. She was not bitter at the time of the divorce in 1965, and kept Weller as her surname. She relocated with the two boys and her stepdaughter Sue to Boston, which was becoming a hub of employment in computers.

In Massachusetts, Maria volunteered for an ecumenical agency that assisted displaced persons from the camps in Europe resettling in a new land. Many were German, and she took a particular interest in individuals and families from regions of Europe where Hitler had inflicted the most destruction. She became very close to a family from Hungary. It's not at all surprising that she became committed to such work. Dietrich had always emphasized the responsibility of disciples of Christ to work for justice and relief among the dispossessed. Maria did the work proudly as a way of carrying on the work that Dietrich started.

The Bonhöffer Society approached her several times over the years to release copies of her correspondence with Dietrich in Tegel, but she wasn't ready. She felt that these letters were very private, a special possession between herself and Dietrich.

Once the family was settled in the Cambridge, Massachusetts, area, their address became known by more people. One day Maria received an unannounced visitor at her front door, a Jesuit priest only 34 years old who had been suffering for six years from a cerebral tumor. He was recovering from brain surgery three years prior and still suffered frightful headaches. He didn't call on her, he said, to learn more of Dietrich's formal theology, but rather to learn more about Dietrich as a human being who seemed to understand how to cope with extreme suffering. They talked in her living room for many hours. Maria couldn't explain how Dietrich often transcended his suffering except to say that he saw his own suffering as something subsumed in the suffering of Christ. Christ bears the suffering with us, so we do not bear it alone.

She also had a visit from Germany by Dietrich's sister-in-law Emmi Bonhöffer, whose husband, Klaus, Dietrich's brother, was executed by the Nazis as well. She humbly apologized to Maria for her part in persuading Dietrich to join the resistance, which led to his arrest and death. Maria was quick to absolve her of any guilt, saying Dietrich would not have joined the resistance unless he himself was motivated by love for his country and driven by his faith in Christ to perform what he called "responsible action."

Meanwhile, the explosive growth of the computer industry opened many professional doors for her. She was hired in the software department of Honeywell. In 1969, she was promoted to the head of the department, which played a major role in developing software for minicomputers in the 1970s. A couple of years later, she was promoted to Group Manager for Software Engineering, the only woman to head a department in the technological field.

"I have to tell you that my life is now happier than it has been in decades, maybe ever," she told Dietrich's best friend Eberhard Bethge. "I have grown to become more than 'Dietrich Bonhöffer's fiancée.' Every morning I wake up looking forward to what's going to happen next. I think this is how Dietrich would have wanted my life to be, even if we cannot spend it with each other as we dreamed and planned. He always said that God writes straight with crooked lines and brings good out of evil."

It was her son Christopher who first noticed that by the summer of 1977 Maria's face had become sallow and uncharacteristically pale. She didn't have her usual excitement about life, not even at their new seaside retreat on the Massachusetts coast.

Her family doctor examined her and sent her as soon as possible to the Massachusetts General Hospital. She was diagnosed with metastatic breast cancer. Upon hearing an unfavorable prognosis, she sent immediately for Ruth-Alice in Hamburg. When Ruth arrived, Maria handed her a simple wooden box and said, "It is time now. I want to share my love for Dietrich with the world. Please take these back to Hamburg with you and find someone to help you organize and edit them. You won't have any trouble getting someone to publish them."

Maria died several days later on November 17, 1977, at the age of 53 years. She was laid to rest in Mount Auburn Cemetery in Cambridge, Massachusetts.

In 1992, Abingdon Press published *Love Letters from Cell 92:*

The Correspondence Between Dietrich Bonhoeffer and Maria von Wedemeyer 1943-45, edited by Ruth-Alice.

A Word from the Author

Dear Reader,

I am honored that I can share Maria and Dietrich's love story with you.

In a work of fiction such as this novel whose primary characters are people who actually lived, the reader naturally wonders, "What *really* happened? Can I trust the story related in these pages to bear any resemblance to real historical events?"

These questions, however, are impossible to answer. This novel is first and foremost a work of the author's imagination. Nevertheless, I maintain that it is *true*. The reader must understand that "fact" and "truth" are not necessarily synonymous. All of the characters and the events portrayed in *Love Out of Reach* are based on extensive historical research, filtered, of course, through the mind of the author. Dietrich's parents, Karl and Paula Bonhöffer; his sisters Ursula, Sabine, Christel, and Suse; his brother, Klaus; his sister-in-law, Emmi; his brothers-in-law Hans von Dohnányi and Rüdiger Schleicher; and other members of his family who appear as characters in the novel all really lived, and their fates are as described. Likewise, Maria's parents, Ruth and Hans von Wedemeyer; sister, Ruth-Alice; brother, Max; and grandmother, Ruth von Kleist-Retzow existed.

The primary exceptions are Corporal Kurt Knobloch, who is a composite of two guards who assisted Dietrich at Tegel Prison, and *Gestapo* officials Franz Sonderegger and Judge-Advocate Röder, who also are composites of multiple Nazi officers.

It is in the dialogue and conversation between characters that most of the fictional material from the author's imagination appears. There are no recordings or transcripts of such conversations between, for example, Maria and Dietrich and, with the exception of a guard in the visitation room, their conversations were private. However, the author was not left completely to his own devices to create imaginary dialogue. Many of their conversations are paraphrases of statements they made to others and emotions expressed in the wonderful collection of the letters they wrote to each other while Dietrich was confined to Tegel Prison, which, fortunately, Maria saved.

I am also grateful to several excellent biographies of Dietrich, written by such scholars as Eric Metaxas and Dietrich's good friend and colleague Eberhard Bethge, who report *verbatim* some of Dietrich's conversations with several of the people who are characters in *Love Out of Reach*.

The depiction of events in Dietrich's final days and his execution at Flossenbürg are historically accurate to the degree that eyewitness accounts by fellow inmates Fabian von Schlabrenndorff (Maria's cousin) and Captain Payne Best, as well as Dr. H. Fischer-Hüllstrung, are trustworthy.

Love Out of Reach is a labor of love, particularly for Maria and Dietrich. I began reading about Dietrich Bonhöffer at the urging of my Lutheran Campus Pastor at the University of Toronto as an undergraduate student and was inspired by what I read about him to become a Lutheran pastor myself. My primary interest originally had been exclusively Dietrich's life and work. I knew of Maria only as the young woman who before his arrest he had intended to marry.

In researching for this novel, however, I was struck—haunted actually—by Maria's remark to Eberhard Bethge just before her death that she was happy that she had grown into someone who was "more than Dietrich Bonhöffer's fiancée." I learned that she was a strong, courageous, resourceful individual in her own right, and I hope that the reader comes away from the novel with that impression.

I hope that you, reader, have enjoyed becoming familiar with two outstanding individuals who are an inspiration to me.

Jack A. Saarela
Wyncote, PA
2019

About the Author

Jack Saarela was born in Finland and emigrated to Toronto, Canada, as a young boy. He studied at Yale Divinity School, and in 1981 moved to Florida. He currently lives in Wyncote, Pennsylvania, and remains a Canadian citizen. He and his wife, Diane, are the parents of two adult sons, Luke of Wyncote, Pennsylvania, and Jesse of Gainesville, Florida.

In June 2015, Jack retired after over 40 years as a Lutheran clergyman. Since retirement, his avocation has changed from scanning the environment for sermon material to viewing the world as a novelist. He'd always wanted to write one since reading *The Great Gatsby* in high school and then studying English literature at the University of Toronto. So far he has written not just one, but now three novels. In October 2016, his immigration novel, *Beginning Again at Zero,* was self-published at Lulu Press. His second novel, *Accidental Saviors,* was published in 2018 by Can't Put It Down Books, which is also publishing his third novel, *Love Out of Reach*.

Acknowledgments

When an author completes the manuscript of a work such as a novel, he or she is filled with the gratitude of accomplishment and for having come to the end of a project that has taken him or her over a year and a half or more to complete.

More than that, however, having brought *Love Out of Reach* to a successful conclusion, I am overcome by gratitude for much more when I think of all the persons who have helped me conceive of and produce the final product. Granted, I was the one who sat in front of a computer screen and keyboard and typed the words and fashioned the sentences, there were many others for whose contributions to the project I give thanks.

This story has been germinating in my mind for many years since I was first introduced to the life and work of Dietrich Bonhöffer as a young adult. It was in conversation with editor-publisher **Karen Hodges Miller** of **Open Door Publications** that we landed on the idea of focusing on the unique semi-tragic love story of Dietrich and Maria von Wedemeyer, which at the time had been an underrepresented facet of the life of the famous theologian. Karen was with me all the way from conception of the novel to its completion and printing. She was hesitant at first about editing and publishing a love story that ends in the death of one of the protagonists. I hope, however, that she and you, dear reader, feel uplifted and inspired by the story of Dietrich and Maria, despite the fact that they don't get to live "happily ever after." I have tried to show how their love for each other is ultimately victorious over the obstacles they had to face with the backdrop of a cruel World War.

Beta readers **Cindy Raff** and **Marty Weiss** were invaluable in pointing out inconsistencies in the plot, grammatical and spelling errors, and weaknesses in the text that rendered the manuscript more eminently readable for the reader.

In addition, published and successful novelist **Sophfronia Scott** (*All I Need to Get By* and *Unforgivable Love*), whom I count as a friend and among my teachers, gifted me with reading an early draft of the manuscript and providing me with invaluable suggestions to improve the story.

As he did for my second novel, *Accidental Saviors,* **Eric Lebacz**, designed the absolutely creative cover.

Fellow writer published by Open Door Publications, **Vivian Fransen** *(The Straight Spouse: A Memoir)* gave the manuscript one final readthrough as a proofreader. **Albert Glenn** produced the flattering author photograph on the back cover.

I would be amiss if I neglected to thank my dear bride, **Diane Saarela**, for protecting my valuable, almost sacred, writing time each afternoon from other tasks and distractions and for not objecting when I informed her that I intend to give writing a novel a fourth shot in the near future.

And thank you, dear reader. You were in the forefront of my mind from the first word to the last.

Jack A. Saarela
Wyncote, PA
2019

Further Reading

About Dietrich Bonhöffer and Maria von Wedemeyer

Barnhill, Carla, ed., *A Year with Dietrich Bonhoeffer*, San Francisco, CA: HarperCollins, 2005.

Barz, Paul, *I Am Bonhoeffer – A Credible Life – A Novel*, Minneapolis, MN: Fortress Press, 2008.

Zimmermann, Wolf-Dieter, and Gregor-Smith, Roger, eds., *I Knew Dietrich Bonhoeffer*, London, England: Harper and Row, 1966.

Giardina, Denise, *Saints and Sinners: A Novel*, New York, NY: Ballantine Publishing Group, 1998.

Glazener, Mary, *The Cup of Wrath: A Novel*, Macon, GA: Smyth and Helwys, 1992.

Marsh, Charles, *Strange Glory: A Life of Dietrich Bonhoeffer*, New York, NY: Knopf, 2014.

Marty, Martin E., ed., *Letters and Papers from Prison: A Biography*, Princeton, NJ: Princeton University Press, 2011.

Mason, Herbert Malloy, *To Kill Hitler: Plots on the Führer's Life*, Middletown, DE: Endeavour Press, 1978.

Dietrich Bonhöffer's Works

A Testament to Freedom: The Essential Writings of Dietrich Bonhoeffer. Geffrey B. Kelly and F. Burton Nelson, eds., San Francisco, CA: Harper, 1990 (second edition 1995).

Dietrich Bonhoeffer's Prison Poems. Edwin H. Robertson, ed., Grand Rapids, MI: Zondervan, 2005.

Ethics. Minneapolis, MN: Fortress Press, 2005.

Theological Education Underground: 1937-1940 from *Dietrich Bonhoeffer's Works*, Victoria J Barnett, ed., Minneapolis, MN: Fortress Press, 2012.

Maria von Wedemeyer's Works

Von Bismarck, Ruth-Alice, and Kabitz, Ulrich, eds., *Love Letters From Cell 92: The Correspondence Between Dietrich Bonhoeffer and Maria von Wedemeyer, 1943-1945,* Nashville, TN: Abington Press, 1995.

Made in the USA
Lexington, KY
13 December 2019